Darkness in Córdoba

Paul S. Bradley

Paul S. Bradley is a pen name.
© 2022 Paul Bradley of Nerja, Spain.
The moral right of Paul Bradley to be identified as the author of this work has been asserted in accordance with the Copyright, Design, and Patents Act, 1988.
All rights reserved.
No part of this publication may be reproduced or transmitted in any form or by any means, electronic or mechanical, including photocopy, recording, or any information storage and retrieval system, without permission in writing from the publisher.
This is a work of fiction. Any resemblance of characters to actual persons, living or dead, is purely coincidental.
Editor: Gary Smailes; www.bubblecow.com
Cover Design: Paul Bradley; Nerja, Spain.
Cover Photo: Stock Images from www.pond5.com
Layout: Paul Bradley; Nerja, Spain.
Darkness in Córdoba is the fifth volume of the Andalusian Mystery Series.
Publisher: Paul Bradley, Nerja, Spain.
First Edition: February 2022.
Contact: info@paulbradley.eu
www.paulbradley.eu
Available in eBook and Print on Demand. See website for details.

The Andalusian Mystery Series

Andalucía is wrapped in sunlight, packed with history, and shrouded in legend. Her stunning landscapes, rich cuisine, friendly people, and vibrant lifestyle provide an idyllic setting for a mystery series. The first four books are linked, the others are standalone cases. The author recommends reading them in numerical order.

1- *Darkness in Málaga.*
2- *Darkness in Ronda.*
3- *Darkness in Vélez-Málaga.*
4- *Darkness in Granada.*
5- *Darkness in Córdoba.*

Acknowledgments

My heartfelt thanks to Jill Carrott, Elizabeth Francis, Fran Poelman, Renate Bradley, and editor Gary Smailes.

Paul S. Bradley

1

The buzzing phone dragged Salvador out of troubled sleep. He yawned, stretched out an arm from under the cozy bedcover, and groped around on the bedside table for the lamp switch. Hazy remnants of disturbing images continued flashing through his mind. Were they an anxiety nightmare or was it an omen?

He shivered, clicked on the light, perched gold-rimmed reading glasses on the end of his nose, picked up the offending instrument, and glanced at the flashing screen. It was a tad after five a.m. The dean of the cathedral was trying to contact him. His light brown eyes were instantly alert because any calls before six implied something out of the ordinary. He sat up and swiped the green icon.

"What is it, Demetrio?" he said.

"Can you come to the cathedral immediately, Eminence," said Demetrio, his voice shaking.

"Why?" said Salvador.

"It's Father Julián," said Demetrio. "He's dead."

"Oh no," said Salvador crossing himself. "Where?"

"In the Chapel of the Souls of Purgatory."

"Have you informed Father Ildefonso?"

"No, let him sleep, he wouldn't have the stomach for this."

"Don't touch anything. I'm on my way."

The Bishop of Córdoba, Salvador Velasco Gumersindo, a tall imposing man in his early sixties with short-cropped gray hair, cast aside the duvet, scurried across the rug, and into the en-suite marble-clad bathroom of his quarters in the grand episcopal palace. Was this the omen? He thought.

He dried off in front of the open wardrobe, threw the towel on the bed for the housekeeper to deal with, and surveyed his wide range of clothing options. Something quick, he thought extracting a full-length, light brown monk's robe from the wardrobe. He slipped it over his head covering his naked hairy body. The rough outer cloth had been lined with cotton making it warm and comfortable in the chill of the ancient cathedral. He pulled on a pair of knee-length socks, jammed his feet into a pair of trainers, and headed out onto the landing. He trotted down two wide flights of stairs to the lobby, unlocked the front door went out into the courtyard and around under the cloisters to the main gate. As he approached the sixteenth-century gothic arch which formed the principal entrance to the palace, he raised the hood over his head and opened one of the heavy, studded wooden doors as quietly as he could.

He peered in both directions, but Calle Torrijos was empty of traffic and people. Opposite stood an ancient building, parts of which were built more than fifteen hundred years ago by Arab invaders. The original Mosque was converted into a cathedral from the thirteenth century onwards but retained much of its Islamic features. It loomed ominously under the glow of halogen streetlights. The modern illuminations appeared incongruous with the ancient Moorish arches and metal-lined doors surrounded by intricate Islamic carvings. He closed the palace door with a dull thud and with a sense of foreboding walked out onto the street. A solitary, anonymous, sinister figure in the stillness before dawn.

He walked quickly past the ice-cream shop and tourist trinket store. Both sides of the street were lined with waist-high barricades of aluminum frames draped with red material printed in gold with a border and single cross. They would restrain the holy week crowds from overspilling onto the processional route. They bestowed an air of warmth, color, and a soft reverence to the hard stone surfaces. Most of the balconies overlooking the street were similarly decorated. He crossed the cobbles toward the Puerta de Los Deanes, the entrance to the Courtyard of Oranges at the northwestern end of the huge cathedral.

Another studded door led into the cloistered courtyard; it was partly ajar. He went through and paused momentarily torn between the urgency to attend Father Julián and racking his brain to decide who would take over the poor man's onerous responsibilities. Was the cathedral ready for the day's processions, had Julián completed his tasks before departing?

He glanced at the Campanario Torre del Alminar, the forty-two-meter-high bell tower the lower part of which during Muslim times had been the minaret. To the right of the tower was the imposing Puerto Perdón through which the processions would enter from the street into the cathedral grounds. The metal ramp covering the steps was in place. Otherwise, entry for the cumbersome Pasos, processional thrones, would prove impossible. In the open-air courtyard, the serried ranks of orange trees had all been neatly trimmed and the brick-lined irrigation channels renowned for tripping up rubber necking tourists had been covered with plywood inserts.

The lull before the storm, he thought, thinking of the masses of penitents, raucous music bands, and even a fully armed detachment of the country's most fearsome regiment, the Spanish Legion, passing this way later in the day.

"I pray the day goes well," he muttered and headed to his right toward the massive double timber doors of the public entrance. One of them was wide open. He rushed past the shelves of multilingual visitor brochures, the counter where audio devices were distributed, and the dormant security scanning equipment into the cool darkness of the interior. He spotted a solitary dim light straight ahead.

The interior illuminations were all controlled by a time clock. They switched on at eight am and turned off at eleven p.m. The bishop wondered how to override the timer, but he didn't know where it was in the complex building. He made a mental note to remedy that.

He scurried past Puerta de las Palmas, the door through which the processions would later enter the cathedral. He stopped dead. The door reminded him of something critical. The route for the processions went straight past the chapel containing Father Julián's body and out at the Puerta de Catalina at the far corner of the North Wall. The bishop's pulse was by now racing at a dangerously high level as he pondered the possible changes to the well-rehearsed route and accompanying rituals. Would the police want to close off access? Will I have to divert the processions, who will supervise, and what about my religious and dignitary responsibilities? But more significantly should I cancel Wednesday?

"God, help me," he mumbled gazing at the heavens.

He continued toward the light, along the inside of the north wall passing several chapels secured by ornately designed, robust, wrought iron railings. Each interior was lavishly decorated with statues, tapestries, artifacts, and paintings depicting biblical scenes. As he neared the light, he prayed for Father Julián to rise again. Then he shook his head. Despite his religious calling, his common sense told him miracles never happened. They were just the creative imaginings of biblical scribes ordered to instill fear and obedience into the heathen masses so the church could retain power.

To his right, ghostly ranks of stone, granite, and marble pillars, many scavenged from Roman ruins, supported double-height rows of Moorish and Roman arches. The spaces between the columns were protected by a timber beam ceiling. The unique blend of architectural features gradually faded into the black abyss of the distant gloom.

The silence was deafening.

He shuddered as if someone was standing on his grave, arrived at the chapel gate, and spotted the single source of light, a large torch jammed between the chapel railings at head height, its bulb fading fast.

The dean, Father Demetrio, stepped forward from leaning against the chapel entrance; a tall, thin man in his early sixties, with bushy black hair and a prominent nose. He was dressed in the customary black jacket, pants, shirt, and white dog collar. They patted each other's shoulders.

"Have you called an ambulance," said the bishop.

"No," said the dean. "He's stone cold."

"He's been murdered?"

"Possibly, or it's suicide. The police need to ascertain the cause before he's moved."

"You're right, where is he?"

"Come and see for yourself," said the dean taking the bishop by the arm and leading him toward the closed gate where he took out his phone and pointed it at the chapel interior. "Prepare yourself, Eminence. It's not a pretty sight."

The dean switched on his flashlight. The bishop peered through the sturdy bars. "My dear Lord," he whispered and fell to his knees in prayer.

2

In October 1612, the space for the Chapel of the Souls of Purgatory was granted to Inca Garcilaso de la Vega by the Córdoba cathedral chapter to establish his chapel and tomb. The famous author was born in Peru as Gómez Suárez de Figueroa but referred to as El Inca. Earlier in his life, he had been the sacristan to the cathedral responsible for the sacristy, and its precious artifacts.

The chapel is roughly thirty meters square. Opposite the entrance, set in a niche on the north wall was the altarpiece consisting of a single vault flanked by two columns and crowned by a pediment divided by a relief of the Eternal Father. It framed a two-meter-high solid timber carving by Felipe Vázquez from Ureta, of the crucified Christ on the cross. It had been donated by the author. The backdrop to the carving was a painting of Jerusalem by Melchor de Los Reyes.

Underneath the painting was a red felt-covered marble table. The six tall solid gold candlesticks usually adorning the table had fallen on their sides; one had landed on the stone floor but remained intact. The unlit candles had been separated from their holders and were scattered around the floor.

The bishop crossed himself, heaved himself up with the assistance of the railings, and examined the tragedy before him. Father Julián's corpse was stripped naked, he lay face down, spread-eagled on the floor with his feet almost touching the base of the marble table. The statue and cross were on top of him and had seemingly crushed him to death. Congealed blood had pooled around his body. It looked black and the faint coppery smell was instantly recognizable.

"Did you check his pulse?" said the bishop.

"Yes," said the dean. "I would say he's been there for some time."

"And who is he?" said the bishop pointing to an elderly, silver-haired, bearded man dressed in a shabby gray djellaba and sandals. The traditional full-length robe indicated the man was from the Maghreb area of Eastern Morocco. The hood was pushed back over his shoulders. He was sitting cross-legged on the floor to the left of the corpse, about a meter from it, and staring at the dead priest.

"No idea," said the dean. "When I asked him if he had seen anything, he said only three words in Spanish. Sólo hablo árabe, I only speak Arabic. I tried French but he didn't understand. He, er… stinks."

"Is the chapel gate locked?" said the bishop.

"It is now," said the dean. "I didn't want our friend to leave while I went outside to call you. Shall I summon the police?"

"In a moment, yes," said the bishop. "But before you do, tell me, how did you come to be here at this time of the morning?"

"I couldn't sleep worrying if the workmen had tidied up properly," said the dean. "They were hard at it when I left last night but assured me, they would stay as late as needed to finish."

"And did they?"

"I don't know. First, the doors being open distracted me then I saw the torch light and discovered this scene. The key had been left in the lock, so I immediately secured the gate and went outside to call you."

"Did you see Father Julián last night?"

"Yes, he was also keeping an eye on the workmen but said he had to go and finish some administration in the office. He left me to it at around nine p.m."

"When did you leave?"

"I went to my rooms a few minutes later."

"And the workmen?"

"Da Rosa, their manager assured me they would finish before ten p.m. Father Julián was to lock up after they'd gone."

"Was the door locked when you arrived?"

"No, it was exactly as you found it."

"How did Father Julián seem last night?"

"On edge, certainly not in his usual good humor."

"Any ideas on how, or why this has happened. I've known him since we served together in Valencia. Such a strong, fit, dedicated, and well-balanced man. This could not have been an accident."

"Like you, Eminence," said the dean. "I have no cause to suspect he would end his life in such a disturbing manner."

"And it is unlikely our Arab friend killed him," said the bishop. "He looks too old and frail to overpower the priest, let alone move the carving. We'll leave it for the police to solve. More earthly matters require our thought and energy. Thanks to our now absent sacristan, the responsibility for the most hectic week of the year falls on you, me, and Father Ildefonso. God help us."

"Should we cancel Wednesday?" said the dean.

"Impossible," said the bishop. "Do you think Julián's death might be related?"

"I sincerely hope not," said the dean. "But being so close to such an important event in religious history, it can't be a coincidence."

"Regretfully, I have to agree," said the bishop.

"I'll call the police," said the dean crossing himself. "Hopefully, someone will answer at this time of a Sunday morning."

The bishop watched the dean head outside to where there was a strong enough cellphone signal. Then he knelt outside the chapel gate, surveyed the scene which without the dean's flashlight was gloomy and full of shadows. He bowed his head and prayed for his late friend and beloved family. When he'd finished, he stood. His movement must have attracted the attention of the old man who stared directly at him without flinching. His bloodshot eyes glistened faintly.

"Did you kill the father?" said the bishop in reasonable Arabic.

"He was like this when I found him," said the old man, his gaze strong, his chin defiant.

"How long ago?"

"About an hour."

"Who are you and what were you doing here?"

"My name is Ibrahim Kamal. I've come from Morocco with my grandson, Faraq Kamal, in a humble attempt at completing the five pillars of Islam before I die. I cannot afford to travel to Mecca, so chose the Mezquita of Córdoba as the nearest alternative. We

Muslims still consider the building to be of Islam, and I desperately wanted to pray in front of the beautiful mihrab. It's one of the finest in the world."

"At this time of night?"

"Ah, yes. I can explain," said Kamal looking down with a sheepish expression. "We er… don't have passports. We arrived on the beach three nights ago near Nerja on a smuggler's boat and walked here during the hours of darkness. Yesterday morning, when we joined the queue to buy our entrance tickets to the Mosque, the police asked to see our papers then arrested us. We were obliged to remain at the Red Cross detention center pending further immigration inquiries. The security is lax and when the guard nodded off, I left my grandson asleep and slipped out to see if I could at least get closer to my goal, fully intending to return before they woke. When I found the Mosque door open, I couldn't believe my luck and came straight in unchallenged, but I hadn't reckoned on almost total darkness. I saw this light, came to see if someone was there to turn the main lights on, and found this poor man. The gate was open, so I checked the pulse on his wrist, but he was long dead. Nobody should be alone in death, especially like this, so I decided his peace came before my pilgrimage."

"Most kind but you realize the police will want to talk to you. They'll be here shortly."

"I doubt they will believe me," said Ibrahim. "Undocumented Muslim immigrant absconded from detention. A perfect profile for a murderer."

"If you tell the truth, they will believe you."

"I doubt it, even though the words of Allah are the truth as are mine, police want to arrest a culprit as quickly as they can, innocent or not."

"A sad indictment of law enforcement," said the bishop.

"Then you have no personal experience of such matters."

"True. If it helps," said the bishop. "Tell them the bishop of this cathedral believes you."

The man nodded and resumed his solitary homage to the dead priest.

The bishop watched momentarily, grateful for the Moroccan's unselfishness but his mind was in turmoil overwhelmed by the challenges facing him. "Sorry, Father Julián," he mumbled. "I have to leave you." He headed off past the chapels toward the cathedral entrance, his heart heavy with grief.

The dean was leaning against the courtyard entrance.

Given the circumstances, he appears remarkably calm, thought the bishop.

The dean stood to attention when he saw the bishop approach.

"The police are on their way," said the dean.

"Including el comisario principal?"

"They couldn't say for sure but will try and contact her."

The bishop paced up and down, his mind racing. "There are six brotherhoods in the procession today," he said. "Six heavy thrones to maneuver around the narrow streets along with their accompanying brass bands and penitents. They assemble at the Roman arch from nine onwards and move off around eleven after which it is continuous for some thirteen hours. The first throne is due to enter the interior of the cathedral at around one o'clock this afternoon. The ultimate, shortly before midnight. If we are to stand any chance of preventing a disaster here today, we'll need the crime scene cleaned up or screened off from public view. If it proves impossible, we'll have to change the route so they cross over to the east door deeper in the cathedral which will add at least another hour to the day's schedule. More importantly, I can't decide anything or inform the brotherhoods until the police have done their work. Dear colleague, this is a recipe for absolute mayhem."

"We must forewarn the brotherhoods as soon as possible," said the dean.

"Do you have their contact details?"

"They are on Father Julián's laptop in the office," said the dean.

"The police are likely to take it. What do you suggest?"

"Could you go now and copy the files before the police arrive?"

"Wouldn't I be interfering with potential evidence?"

The dean glanced upwards. "For the greater good?"

"Or else pandemonium and an irate cardinal," said the bishop trotting away in the direction of the palace looking back over his shoulder. "I know which I prefer, I'll see you shortly."

"Shall I ask the police to await your return before beginning their investigation?" said the dean.

"No, I'll join you as soon as I've copied the files. Don't tell them where I am, or what I'm doing. Just advise them I'll be there as soon as I can." The bishop waved, turned toward the palace, and observed a movement near the far end of the cathedral wall. A dark figure looked to be cleaning the stonework. The bishop increased his pace and as he approached, the person became clearer. It was a man in black clothing wearing a hoodie and holding something cylindrical in his hand.

"Can I help you?" called out the bishop.

The person, face hidden by the shadows, jumped with surprise. He dropped the metal cylinder with a clatter, leaped over the barricade like an Olympic hurdler, and ran toward the river. The bishop followed in hot pursuit.

My sprinting days are long gone, he thought as he arrived at the cathedral corner, his breath rasping. He stopped, leaned against the wall, and surveyed the rows of viewing galleries between the massive Puerta del Puente, Roman Arch, and the cathedral. To the left against the cathedral wall stood the imposing dignitary platform. They were all fronted with red material and gold crosses. The vandal could be hiding behind or under any of them, he wondered, frantically moving barriers as he began to search, but there was no sign of him.

The bishop scratched his head, looking back and forth. "It's pointless to waste further time," he muttered. "I have more pressing matters to attend to, the police can deal with it." He crossed the road to the palace entrance, extracting his keyring from the deep pocket of his robe. He paused at the door and regarded the wall where the man had appeared to be cleaning. Then he saw and understood what he had been doing. The word 'MEZQUITA', Mosque, had been sprayed in giant red capital letters onto the wall. The bishop's surprise interruption meant the man hadn't been able to complete his task. The final 'A' was only half complete. Underneath the letters, the wet paint dripped slowly down the wall leaving a trail. It reminds me of Jesús on the cross, he thought, like the blood flowing from his wounds.

"Is this mindless act connected to Father Julián's death?" he mumbled. Then it twigged. Dear God, he thought, his heart pumping madly. The graffiti is directly opposite where the film crew will later be located on their raised platform. Its message would be broadcast all over the world and might upset the delicate accord being signed on Wednesday. It has to go.

He looked up and down the street but could only see the distant shadow of the dean waiting at the cathedral gate enjoying a surreptitious cigarette. He walked back across the road and peered over the barricade for the spray can. He spotted it nestling against the base of the wall, clambered over the barricade, picked it up with his fingertips by the rim, and slipped it into his robe pocket. The police could check it for prints but as the street cleaners were due imminently, he thought it best to keep it safe.

He returned to the palace gate and went through to the office, desperately thinking who could be available at this hour on a Palm Sunday to clean graffiti off a wall.

3

The General Office was on the ground floor at the southern end of the palace cloisters overlooking the garden and central fountain of the bishop's palace. The magnificent medieval building had been constructed between the sixteenth and nineteenth centuries on top of some of the original Arab walls. Previously, there had been palaces on the site for well over fifteen hundred years. The first was built in the Seventh Century by the Visigoths. From the Eighth Century, the building was converted into a castle by the Umayyads who named the Iberian Peninsula, Al Andaluz with its capital as Córdoba. The Arab dynasty and their successors had ruled for over four hundred years until the Thirteenth Century when the Christians under King Fernando III of Castile and Leon had laid siege to the city and recaptured it.

The bishop unlocked the general office door, went inside, and turned on the lights. There were four modern timber desks in the large rectangular space with a restroom at the far-left hand end. The one in front of the restroom was used by the dean. Two central desks faced the door used by Father Ildefonso, secretary to the three senior clerics, and Cora, the office assistant who worked in the afternoons. Father Julián's was to the right in front of a single four-drawer metal filing cabinet. Mounted on the wall next to the cabinet was a large cupboard holding sets of keys for every chapel and lock in the cathedral and palace. To the right of the cupboard was the ever-open door to the stationery and photocopier room. The white painted walls were covered to half-height with Andalusian green and cream ceramic tiles. A large wooden cross was opposite the entrance. On either side were framed prints of the palace depicting its development through the centuries. Timber beams supported a white ceiling.

A laptop was parked in the exact center of Father Julián's oak worksurface, just as it always was. A meticulous, organized man, the father possessed the ideal skillset for a modern-day sacristan. From this desk, he had his fingers on the inventory of ancient and valuable religious artifacts. However, because of his engineering studies prior to taking holy orders, he was also responsible for the never-ending restoration projects. His most important job though was organizing what were, since the Sixteenth Century, the devout soul of this beautiful historic city, the Easter processions.

On the desk, behind the laptop, were three wooden trays, perfectly aligned and spaced equally apart. One for work to be done, another for filing, and the final one for pending matters. All three were empty, just as every morning. The father never left his post until his daily tasks had been completed and all digital files had been printed out on cathedral notepaper and filed. Thanks to his initial experiences with the early versions of the Windows Operating System, no matter how often he was reassured by modern-day computer technicians, the priest had a deep suspicion of cloud storage. Paper remained to him the best and safest method of retaining data. However, he did agree the laptop was convenient for browsing or email and when pushed, would reluctantly concede the occasional round of virtual golf was most pleasurable.

The bishop slid out the leather and chrome chair from under the desk and sat. He dragged the laptop nearer and pushed the on button. It booted up and asked him for a password. All the cathedral devices used a common password. The bishop tapped in 'Crónicas1', and the Windows Ten desktop presented itself.

He clicked on documents.

It was empty.

Panicking, he looked at every file, software program, browser history, and trash.

The machine had been wiped clean.

He rushed over to the filing cabinet.

All the file wallets were empty.

He closed the machine down, turned out the light, locked the door, and ran around the cloisters to his own grander office on the north side of the palace panicking his computer had been tampered with. Thankfully, his laptop was fine. He checked his inbox. There were twenty or so blank emails, mostly from Father Julián sent at ten-forty the previous evening. To each was attached the files detailing the full program for the week and the contact details of the brotherhoods.

The final email contained a message.

Eminence,

Thanks to those behind the mask, lives are at stake on Wednesday. For your safety, delete this now. God be with you.

Julián.

The bishop was grateful for the files and uploaded them to the cathedral's secure server but the final message he read through, again and again, racking his brain to interpret the cryptic content. What mask? Whose lives and why my safety? Then, as instructed, he deleted it and cleared his wastebin.

He shut everything down and trotted upstairs to the top floor but instead of heading for his rooms, he turned left toward the rear of the building where the dean and Father Julián had their private quarters. He let himself into Julián's unlocked suite and turned on the light. He surveyed the living room, then moved into the bedroom, bathroom, and kitchen. Everything was exactly as it always was; meticulously tidy, nothing out of place, and no hint of anything suspicious. The charger for his phone was still plugged into the wall near the giant flat-screen TV but after rummaging through drawers, cupboards, and the contents of his wardrobe, there was no sign of the phone itself. He let himself out, shut the door behind him, and returned to his accommodation where he threw his robe on the bed and changed into his usual day wear of black suit, purple shirt with a dog collar, and prayer beads. He exchanged the knee socks and trainers for more formal black socks and shoes before heading back to the cathedral.

The content of Father Julián's message haunted him as he walked. During Holy Week, hundreds of people would be wearing masks. Did his death in the chapel of the Souls of Purgatory imply a hidden meaning? Is he trying to tell me something about Wednesday? Was the omen in my nightmare coming true?

Two police cars were parked outside the courtyard entrance, blue lights flashing. An unmarked Mercedes stood alongside. They were all empty.

A female officer in uniform was guarding the courtyard gate and another the main cathedral door. Recognizing the bishop instantly, the one on the main door escorted him to the crime scene.

The bishop found the dean standing next to a man and woman. All three were outside the chapel looking at the scene within. The gate was still locked. The Arab hadn't moved and ignored them, his concentration on the corpse relentless.

"Ah, bishop," said the dean indicating the man. "This is Detective Inspector Humberto Tobón." He was a smartly dressed medium height slender man in his mid-forties wearing a black suit and white open-necked shirt. With swept-back, jet-black longish hair, he resembled a rock star, not a detective.

The bishop regarded the man's chiseled features. During his short time as bishop, he'd met several senior police officers but had only heard of Tobón by his reputation for solving whatever case he was given. The policeman's hazel eyes flittered from right to left but he couldn't bring himself to look directly at the bishop.

"Buenos días, obispo," said Tobón, nodding his head at the woman. She was in her late thirties with long dark hair arranged in a French plait. She was also dressed smartly in a black jacket and pants. "This is Sarjento Natalia Chavez, my assistant. Please be assured bishop we will have this case wrapped up within hours and you may continue with your hectic schedule. Nothing should interfere with Semana Santa, and particularly not the event on Wednesday." Still, he couldn't look the bishop in the eye.

Was this his usual manner? Thought the bishop. And how does he know about Wednesday?

"I agree with the Inspector," said Natalia who had no trouble with eye contact and smiled. "Forensics will be here shortly. We'll check the scene and speak with this man. After we're done, we'll need to search Father Julián's accommodation and office."

"Of course," said the bishop. "The dean will escort you and help access his computer. What will happen to the corpse?"

"The pathologist will take him to the police morgue for a postmortem," said Chavez. "His staff will clean up the mess."

"Who will inform the father's family?" said the bishop.

"Normally, it's our responsibility," said the inspector gazing through the bars at the corpse. "Do you know them, bishop?"

"Yes," said the bishop. "His aging parents and siblings live in Sevilla. We've met frequently, and I presided over the marriage of his youngest sister, Irena. It would be kinder if they heard the news from me but don't let me intrude on your procedures."

"You're right," said Tobón still staring at the corpse. "In this case, it would be appropriate for you to inform them. Please keep me informed."

"When do you think his body can be released?" said the bishop.

"In a few days," said Tobón. "We'll know better

after the postmortem."

They all turned as a loud noise clattered around the cathedral from the entrance. Two members of the forensics team had arrived wearing white overalls, hoods, masks, and carrying metal briefcases.

The dean unlocked the gate, handed the key to the sergeant, and after donning protective gloves and shoe-guards the police team entered the chapel. The young women went about their work with a well-practiced routine. While one forensics officer photographed every aspect of the scene in intimate detail, the other scanned for fingerprints, blood splatter, and other evidence. The bishop observed the inspector as he prowled about the chapel. Something was irritating him. His movements suggested urgency even desperation as if the death of Father Julián had interrupted something. He stopped frequently to proclaim something to his team.

Natalia dogged her boss's every step, speaking into a recorder as Tobón barked out his instructions and observations before strutting over to the wall where the statue and cross had been mounted. As he passed the Arab, the bishop noticed the quick expression of what appeared to be distaste. Satisfied with the fixings, Tobón visually examined the massive solid gold candlesticks. He picked up the one on the floor and seemed surprised at its weight. He gave it a cursory glance and returned it to where it lay.

He moved to the corpse, squatted opposite the Arab, ran his finger over Julián's almost solid blood, sniffed it, and continued studying how the corpse had been strapped to the heavy ancient carving which, other than a few flakes of paint scattered around the body, had remained intact. The muscular frame of the dead body had broken its fall.

The scanning forensics officer stooped down by the Arab and turned up her nose as she appreciated the full blast of his body odor, despite the filter in her mask. She indicated he should open his mouth, which he did while she dabbed a sample of the man's saliva. She scanned his fingerprints and extracted samples from under his nails. After one look at his disgusting sandals, she shook her head and stood.

"Enough," she said. "OK, boss, they can take him now."

The inspector indicated to the officer guarding the chapel gate. She stepped forward, heaved the Arab off the floor, handcuffed him, and led him away for interviews. The Arab made no attempt to resist and as he passed the bishop, shrugged as if to say, 'I told you so'.

"Thank you for your kindness," said the bishop in Arabic.

"Al·lahu-àkbar, god is great," said the Arab grimacing at the discomfort of the cuffs and being dragged along by a female officer after his elderly frame had been seated for so long. "Please inform my grandson."

"Where did you learn Arabic," said the inspector, joining him.

"At university and my first church in Casablanca," said the bishop.

"I wasn't aware there were Christians in Morocco," said Tobón.

"There are some fifty thousand Catholics, mostly of European origin," said the bishop. "Will you be requiring any help with interviewing the man?"

"No, we have our official interpreter," said Tobón.

"I don't expect it to take long for the man to confess."

"Really," said the bishop. "From my brief conversation with him, I was convinced he had nothing to do with Father Julián's death."

"What did he say, exactly?" said Tobón.

"He was hoping to pray in front of the mihrab."

"At this time of night?"

"He was an illegal immigrant. He and his grandson landed by boat in Nerja a few nights ago. They were on a pilgrimage to the Mezquita but were arrested when queuing for entrance tickets. The security at the Red Cross detention center was lax, so he slipped out when everyone was asleep to at least soak up the atmosphere of the building, but on arrival, he spotted the doors open and came in. The chapel light sparked his curiosity, he found the body, was concerned about the father being alone in death and decided to watch over him."

"Foolish thing to do, especially for an Arab," said Tobón. "Where is his grandson now?"

"I assume he's still sleeping at the center," said the bishop. "Will you inform the boy?"

"I'll have to interview them both. This could have been a planned terrorist operation."

"He thought you would say that, but still he sat down and prayed for the father. Not the typical action of a guilty man, I thought," said the bishop.

"Best you stick to your work," said Tobón raising his voice and for the first time looking directly at him with a glare of anger. "Leave the detecting to me. The pathologist will be here shortly, now show me the father's office and accommodation."

"The dean will escort you," said the bishop. "And on your way, look at the freshly applied graffiti on the west wall. I nearly caught the culprit, but he was too quick."

"Graffiti?" said Tobón.

"A hooded man sprayed 'Mezquita' in two-meter-high letters right in front of where the TV cameras will be."

The bishop watched as the veins in the inspector's nose swelled with blood and his lips tightened so much, they almost disappeared inside his mouth.

"Somehow," said the bishop. "I have to find someone to clean it off before the TV cameras are set up."

"You're right, bishop," said Tobón reverting to his dour self. "And I have just the person to remove it." He extracted a phone from his jacket pocket and for the first time smiled.

"Don't you need to test the paint or something?" said the bishop.

"Why?" continued Tobón while swiping his phone. "You failed to apprehend the culprit and the cameras will have only seen a disguised figure. The only useful thing I can do is clean off the mess as soon as possible."

"Thank you. One less thing to worry about on my increasingly long to-do list, and by the way the phone signal in the cathedral is feeble. You'll need to go outside to make your call," said the bishop as the inspector stabbed frustratingly at his screen.

"I'll do it later," said Tobón turning to the dean. "The father's computer?"

"This way," said the dean.

4

Despite the overwhelming pressures of the day ahead hanging over him like a pall, the bishop remained with Father Julián's body until the white-suited and masked pathologist and his two male assistants arrived with a mini mobile crane some ten minutes after the inspector and his glamorous female team had departed. He hovered near them as they worked and was impressed by their respect and professionalism as they winched the carving gently off the body and suspended it vertically. The pathologist kneeled and examined the corpse paying particular attention to the back of his skull. All three lifted the father into a black plastic body bag and heaved him onto a trolley which they parked outside the chapel and resumed their examination of the scene.

"Can you share your initial observations?" said the bishop watching the pathologist examining the bloodied front of the statue with his magnifying glass.

"I shouldn't say anything until I've completed the postmortem," said the pathologist without pausing his work. Underneath the protective gear, he was a short, overweight man in his early fifties with a bushy walrus mustache and balding hair. "But as it's you bishop, I would estimate the time of death between eleven p.m. last night and one a.m. this morning."

"Was it painful?" said the bishop.

"No, the landing would have rendered him unconscious instantly," said the pathologist. "And despite appearances, there isn't much blood, so the heart must have stopped beating within minutes. His skull is badly crushed, and I suspect those injuries are likely to be the cause of death."

"The inspector has asked me to inform his family," said the bishop. "From your experience and brief inspection, could this have been suicide, or was he killed? They are bound to ask."

"It could be either," said the pathologist. "But to be frank, I've never seen a suicide like this. There is too much work involved, too many things to go wrong and the risk of failure was high."

"Can you explain?"

"The carving was unbolted from the wall brackets, lowered onto the top of the marble table, and leaned against the wall. The deceased's arms were then strapped onto the carving's arms, almost impossible to do by oneself, and then he had to heave the statue onto his back and jump forward. The weight of the carving would have made it extremely difficult. Only the strongest of men could have managed it alone."

"So, you're inclined to murder as against…?" said the bishop.

"It's certainly the most logical conclusion," said the pathologist. "Now I must double-check the forensics, take all this to my lab, and begin my examination. Our heartthrob inspector detests being kept waiting for my findings. My team will clean up this mess, but the scene will remain under our control until the inspector is satisfied it serves no further purpose. An officer will remain on guard by the chapel entrance, she will need the key in case we have to return."

"I gave it to the sergeant," said the bishop. "What about the area in front of the chapel? The procession is due to pass this way from around lunchtime. If we can't use it, I will have to divert everyone deeper in the cathedral, or not let them enter at all."

"The inspector will decide."

"When? Only there isn't much time to inform all the brotherhoods. Procession routes need careful planning well in advance."

"Again, the inspector will decide."

"One more thing. The chapel owners will ask when they can have their carving back?" said the bishop. "It's their family legacy and a rare antiquity."

"Ask them to contact me," he said handing over his card. "I will clean off the gore, but it needs some attention. Several flakes are missing from the paintwork and the front requires some minor repairs. I suggest they send the restorers to my lab to collect it in a few days."

"Thank you, I'll leave you to it," said the bishop heading out the chapel gate toward the southern end of the cathedral to inspect the building works.

He checked his watch and was surprised to find it was barely eight o'clock. He'd assumed it would be later. Dawn was approaching, and the rows of columns were now visible as the light penetrated through the stained-glass windows into the cathedral set in the middle of the Mosque. The café opposite would be opening shortly. The lure of espresso and pitufo, bread roll caused his stomach to rumble but he had more pressing matters to attend to.

From his previous assignments, the bishop was well accustomed to the maintenance of ancient buildings, it was a never-ending and expensive process. While he had often visited Córdoba cathedral before his appointment, he hadn't fully appreciated the restoration challenges its magnificent combination of architectural styles presented.

When the Christians reconquered Córdoba in 1236, they'd immediately set about building a church in the center of what by then was one of the largest and finest Mosques in the world. Over the centuries, this evolved into a substantial and beautiful cathedral with a central tower, an imposing altarpiece underneath, facing a choir made of intricately carved timber, and an impressive organ above. Wooden pews lined the space between choir and altar. Its bright, airy, and spacious ambiance was a dramatic contrast when compared with the cool, gloomy surrounds of the open-plan Mosque.

The outer walls were over a meter thick, the foundations solid and deep, but the structure had been built into the side of a hill. Over the centuries, earth tremors, rainstorms, and soil erosion had undermined the inherent robustness of the foundations, and stonework was crumbling in places. Consequently, the southern end had been gradually slipping down the hill causing large cracks to open in the floor and roof in front of the chapels and sacristy. Between these catholic features stood the exquisite mihrab. A niche in the wall of a Mosque indicating the qibla, the direction of the Kaaba in Mecca, where Muslims should face when praying, which is usually just to the south of east. However, in Córdoba, the qibla faces due south causing much debate among historians as to why. The bishop considered it an incredibly beautiful Islamic structure to be protected for future generations of all religions, yet thanks to the condition of the foundations, it was in danger of collapsing. Father Julián had been overseeing the complex, lengthy, and expensive building project to prevent such a disaster.

Specialist contractors had been working around the clock for over ten months to reinforce the roof and foundations using the latest underpinning technology. Everything was to be completed and accessible by Easter and if the dean was right, the workmen had finished last night, just in time.

As he passed through the cathedral the bishop looked up with a sense of wonder. The soaring tower never failed to bring him closer to God as the deep toll of the cathedral bell struck eight o'clock and the automatic timer switched on the lights.

The bishop entered the Mosque area through the soaring archway and began searching for signs of the repair work. As he approached the mihrab he had to peer closely at the floor to see where the crack had been repaired. Most visitors wouldn't have spotted anything but because he knew it was there, he found it eventually. The repair work appeared most professional, and the surrounding area spotlessly clean, but he knew these works were superficial and cosmetic only. The real substance was in the basement underneath the mihrab but would be pointless for him to inspect. He had no idea about engineering and would just have to trust the contractors had done their work. What was important for him was the cathedral interior looked fine and more critically, safe to use.

"If the police can release the crime scene before

lunch," he muttered. "We should be OK."

He went back to his office the aromas of toasted bread and ground coffee beans still tugging at his tastebuds as he reluctantly passed the café.

He had a difficult call to make. And it was not something he felt up to doing on facetime. He checked his contacts on his mobile, picked up the desk phone, and pressed the buttons for Father Julián's family.

"Dígame," said a male voice.

"Hola José María. Salvador."

"Obispo, your timing is impeccable."

"Sorry, why?"

"Irena has been returned to us, only minutes ago."

"Forgive me, I don't understand."

"Has Julián not informed you?"

"About what?"

"Irena disappeared during Thursday night. The police, her husband Javi, and all the family were searching for her but when we opened the front door only minutes ago, she was lying on the porch."

"Is she OK?"

"No, she's unconscious, dehydrated, and stinks of urine. We're assuming she's been drugged but otherwise seems unharmed. We've called the ambulance and police. We are so relieved she's back with us but wait… if Julián hadn't told you about her, why have you called?"

"Listen, José María, I am so happy you have Irena back in the bosom of your family, but I have some terrible news for you and there is no possible way I can soften the blow."

"Is it Julián?"

"Yes, I am so sorry, but his body was found in the cathedral a few hours ago, he'd been crushed by a cross."

"He's dead?"

"Yes."

There was a pause. The bishop heard a stifled sob, then José María hung up.

5

The bishop looked sadly at the purring handset and replaced it deliberately on its base. All he could think of was to pray for the poor Father's family. Such loving people did not deserve the double whammy of a missing daughter followed by the brutal demise of their eldest son. José María would call him back when he felt stronger, but why did Julián not tell him his sister was missing? Were the two events connected in some way?

He turned his laptop back on, clicked on the file named Domingo de Ramos, and forced his mind to concentrate on the Palm Sunday procession.

The brotherhood leading the procession celebrating Christ's entry into Jerusalem was Hermandad de la Entrada Triunfal. He looked up the contact details, picked up his mobile phone, and was about to dial el hermano mayor, the senior brother when the thought struck him. He had no hard information to tell them about any changes in route or even if the event could go ahead, and it was far too early for the police to have completed their investigation.

He picked up his mobile phone and called the dean. "Where are you," said the bishop when the dean answered.

"In the café. The police left a few minutes ago so I thought I'd grab some breakfast before checking the building works. Father Ildefonso is with me, care to join us?"

"Good idea, we seem to be in limbo until the inspector has finished his inquiries."

The café was full but not with its regular early morning clientele of shopkeepers, taxi drivers, and tour guides. Most nearby businesses were closed, and the café was catering to those about to participate in the procession. Nazarenos, originally citizens of Israel during the first century now the name used to describe penitents, were dressed in a variety of full-length tunics of pure white with cloaks in rich colors of purple, green, blue. Some were in all black. They were carrying tall conical hats, capirotes, and facemasks chatting animatedly. Costaleros, the men who carried the heavy thrones were stocking up on energy for their marathon session underneath in claustrophobic and sweltering conditions. They had shorter tunics with shoulder pads and wore matching trainers. A few uniformed bandsmen, trumpets left standing vertically on the table, added to the buzzing atmosphere.

The dean was standing by the bar talking with the waiter. The bishop overheard him say, "So sorry for your loss," as he approached. "The father was a fine man. We'll miss his terrible jokes. The usual, bishop?"

The bishop nodded and they adjourned to a table by the window grabbed for them by Father Ildefonso and sat down.

"I am so sorry for your loss," said Father Ildefonso as they took their seats. The father was a good-looking young man in his early twenties with a slender physique, angelic face, and light brown hair and eyes. He was dressed in his customary black day suit and black shirt with a dog collar.

"Thank you," said the bishop. "You realize this has placed an enormous burden on all three of us?"

"I do, bishop and I'll do anything to help," said Father Ildefonso.

"I examined the building works," said the bishop. "They seem OK to me but I'm hardly an expert. What did the police do in the office?"

"They searched Julián's quarters and found nothing but took his laptop and asked where all the files were. Had you noticed the filing cabinet was empty?"

"Yes, and his laptop had been wiped. Thankfully, Julián sent me the digital files we needed for the processions last night."

"Did he say anything to explain his death?" said the dean.

The bishop thought for a moment. "Nothing at all," he said. "It's a complete mystery."

The waiter served their coffees with toasted bread rolls smeared with garlic and grated tomato. They drizzled local olive oil over the top and ate.

"More Nazarenos," said the dean sipping his coffee as new arrivals squeezed into the café. "They are keen, there are still four hours to go until the first brotherhood is due off. Shouldn't we be warning them of a potential delay or cancellation?"

"We're in the hands of the police at the moment," said the bishop. "I have no idea what to tell anyone."

"Then all we can do is check the building is safe and ready," said the dean. "By then perhaps Inspector Tobón may have something to tell us."

The three men stood, the dean went over to the bar,

paid the bill, and they headed to the cathedral.

Crowds were beginning to assemble behind the barricades bringing their chairs, picnic boxes, and shade umbrellas, settling in for a long day and evening. The same people were in their usual front-row positions year in year out. They were experts on the proceedings and fully conversant with the nuances of what made a good procession. Many had family participating.

The bishop noticed the camera crew were setting up their equipment on the scaffold tower and the graffiti team was halfway through cleaning off the 'MEZQUITA' paintwork.

"I didn't know the council had such resources," said the bishop nodding towards the men scrubbing the wall.

"Me neither," said the dean. "Thankfully, they should be finished before the cameras roll."

"To deter any other budding spray can artists, we should beef up our security to include the surrounding streets until next Sunday night," said the bishop. "Will you arrange it?"

"Fine. I assume you mean twenty-four-seven?" said the dean.

"Of course."

"One other thing. The previous bishop used to interview the TV presenter. Will you be doing the same given the extraordinary circumstances?"

"Yes, I'm due to meet her at eleven by the Roman Arch."

"Will you say anything about Father Julián?"

"I might do. It depends on what we hear from his parents or the police. I don't want to broadcast something they prefer to keep private or might spoil the investigation."

The cathedral security team was in place as they walked up to the main entrance. As only participants in the processions were allowed entry during Holy Week, their job changed from scanning visitor bags to escorting each brotherhood through the building. The chief, Guillermo Rojas, a burly man in his mid-fifties with cropped hair and an erect military bearing was standing just inside the door. He walked up to them with a grave face.

"So sorry, to hear about Father Julián," he said. "He was much loved."

"Thank you, Guillermo," said the bishop. "Are the police still here?"

"They left about ten minutes ago. They asked me to take over guarding the chapel gate and gave me the key. I'm to take you there. They were keen you approve their work."

"Am I to take it the processions may now proceed?" said the bishop.

"Yes, Eminence," said Rojas checking his watch. "The inspector told me personally the day's events can proceed as scheduled."

"He was here?" said the bishop.

"Briefly."

"Alone?"

"Yes."

As Rojas escorted them toward the crime scene, they passed sound engineers setting up the PA system opposite the procession entrance. This was where a succession of priests, including the bishop, would take turns accompanying each brotherhood with prayers as they passed through the cathedral.

They arrived at the chapel gate and observed the

cleanup team had hung white drapes inside the railings, so it was impossible to see inside. A discreet sign was mounted on the gate, saying, 'No Entry', without any reference to a crime scene. Rojas took the key from his pocket, opened the gate, and led them through.

The bishop gasped with astonishment. The chapel was spotless. Not a blood stain in sight and it smelled faintly of bleach. He looked around, taking an inventory. Other than the missing carving everything was as it should be, even the candlesticks had been replaced on top of the marble table, candles back in situ.

The dean and bishop exchanged puzzled looks.

Instead of six candlesticks, there were only five.

They went outside where the bishop dialed Córdoba comisaría. When they replied, he said, "Comisario principal, por favor."

"Digame," said a female voice after a slight pause.

"This is Bishop Gumersindo," he said.

"Hola, bishop, Sergeant Chavez, how can I help?"

"Is el comisario principal, not there?"

"Not as yet," said Chavez. "But she would refer you back to us even if she were."

"Oh, I see. I just wanted to confirm the Inspector has completed his work at the crime scene and we can proceed with the Easter processions as mentioned to our chief of security?"

"Yes, I can confirm," said the sergeant.

"Good, please convey my thanks to everyone for the speed and efficiency of your investigation. The chapel is now cleaner than it's been for months, but we seem to be a missing candlestick."

"It's our pleasure, bishop," said the sergeant. "I'll pass on your kind words to all involved and not to worry about the candlestick, it's here, safely locked up in the evidence room."

"Why?"

"It was the murder weapon."

"Sorry," said the bishop. "How?"

"I'm not authorized to discuss this further," said the sergeant.

"I understand, but Father Julián's family deserves a more detailed explanation. I have to tell them something."

"Wait, please, bishop. The inspector is here, I'll pass you over."

The bishop heard bumps and distant whispering.

"How can I help you, bishop?" said the inspector.

"I just wanted to thank you, detective inspector, for your prompt release of the crime scene and the excellent condition in which it was handed back to us. We are now proceeding with the processions as scheduled."

"Just doing our job, bishop. Thanks for your kind remarks. Anything else?"

"I've informed the deceased's father about his son's death."

"Thank you, bishop. How did they take it?"

"Not well, which is hardly surprising given what else was going on at their house."

"What do you mean?"

"Their daughter Irena had been missing for three days, she was found unconscious on their doorstep this morning."

"Were the police informed?"

"Of course."

"I'll speak with them."

"Will this new information have any bearing on

your investigation?"

"I can't tell you anything other than charges are about to be made against a young undocumented Moroccan immigrant."

"What about his grandfather?"

"He died in his cell."

"What?"

"I said he died."

"But I don't understand, yes, he was old and frail but seemed…"

"Bishop," said the inspector. "The man is dead, and his grandson is being charged, goodbye."

The phone went dead. The bishop stared at the screen, completely flummoxed by what he had heard and the disrespectful attitude of the policeman.

"Unbelievable," he muttered heading for the chapel gate. "Excuse me dean, Father Ildefonso, but I must make a private call. I'll leave you to lock up."

The bishop headed outside to the courtyard and stood next to an orange tree. He flicked through his contacts and dialed a rarely used number.

6

Detective Inspector Leon Prado of Málaga National Police opened the front door of his townhouse located in the old part of Ronda. A beautiful historic city high up in the mountains to the northwest of Málaga and famous for being the birthplace of modern bullfighting. Prado was medium height, well built, and in his early fifties, with a thick head of silver hair, round friendly face, and brown eyes. Strangers often confused him with a friendly schoolmaster rather than one of the most successful of Málaga's veteran crime solvers. Especially when dressed in his Sunday best of an elegant gray suit, lilac shirt, and sporting a Panama hat. He and his wife Inma were about to leave to meet other family members for morning coffee in the Parador Hotel before watching the first of the Easter processions cross over the New Bridge. His cellphone rang. He took it out of his jacket pocket and glanced at the screen; it was his boss, Jefe Superior, Provincia de Málaga: Francisco Gonzalez Ruiz.

"This better be important," he answered. "The family beckons."

"If I recall rightly," said Gonzalez in his usual

clipped tones. "You're a Córdoba boy."

"Yes, but I left when I was eighteen to serve in the military. I pop back occasionally but only to visit my parents, four sisters, and their expanding brood of mini-Prados."

"So, it's safe to assume you know the city well?"

"Like the back of my hand."

"Do you have contacts in the police or Town Hall?"

"Where is this going, sir?"

"Just bear with me, contacts?"

"None, although some of my school acquaintances might work there."

"So, if asked to swear in court you have no vested interests in Córdoba, other than immediate family, you'd be telling the truth."

"Yes, but…"

"One more question," cut in el jefe. "Are you, or have you ever been a member of a cofradia, brotherhood?"

"Never, sir. I'm not a club member type and only play at being pious during family events. Sorry, sir but have you called me on Palm Sunday for a debate about religion?"

"Of course not, but before I confirm your availability for a special assignment, I need you to be independent of anything Cordobesa."

"Special assignment?"

"You'll be investigating a death in police custody. You know what that means."

"The local force will do their best to obstruct my work."

"Under the guise of protecting their own."

"It's a human thing, let's hope there is no skullduggery behind it all. How long do you need me?"

"Pack enough clothing for a week, then start driving toward Córdoba. I'll explain the rest when you're on your way, and Prado."

"Sir?"

"Be fully prepared just in case they turn nasty against you. Take your surveillance box of tricks, two phones, and both weapons with plenty of ammunition."

"Sir," said Prado rubbing his earlobe. His usual nervous habit when tension was rising.

"One more thing, don't tell anyone where you are going."

"Not even, Inma?"

"Especially, not her."

Prado shut his front door and turned back to face his wife. She was standing at the bottom of the stairs with an enquiring expression, her curves enhanced by a figure-hugging, medium-length royal-blue, sleeveless dress. Her graying dark hair was cut in a short pixie style framing her pretty face and brown eyes. Prado admired her, then shook his head. This was one of those moments when his dedication to duty pissed him off.

"That bad?" said Inma.

"On the contrary," said Prado waving his phone. "For an old bird, you look stunning. The boss has given me an urgent assignment elsewhere for at least a week. Sorry, darling but I have to pack and go now."

Her shoulders slumped.

"You fetch the suitcase," she said turning toward the stairs. "I'll sort out some clothes. Smart or casual?"

"Smart."

How different, thought Prado. Twenty years ago, she'd have thrown a wobbly when his work interfered with family life, as it so often did.

Prado went through to the study, unlocked the safe, extracted a pair of cuffs, a recorder, and one brand new phone with no personal data he would use only for communicating with the police in Córdoba. The other, his usual work phone was for keeping his colleagues up to date. Three small digital scanners would be his additional eyes and ears. One to protect his communications, another his room and vehicle from interference, the third for feeding fingerprints and photos into the police database. He regarded his two pistols wrapped in muslin cloth, spotlessly cleaned, and well oiled. He hated them. Thankfully, he'd only had to use them on a couple of occasions, his words and physical stature were usually enough to gain compliance. He picked them up along with their respective holsters. The small Glock nine-millimeter was his backup weapon, a Heckler and Koch USP compact nine-millimeter, the main. He placed two large boxes of ammunition on the desk and relocked the safe before packing everything into his well-worn leather briefcase along with a laptop, cables, and chargers.

He gazed out of the window. Painted ceramic pots hung from the yard wall sprouting various colors of geranium. His hardly touched brick-built barbecue with integral chimney was in the far corner adjacent to a timber table surrounded by cane chairs.

"One day," he mumbled. "I'll have time to enjoy all this." He shrugged, picked up the briefcase, and left it at the bottom of the stairs. He went down to the cellar, collected his blue plastic shell suitcase, and took it up to his wife.

Inma was bending over the bed folding his

underwear. He couldn't resist and stretched out his free hand.

"Don't even think about it," she said. "I'm not redoing my hair for anyone, and I'll be late for the family as it is. Now give me the case."

Prado handed it over. Inma packed his clothing and wash gear, fastened the straps, tightened them, closed the lid, and twiddled the numbers on the combination lock.

"Where are you going?" she said turning and pushing the case toward him.

"Not sure, big hush job. The boss will call the instructions through when I'm on my way."

"You'll call me every day?"

"Of course, as always."

They hugged and kissed.

"I hate goodbyes," said Inma. "Just go."

Prado picked up the case. At the door, he turned and looked at her.

"Go," she said, her eyes watering. "Just go."

Prado locked the cases into the trunk of his Mercedes saloon parked in the short driveway and headed out of town. He took the southerly exit route, past the Puerta de Almocábar, the thirteenth century stone gate into the then walled city. It avoided the town center being closed by the processions. He turned northeast toward Córdoba. As he sped over the rolling countryside dotted with majestic rotating wind turbines, olive groves, fruit trees, and wheatfields Prado checked his phone signal. It was spasmodic. About an hour later, just outside Osuna, a bustling town of some eighteen thousand inhabitants renowned for its ancient monuments and quarry, he stopped at a gas station, filled the tank, and parked outside the adjacent hotel café. His stomach rumbled, it was approaching noon and he'd missed his usual coffee and mollete.

He went in, ordered up the bread roll plus a plate of fried eggs sprinkled with crispy garlic with thin slices of serrano ham. Full stomach and two coffees later, he returned to the car.

The phone signal was showing five bars, so he called his boss.

"Where are you?" said el jefe.

"Osuna," said Prado. "First place I've had a decent signal."

"Did Inma give you a hard time?"

"No, but she was upset."

"Sorry, but you were the only officer available who matches the profile requirement."

"Which is what exactly?"

"Seasoned professional, not easily bullied and accustomed to working alone."

"You mean, never follows orders?"

"Exactly."

"So, who died in Córdoba police station?"

"I'll start at the beginning. A priest was found dead in the cathedral early this morning. The local police have arrested a young Arab man under suspicion of murder."

"Then why do you need me?"

"It's complicated but the Arab was an undocumented immigrant who had traveled from Morocco a few nights previously with his grandfather by smuggler's boat via Nerja. The grandfather was found next to the priest's body and claimed to be watching over him. He died later in his cell shortly after interrogation."

"Who requested us to investigate?"

"The comisario principal called me to inquire if I had an officer available. Initially, I was going to send someone else but then I had another call which changed my mind."

"Go on."

"The call was from national police headquarters in Madrid, the head man himself."

"Wow, how did he become embroiled in what is the death of an elderly foreigner?"

"The Bishop of Córdoba requested it."

"The bishop, how?"

"Like most senior clerics, he has friends in high places and I'm not implying anything spiritual here. He was at university with the Minister of the Interior."

"Exalted."

"Exactly. Your first appointment is with the bishop at the Episcopal Palace, he will explain the detail. What is your likely time of arrival?"

"I'm about ninety minutes away, but as it's Palm Sunday, it could take longer to reach the city center and find a parking place. I'll probably have to walk the last two kilometers."

"No, you won't. There's a suite reserved for you at the Eurostars Palace Hotel. It's central and on…"

"I know where it is, and they have parking. Pushing the boat out, aren't we, five-star hotel, suite?"

"I know you love being pampered, but it's for your safety. It's a chain hotel. The manager is a friend of the bishop. You'll be on hospitable territory and the staff is under orders to watch over your room and vehicle."

"When do I meet the local boys?"

"The murder case is being handled by DI Humberto Tobón. The comisario principal will introduce you."

"I've heard of Tobón," said Prado.

"Meant to be invincible but a bit of a prima donna. Likes the ladies, I understand. When you're done with the bishop, report to the comisario principal at her office at the comisaría on… sorry, you know where it is."

"Of course, who is the comisario principal, nowadays?"

"Conchie Ortiz Nieto."

"Should be interesting," said Prado."

"Why?"

"We were in the same class at school."

"Let's hope it won't be a problem. Were you-er… friendly?"

"She was, I wasn't interested but come on, it was nearly forty years ago."

"Teenage emotions run long and deep. Some people carry a grudge, just be sensitive."

"I'm not a monster. Is she expecting me?"

"Yes, sometime this afternoon. She doesn't know about your meeting with the bishop, of his high-level contacts, or where you are staying. I suggest you don't disillusion her."

"Fine. What about a translator for when I talk to the Moroccan boy?"

"Don't use the locals, they may be biased against you. Doesn't Amanda speak Moroccan Arabic?"

"Perfectly, but she and Phillip are tying the knot in Vélez-Málaga next Saturday, she'll be busy with wedding arrangements."

"You'll only need her for half a day, you could ask but if she can't, we'll find another solution, but I prefer we work with our established team. Trust will be a big issue in this case."

"Are you implying the Córdoba force is bent?"

"No idea, I'll leave you to draw those conclusions. I just want to add, as this is your first time leading an internal investigation, may I remind you how it felt when on the receiving end of one."

"Nervous, guilty, and resentful against their intrusion on our patch, even though I was clean."

"Exactly, and the Córdoba team will feel the same. Keep me posted."

"Yes, boss," said Prado and ended the call. He started the engine and headed out toward Ecija then joined the A-45 highway into Córdoba. As he drove through endless olive groves, his mind raced with the possibilities he might face. The only clarity standing out among the spinning brain clutter was a sense of dread.

7

Prado was surprised at how quickly he arrived at Córdoba center. The pavements were jammed full, but the road traffic was light. He crossed the bridge over the river Guadalquivir and shortly after spotted the modern hotel ahead, its unusual rusty iron cladding instantly recognizable. He stopped outside the stylish front entrance and was immediately surrounded by porters insisting on carrying his luggage and taking his car to park in the underground garage. He was escorted into the lobby where the hotel manager, Sr. Marin, a tall, balding, overweight man in his late fifties was waiting for him by the reception desk. They shook hands, waived the registration procedure, and headed toward the elevator.

"Your room is registered to the bishop's palace," said Marin as the elevator door closed. "So, any police checks will keep your name out of the loop. We've put you on the first floor opposite the fire exit should you need a quick and discreet departure. There's a security camera watching your room door activated by any exterior movement and your vehicle will be monitored all the time it is in the underground car park."

"Impressive," said Prado.

"The bishop was most insistent," said Marin. "Room service will be available whenever you need anything, and our office staff is at your disposal for any assistance you may require."

"Thank you, Señor Marin. I'm not expecting any problems, but it is comforting to know you have my back."

"Now you've arrived, I'm to inform the bishop," said Marin opening the suite door and handing Prado the keycard. "The priest who died was a key member of the cathedral staff, meaning the bishop now has more than his usual hectic Easter schedule to cope with. He'll drop whatever he's doing to meet you in the palace office. You are to ring the main doorbell, and his secretary will open it for you. Now let me show you the main features of your room."

Marin's instructions on how to operate the aircon and TV wafted over his head as Prado glanced around the luxury suite. He'd have rather been at home but the spacious lounge, small kitchen, master bedroom, and exquisitely tiled bathroom almost compensated.

His only interest was the room safe. Thankfully, it was idiot-proof and large enough.

The two porters arrived with his luggage. He made to tip them.

"Not necessary," said Marin. "It's our pleasure to welcome such a distinguished guest."

"Thank you," said Prado. "I'll unpack a few basics, then walk over to the palace. Please inform the bishop I'll be there in about half an hour."

"With pleasure," said Marin shooing the porters out in front of him.

Prado took off his jacket, then locked most of his

equipment and weaponry into the room safe. He hung his shirts and spare suit and went into the bathroom where he splashed some cold water over his face. He regarded himself in the mirror while reflecting on his new circumstances. Security sounded good, the room was comfortable, and he could eat whenever suited.

"Let's hope it all works out without anything too sinister," he mumbled to himself, went back into the lounge, turned on his laptop, and logged into the police database. He searched the Córdoba folder, found the files for Father Julián but as soon as he clicked on the access button a warning window popped up informing him, he did not have security clearance for these documents. He searched further but found nothing about the Arabs. He shrugged, slipped back into his jacket, and headed out to see the bishop, his briefcase gripped tightly in hand loaded with cuffs, recorder, scanners, and phones.

It was impossible to walk quickly on the crowded pavements. He shuffled along with the chatty carefree crowds and edged through the Puerta de Almodóvar, the old west gate into the city. The ancient narrow streets of the Jewish Quarter were usually lined on both sides with trinket shops, but they were closed for the day.

He was forced to pause while the procession blocked the way ahead. He was too far back to appreciate the colorful spectacle but the raucous music from the brass band echoed hauntingly off the stone buildings. When a space appeared, he crossed the street into a busy passageway leading down to the cathedral and palace.

His progress became slower and slower and although his destination was only seven hundred meters from the hotel, it was taking longer than anticipated. Finally, he arrived.

He checked his watch as he rang the palace entry phone and announced his name to a male voice. It was shortly before one-thirty. Twenty minutes later than estimated. He hoped the bishop was a patient man.

After a brief pause, he heard the huge door being unlocked and was beckoned in by a young priest. "Father Ildefonso," said the young man. "Secretary to the senior clerics. I'm to show you to the general office where the bishop is waiting for you." The priest closed the heavy door behind them, locked it, indicated he should follow and led Prado to an open-plan office under the cloisters.

The bishop was seated at a corner desk dressed in his magnificent robes and miter, his crook resting against the filing cabinet to the rear.

"Detective Inspector, Prado," said the priest taking a seat at his desk.

"Thank you, Father Ildefonso," said the bishop. "I prefer to be alone with the inspector."

"As you wish bishop," said Ildefonso heading for the door trying to disguise his annoyance. "Don't forget you promised to attend the next brotherhood starting its procession. In twenty minutes."

The bishop stood as Prado approached looking calm and relaxed despite his stressful day.

"Thank you for coming at such short notice," said the bishop shaking hands. "Sorry to disturb your weekend. Let us pray we can find a quick solution to these puzzling events."

"You must be in demand, today of all days," said Prado.

"It's hectic, to say the least," said the bishop sitting

down, removing his hat, and placing it on the desk.

"Then let's crack on," said Prado taking out his recorder and switching it on. "Tell me everything you think is relevant."

"The dean summoned me to the Chapel of the Souls of Purgatory just after five this morning. I rushed over and found the naked body of Father Julián, our sacristan, lying prostrate under a heavy carving with congealed blood pooled around him. An elderly and frail Arab who spoke no Spanish was sitting close to the corpse watching over him. The dean assumed the Arab had killed the priest so locked the chapel gate to ensure he didn't escape while he stepped out to call me. The signal is poor inside the cathedral."

"Deliberately so?"

"Yes, it deters tourists from disturbing those wanting to pray. It is after all a place of worship. After the dean left to call the police, I spoke with the man in Arabic and asked him if he had killed the priest."

"How good is your Arabic?"

"I'm fluent in six languages," said the bishop. "The Arab answered, in my opinion truthfully, denying anything to do with the death. He'd only come to the scene an hour earlier, found the father dead, and decided to stay with him."

"How did the Arab come to be there at that time of the morning?" said Prado.

"He and his grandson had come from Morocco on a pilgrimage to the Mezquita," said the bishop. "They had no passports and had traveled with smugglers landing in Nerja from where they had walked to Córdoba under cover of darkness. It took them three nights to reach the city. While queuing to buy Mezquita tickets, the police asked to see their papers. They were arrested and taken to the Red Cross detention center pending immigration procedures. Their security was lax so while the grandson slept, he slipped out to take a walk around the building of his dreams. He found the entrance open and came inside. However, it was too dark to see his way to the mihrab and the only source of light was a torch stuck in the railings of the chapel. He went to look, found the gate open and the father lying on the floor under a heavy carving. He was concerned about the father being alone in death so sat down and prayed for him. The dean found him and informed me. We called the police immediately."

"What was the dean doing there so early?"

"He was nervous about the restoration project. He wanted to check the builders had finished and cleaned up behind them so the processions could proceed."

"Did you wait by the scene?" said Prado.

"Momentarily, but I had more pressing concerns. Father Julián was responsible for arranging the processions with the brotherhoods. He knew the timings, order of play, and the accompanying logistics which he kept on his laptop. I desperately needed his files if I was to stand any chance of avoiding complete chaos. While the dean waited for the police, I returned to this office where Julián kept his laptop on this desk. On the way, I spotted a hooded vandal spray painting graffiti onto the cathedral wall. I chased him but was too slow. However, I did manage to recover the can."

"Did you give it to the police?"

"Er, no," said the bishop reaching for the desk drawer. "I forgot. Can I give it to you?"

"Yes, but later," said Prado. "Could you understand the graffiti?"

"Mezquita with the final letter only half complete."

"Did you think the graffiti and the murder were connected?"

"I did wonder."

"What happened after you collected the can?"

"I came here. To my horror, the father's laptop had been wiped clean and his filing cabinet emptied. Without the information, I had no way of contacting the brotherhoods to make any possible rearrangements. I went to my office in shock."

"Was this when you called your friend in Madrid?"

"No, at this stage I was only concerned with the missing files."

"I can only see one cabinet, surely it can't hold all the files?"

"The current year's documents are filed here; previous years are in the archives along with artifacts too vulnerable to display."

"Where?"

"In the basement in a controlled atmosphere."

"Who has access?"

"We all do. Sorry, inspector but the paper files aren't important, the business of the cathedral can continue without them. Thankfully, the father emailed me copies of the holy week details so the processions could continue as planned. What worried me more is along with the files, Father Julián sent a mystifying cryptic message. It's had me racking my brains ever since."

"Can you send me a copy?"

"Julián advised me to delete it, so I did."

"Do you remember what it said?"

"Precisely, I'll write it down for you."

The bishop extracted a notepad from inside the desk drawer and a pencil, scribbled a few lines of text, and passed it over.

"Eminence," Prado read out loud, "Thanks to those behind the mask, lives are at stake on Wednesday. For your safety, delete this now. God be with you. Julián."

Prado looked at the bishop, eyebrows raised.

"What?" said the bishop.

"You want to tell me about Wednesday?"

"I'm not sure if I'm allowed," said the bishop. "It's classified as top secret."

"It may well be," said Prado. "But only two days before your secret Wednesday, a priest has died in unusual circumstances. An elderly man has died in his cell and an Arab has been charged with the priest's murder. It's highly unlikely these are not coincidences. Whatever is planned for Wednesday could well be in jeopardy. If I'm to stand any chance of solving a case for which you requested our assistance, I need to know now, bishop."

The bishop looked at him long and hard, sighed, and leaned forward.

"On Wednesday morning," said the bishop. "Most of the world's religious leaders are gathering in this palace to sign an accord expected to have a profound effect on relationships between people of all religions. It's the culmination of six years of difficult negotiations to put aside all differences and unite under a banner of peace. The signing will be followed by the first example of a new form of communal worship in the Mosque-Cathedral. Christians, Muslims, Jews, Hindus, Sikhs, Buddhists, and others have agreed to common words of creed and prayer to be used by all. The event will be filmed and the resulting documentary broadcast around the world in one hundred and sixty languages. For the first time, everybody will be welcome and can participate in any place of worship."

"About time," said Prado. "But why here in Córdoba? Why not Rome, Jerusalem, or Mecca?"

"This year is the thirteenth hundredth anniversary of the first Mosque built in Córdoba on the site of the current Mosque-Cathedral. Previously, it was home to a Visigoth church and possibly before, a Roman temple. It's the only active religious place in the world still standing with a history of different religions from Pagan to Muslim to Christian and is the only weatherproof building with a mihrab and an Altar. It's also big enough to accommodate a large group of worshippers, is not in a war zone, and has easy access by airport, road, and train. Believe me when I say the longest and most difficult debate in all the leaders' discussions was the choice of venue. Nothing can change it."

"I understand, but why Wednesday morning during Easter week in Spain? Surely, it's the busiest time of the Christian religious calendar?"

"I'll try not to bore you, inspector but let me explain the origins of Easter. Pagans used the Vernal Equinox as the basis for deciding what date to hold their festivities to celebrate the first day of Spring. Christians use the same natural event to set the date to mourn the death of Christ on the cross and celebrate His rise from the dead. Muslims dropped Easter, but others continued using the Equinox to set their celebrations. The Jews remember the exodus of the Israelites from slavery in Egypt which they refer to as Passover. It's Wednesday morning because it was the only time the Pope could be released from his duties in the Vatican."

"In other words," said Prado. "There is no possibility to change anything."

"It's set in concrete, Inspector. If something or someone interferes to prevent it from happening, we can forget about any pretense of saving humanity and can join the lemmings on their inevitable journey to apocalypse cliff."

Prado looked at the bishop with new respect and said, "Were you involved in the negotiations?"

"Some of them."

"So, this is not just another event for you?"

"Exactly, inspector. It's a personal crusade to slow the decline in believing in something bigger than our pitiful selves. I don't care if you call it God or Auntie Mary. But unless most humans share a common behavior united by love, peace, and respect for the planet, we are doomed. Look, inspector, I don't wish to lecture you about my beliefs when you no doubt have your own but I'm curious. What do you think of the event?"

"Why ask me?"

"I haven't had the opportunity of discussing it with anyone outside of my narrow religious circles."

"It sounds like a good idea," said Prado. "But I think the appeal is limited to the religious and maybe some media. What makes you think ordinary people will care or take any notice?"

"Why do you say that?"

"Politicians and religious leaders have lost any credibility they may have had among the masses. They're judged to be puppets of the wealthy, the true holders of power who only want to continue exploiting and repressing them. Decades of lies, false facts, and abuse have desensitized most against anything they might say or do because none of it helps them. Add religious differences as the biggest cause of terrorism and I just see people yawning and ignoring it."

"That's a cynical outlook."

"Not when you sit where I do. After more than thirty years investigating crimes, I see the world through completely different eyes to you. Only a few people commit a crime to quench their greed, most criminal acts are just to survive. Ridding the world of poverty is the only solution to making lives worth living and forgive me bishop but I don't see a more harmonized, streamlined religion putting more money in people's pockets."

"Is this how you measure life in today's world, money?"

"God does not put food in starving people's mouths, bishop."

"So, if religions unite with the common goal of ridding the world of poverty, the masses may be better disposed to our announcement."

"They'd struggle to believe it but yes, some might be persuaded."

"What should we do?"

"A united religious front could be a formidable group to lobby governments to share wealth more equitably."

"An interesting perspective, inspector," said the bishop. "I'll keep it in mind."

"Why is the event being kept secret?"

"Most religious institutions are controlled by old men who feel faith is a deeply personal matter and should remain so. They don't recognize their reticence to modernize is killing it off. The wealthy, who own most of the world's media support these divisions, they keep them in power. If our plans are published ahead of the event, these same powerful barons will bombard the airwaves with negativity before we've even started. Whereas, if we surprise everyone, there will be time for it to take hold. The documentary will be launched with a massive social media campaign to spread positivity before naysayers can respond. Afterward, anything they say will sound like sour grapes."

"Sounds sensible. Who is in charge of the security arrangements?"

"My friend at the ministry of the interior is ultimately responsible but General Quijano, head of the anti-terrorist division is running the show. He's using a combination of military, secret service, Spanish Legion, and local police but it's complicated because every leader is bringing their team."

"The General is a capable man," said Prado. "But I wonder how familiar he is with the local force."

"I know the General and his experts have vetted and validated everyone participating. However, they want to keep everything low-key so there will be no obvious police presence. It is a secret occasion after all. Delegates will be arriving at Córdoba airport early on Wednesday. Most are flying down from Madrid, a few others such as the Pope are coming directly. They will be transferred to this palace by normal tourist buses and dressed in business suits. Anybody watching will conclude it's just another of the many conventions we hold here."

"We'll have to hope Father Julián's death has nothing to do with all this."

"I fear it may, especially after the actions of Inspector Tobón."

"In what respect?" said Prado.

"Several. Having the crime scene released so quickly is a Godsend for our important day of processions. We didn't have to change the itinerary or worry the brotherhoods about it. While it made me happy, it also seemed too convenient. Surely, more laborious, and in-depth work would be required for an unexplained death. My initial estimate was it would take at least a day or two, and we would probably have to cancel some of the processions but lo and behold, four hours after the body was found we are back to normal service."

"It does sound suspicious but still possible."

"I'm also concerned about Tobón's attitude. Within minutes, he'd concluded the Arabs had murdered the priest with a candlestick. No other possibility was muted such as suicide for example."

"Was the father prone to depression?"

"Quite the opposite, he was an outgoing, content person loved by all."

"You mentioned the priest was naked. I cannot imagine he walked from the palace without any clothes, did you see any?

"Good point, no. There were no clothes."

"What about the chapel itself. Souls of Purgatory, does it have any theological significance?"

"Maybe? Purgatory in the Catholic Church refers to an intermediate state after physical death for expiatory purification. In other words, it's a halfway house between heaven and hell, where your soul goes for cleansing before being allowed in. Meaning it's up just below God, not down in the fiery depths."

"If it was a suicide, why might he have chosen this chapel over thirty others."

"Are you suggesting he is trying to tell us something?"

"Exactly."

"The truth is I have no idea," said the bishop. "I'll think on it and speak to the dean. He has far more cathedral history knowledge than I."

"Please keep me posted with what he says. Did Tobón say anything to you about the murder weapon?"

"It was most odd," said the bishop. "On our arrival at the chapel all six candlesticks were scattered about the table, one was on the floor but none of them showed any sign of blood. The forensics officers showed no interest or the pathologist. I left shortly before the pathologist had finished and all six were still there. Yet when I returned later with the dean to inspect the cleaned-up scene, we spotted only five. One was missing and nobody knows how it left the premises. I learned later Tobón had returned for a second visit, but nobody saw him take it. I called Tobón to report it missing and was unceremoniously informed it was the murder weapon and was being kept in the evidence room. That's when I learned the old man died in his cell, and the grandson, who I suspect has never been near the chapel, was being charged."

"What was your impression of the Arab?"

"A God-fearing and kindly man but frail and incapable of overpowering the father who was a fitness freak and as strong as an ox."

"Did you meet the grandson?"

"No."

"Will I be able to see the crime scene today?"

"No but come back early tomorrow morning and take as long as you need."

"I will be there at precisely eight o'clock, thanks. Just one more thing for now. I'm most grateful for the hotel suite and excellent security arrangements but may I inquire as to why you thought they were necessary?"

"It comes back to the Arab," said the bishop. "I've seen more sick people in my career than most and can gauge with some degree of certainty if people are about to die of natural causes. This Arab, this Ibrahim Kamal may have been elderly and frail, but he was mentally tough and physically capable of walking from Nerja to here, and he would never abandon his grandson in the middle of a foreign land. Something else spurred his death and without wishing to point the finger, I was concerned about Tobón as soon as I met him. It wouldn't surprise me if he was possibly covering something up."

"Thank you, bishop," said Prado. He made to stand.

"Please remain seated, Inspector," said the bishop. "I haven't finished yet."

Prado sat.

"Tobón agreed I should inform the father's family of his death. I know them well and officiated at Irena's, their youngest daughter's, wedding. They live in Sevilla. The father informed me Irena, had disappeared a few nights ago but had been found on their doorstep unconscious just after seven am this morning."

"Did they report this to the police?"

"They were too upset to say anything when I first contacted them, but José María, the father, called me about an hour ago and updated me."

"Has Irena recovered consciousness?"

"Yes, but she's shaken and weak. All she remembers is going to bed as usual on Thursday night and waking up on her parents' doorstep this morning. Her husband was away on Thursday night on business and was concerned she wasn't answering her phone. Her father went to their villa and found it empty. The bedclothes were rumpled and there were two scuff marks on the rug next to the bed as if someone had drugged her while she slept and then dragged her over the floor. The police doctor examined her and found needle marks in her right buttock and heavy traces of opioids. They're keeping her in hospital tonight to balance her fluids and check for addiction possibilities. All being well she'll go home tomorrow."

"Did father Julián know about this?"

"His father informed him on Friday, but Julián never mentioned it to anyone here."

"Is it possible his sister was taken to force Julián to cooperate with something he didn't want to?"

"Maybe, but why wouldn't he tell me? We shared everything," said the bishop.

"Perhaps he was warned not to, or she would be killed."

"Preposterous, inspector, this is the Catholic church, not a gangster movie."

"Desperate times call for desperate measures," said Prado.

"I fail to understand why?"

"Somebody wants to prevent Wednesday from going ahead."

"Nonsense, this is the best thing for religion in centuries. Why would anyone want to stop it?"

"I can't imagine," said Prado. "However, no matter if it was murder or suicide, people don't die violently without a pressing reason. Julián must have discovered something and killed himself to draw our attention to it or was killed to keep him quiet."

"Why didn't he tell me?"

"It might jeopardize his sister's life."

"Possibly but he was also unbelievably stressed out with the pressure of work."

"With Easter?"

"Plus, the building project," said the bishop.

"You mentioned it earlier, tell me about it."

"The southern end of the cathedral was slipping down the hill. We've had the foundations completely underpinned and the roof reinforced. Julián is also a qualified engineer and was responsible for the project. The builders only finished around ten pm last night. He was meant to check their work and lock up after they had gone, but as I said earlier, the outer gate and public entrance were left open all night."

"Don't you have security?"

"During the day, yes, but with men working all hours, our night monitoring service was stood down. Perhaps we should have reactivated it yesterday."

"Too late now, bishop. I'll need to talk with the builders. Are they a local firm?"

"Yes, Construcción Artesanos SL. They specialize in ancient monuments bringing in experts when needed. Father Julián handled all dealings with them. Sorry, Inspector, perhaps I should have shown more of an interest, but I have no understanding of engineering or construction whereas Julián was fascinated by it."

"Me neither, bishop. Do the police have Julián's cellphone?"

"I don't know but it wasn't in his quarters."

"Where are those exactly?"

"Here at the palace, would you like to see them, they haven't been touched other than by Tobón and his team?"

"If I may."

The bishop stood, led Prado out the office door.

Father Ildefonso was standing closely outside the

door looking flustered.

"Sorry to interrupt, Eminence," he said. "Have you finished with the inspector?"

"Not yet."

"Shall I ask the dean to stand in for you with the next brotherhood?"

"Good idea, thank you, father."

The bishop led Prado to Julián's quarters and opened the door. Prado followed him in.

"No locks?"

"Downstairs yes, but up here, no. We don't feel the need."

The sacristan's spacious one-bedroom apartment was traditionally decorated with white walls, timber furnishings, and rugs. There were a few family photos on the bedroom dresser which was next to a cross-mounted on the wall above a small prayer station. A large, framed copy of the last supper was on the living room wall. Prado strode around, looked inside cupboards, drawers and checked the kitchen trying to gauge the father from his possessions. Other than Julián being frugal, spotless, and immaculately tidy, he learned nothing.

"Does Father Ildefonso also live in the palace?" said Prado.

"Yes, he has a room on the ground floor next to the office."

"How many staff do you have in the palace?"

"Three priests and seven novices but only four of us live in. The remainder attends as needed.

"Is there a housekeeper?" said Prado.

"Yes, Cora, she comes on weekdays. She looks after the four of us. Mornings she does laundry and domestic work, afternoons she helps in the office."

"What about security, maintenance, cleaning?"

"We have four full-time security officers under Guillermo, everything else is outsourced. They are part of the dean's responsibilities."

"What else does the dean do?"

"He's my number two. He's in charge of administration, ensures all staff stick to the rules, and manages the religious calendar. For example, if you qualify to marry in the cathedral, he will make the arrangements."

"You referred to the father as being a fitness freak," said Prado. "Where did he work out?"

"Every day he spent an hour in the gym and went jogging along the river three times a week."

"A man of habit?"

"Like clockwork, I always knew where he was and what he was doing."

"Except last night."

"Except then, yes."

"Where is the gym?"

"We have our own, it's by the swimming pool in the basement."

"May I have a quick look at your quarters and the dean's?" said Prado. "It will help me put Julián's in context."

"May I ask why?"

"Priests live differently from policemen. I don't know if the father's rooms are typical or not. It should help me understand more about your way of life."

The bishop looked at him with eyebrows raised. Decided Prado was being serious, turned, and led the way.

The dean's apartment was identical to Julián's, except with different family photos and several smaller religious paintings Prado didn't recognize. The bishop's apartment was enormous, exquisitely decorated, and fitted with dark timber furnishings, Persian rugs, a marble-clad bathroom, a sizeable wardrobe, and several tall chests of drawers. There was a separate TV room, dining room, kitchen, study, and a small chapel. Prado came to one conclusion. They were comfortable places to live but they didn't feel like homes, just a place to sleep and keep their stuff.

"Seen enough?" said the bishop.

Prado nodded.

"Then we'll return to the office. I have to give you the spray can."

Father Ildefonso was hovering by the general office door as the bishop and Prado returned from upstairs. He was still agitated and came toward them.

"Not now, father," said the bishop waving him away. "We've nearly finished."

Ildefonso looked devastated but stopped, opened the door for the two of them, and closed it behind them.

The bishop returned to the same chair, opened the desk drawer, and extracted a spray can wrapped in a clear plastic bag.

"It might have some fingerprints," said the bishop.

"I didn't see any graffiti," said Prado picking up the bag and transferring it to his briefcase.

"Miraculously," said the bishop. "Tobón organized for it to be cleaned off almost immediately. Normally, it takes weeks for the council to act about anything. Maybe, I'm becoming paranoid, Inspector but to me, it was unusually quick."

Prado nodded and looked into the bishop's eyes. "What do you think Julián meant by his message?"

"No idea," said the bishop. "But bearing Wednesday in mind, it terrified me. It's why I called Madrid, and the reason you are here."

8

The bishop handed over his card, repositioned his miter, grabbed his crook, and rushed off to his next engagement. Father Ildefonso escorted Prado to the palace gate. Prado slipped into the crowd and wormed his way down toward the river where the next brotherhood was readying themselves to take their place in the procession. Prado was forced to stop while they lifted the throne and shuffled it into position pointing in the direction of the Roman Arch, the starting point of their long parade through the streets.

While the biblical significance of the throne went right over the policeman's head, he never failed to marvel at the attention to detail and incredibly lavish and high-quality workmanship. This one was Jesús on the cross with two figures kneeling before him. The surrounding gold leaf ornate décor was elaborate and beautiful. Black skirts were draped around the edge of the platform under which were stood the costaleros. At least four rows of eight crammed under the skirts. When lifted, their identical sports shoes could be seen taking tiny steps in perfect unison as they swayed from side to side slowly moving forward. Unlike those of

Sevilla or Málaga, none of the thrones in Córdoba were large as the streets were too narrow and the turning points tight. Negotiating corners was a skill on its own requiring one side to shuffle while those on the other took long strides. There was black netting in the skirts providing some vision to the outer carriers but those in the middle were working completely blind and put their implicit trust into the throne guide. Instructions to lift, stop, go, or park up for a while were given by the guide striking a small bell mounted on the front of the throne. More modern thrones were electrified and steered like a model car with remote control. However, it was considered the ultimate brotherhood privilege to physically carry the throne which required peak athleticism, endurance, and mental toughness.

The brotherhood band was forming up dressed in smart blue uniforms, their spotless brass instruments sparkling in the warm sunlight.

The remaining members of this brotherhood were dressed in black capirotes and masks which covered their faces completely except for two slots for the eyes. These were the Nazarenos and would parade in front of, to the side and rear of the throne acting as penitents. The mask allowed them to serve penance in public without revealing their identity. Depending on their seniority in the brotherhood, some would carry an ornate staff, others' candles, the wax dripping onto the cobbled streets as they ambled along at a snail's pace.

As soon as Prado could find a way through, he headed down to the riverside, where the crowds thinned out and he could make reasonable progress along the promenade. He went past the magnificent Roman Bridge crossing over the river Guadalquivir in the direction of the comisaría.

The ancient toll house at the far end of the bridge and superb views over the river usually never failed to impress Prado but today his mind was preoccupied with the message from Father Julián to the bishop. Who was behind the mask, whose lives were in danger on Wednesday, and where? Should he even take the words of warning seriously?

By the time he arrived at the comisaría just over a kilometer later, he'd drawn no conclusions. He paused outside the ochre-painted three-floor police station with rusty red windowsills. He'd passed it often as a boy on his way to school but had never been inside. He stood outside the exterior gate for a moment thinking ahead to his meeting with his old school friend wondering how he would be received.

He entered the open gate, went up the steps to the main door, showed his identity card to the female officer behind the reception desk, and announced his appointment with the comisario principal. After a cursory telephone call, she nodded to the side and a young muscular male officer came out of the reception office, escorted him up the stairs to the first floor and along a corridor lined with photos of previous senior officers to the far end.

The officer knocked and went in without waiting. Prado followed. "Detective Inspector Prado," he announced and left.

The comisario principal was sitting behind her desk typing something into her desktop computer. She didn't look up but indicated Prado should take a seat opposite. He put his briefcase on the floor, pulled the chair to the side, sat, and waited patiently looking around the room. Mounted on the wall behind the desk were the Spanish and Andalusian flags on either side of the national police emblem. Scattered randomly on the wall to the left were framed photos of the comisario shaking hands with various dignitaries.

Prado regarded her as she tapped the keys. She was in full uniform, her peaked hat resting on the side of the desk, dark hair swept back and pinned behind her ears. She stopped typing, looked directly at him, and smiled warmly, her brown eyes twinkling.

Prado was shocked, facially she looked almost identical to when he last saw her, except with far more make-up. She was more alluring than he recalled.

She stood up, came round the desk, and held out her hand. She was still petite and had gained a little weight but moved athletically in flat black shoes.

"How long has it been, Conchie?" he said grasping her hand firmly and exchanging cheek kisses.

"I hate to admit it, Leon," she said. "But the last time was when you left the Instituto having scraped through your exams. You were eighteen so thirty-five years ago."

"You haven't changed a bit," said Prado.

"Most generous. I struggle to keep my waistline to where I'd like it though which becomes harder with each passing year, but other than your silver hair you still look the same handsome fellow. How is your family?"

"They are fine, parents are slowing down but there are nine grandchildren now. My sisters have been busy."

"Will you be staying with them?"

"Not sure, but I'm seeing them after I'm done here and will see what is available. How are your family?"

"I lost my father and elder sister, but my mother

and younger brother are still with us, he's married with three girls. They keep me busy when I can occasionally escape from here."

"You've done well," said Prado letting go of her hand.

She returned to her seat and indicated he should sit.

"After Instituto, I went to university, then signed up to serve."

"I don't recall you showing any interest in policing."

"I wasn't but events nudged me in this direction. You didn't hear about my elder sister, Maribel?" Prado shook his head. "She was raped at the annual Feria and poorly treated by the then all-male force. Do you remember Dani Lopez?"

"Vaguely, wasn't he in the class below?"

"Maribel accused him, but all he was charged with was assault because my sister was drunk. Four months in jail is all he got, only four months. I was furious and swore I would not let the same happen to any other poor girl. It's what motivated me to join up. My determination to protect women has earned me this position. I also serve on several committees advising lawmakers on their policies toward women."

"How is your sister?"

"Sadly, she never recovered mentally and killed herself."

"I'm so sorry."

"It was over thirty years ago now, but it still hurts. What about you, why did you join?"

"For my national service, I was posted to the Spanish Legion base outside Ronda, where I joined the military police. After several small successes, I decided solving crimes was my thing. When I left the army, I joined the national police in Málaga, where for the last twenty years I led the serious crimes division. Last year I opted for a quieter life and set up a new department handling crimes involving foreigners. It's not so hectic and I can do much of it working from home in Ronda where I live with my wife. Did you marry?"

Conchie looked momentarily unsettled. "No, I was engaged for a while but after what happened to my sister, I became somewhat obsessed with protecting women. Since then, I've had no time for relationships. Do you have children?"

"Two fine sons, both away at university in Madrid."

"You are so lucky," said Conchi looking down briefly.

"I am now but for twenty years my wife and I lived separately. Like you, I gave myself to the job. She couldn't handle it and until I started this new role, I wasn't prepared to compromise but we're both over it now and happily back together."

"Shame our paths didn't cross," said Conchie looking at him. "I mean during your separated years."

Prado didn't react.

Conchie continued looking at him, then shook herself, picked up a file, and opened it. "This is from your boss," she said after skimming through it. "My only observation is administration seems not to be your strongest point."

"I can't disagree. I prefer to focus on solving crimes. I find the paperwork and too much protocol interferes."

"I agree, but it's crucial if we are to win court cases and punish culprits which brings me on to this death in police custody."

"I understand DI Tobón is responsible for the case?"

"Correct. He's a fine officer with an exemplary record, however, like you, he skips on the admin. I'm always berating him about it, but he takes little notice. I tolerate it because his failure rate is practically zero. On the downside, many of his cases don't reach the court because of his poor record-keeping. Last year, I gave up and surrounded him with some of my best girls who have improved his conviction rate."

"Is this his first death during custody?"

"No."

"Should I be concerned?"

"He's had an unusually high number, but they were investigated, and he was exonerated."

"I trust I can have access to all the case files, forensics, and pathology on this and his previous cases."

"Of course, would you like a quick look at what's been uploaded so far on this case?"

"I'd be better prepared for the briefing if I could. I tried to look earlier but my security level wasn't high enough."

"Correct, I deliberately set it high until we'd met and talked first. Bring your chair round here," said Conchie tapping her keyboard. "We'll log in to the file using my details."

"It would help cover my tracks," said Prado moving to sit next to her. "If your officers didn't know what I was checking out. Would you object if I continued to use your account to browse?"

Conchie studied him for a moment. "An unusual request," she said. "It means granting you access to everything, including personnel files."

"Should I need to access any, I'll ask you first and at least you will be able to track where I have been."

"May I ask why?"

"It's probably nothing, but in my experience, causes of death in custody can fall into three categories: most are accidental, some suicidal but a few are at the hands of the police. Until I'm sure which this is, I need to keep my distance from your team. I want to observe everything they are up to but prefer them not knowing what or whom I have my eye on. In the unlikely event, someone is up to something sinister, it will give me a better chance of spotting it while protecting myself and your reputation."

"You make it sound dangerous."

"I appreciate it sounds dramatic but at this early stage and until we are confident of the facts, caution is the word."

"I appreciate your concern, Leon, however, we should try and keep things in proportion. The only thing going on here is an elderly Arab dying of natural causes in one of my cells. He was alone at the time and the pathologist has not signaled any reasons for alarm. Your job is to confirm it, not make a crisis out of nothing."

"If only it were so simple. Regrettably, the Arab's death cannot be investigated as an isolated incident. The old man was present at the priest's place of death; therefore, I need to know his state of mind and health before he arrived at your police station not just while he was here."

"Now I understand," said Conchi scrutinizing him. "So, you need access to both cases?"

Prado swiveled his chair causing his knee to brush Conchie's thigh. He left it there and looked into her eyes. "Yes," he said.

She reached over and picked up a lined notepad,

tore off a single sheet, and wrote down her access codes.

"You are the only person, I would do this for," she said handing it over and returning her thigh to touch his knee. "I trust you will return my faith in you and share what you discover with me as much as protocol allows."

Prado took the paper, folded it in half, and slipped it into his jacket pocket. "Of course," said Prado smiling at her.

Conchie tapped on the mouse. "Here are the images from the cathedral," she said.

"Just flick through them quickly. I only need to visualize the scene. I'll go there tomorrow morning and check it out personally. Is it still sealed?"

"No, but it is not open to the public or owners. The cathedral security has the key."

They spent a few minutes looking at the photos.

"Any theories as to how the priest died?" said Prado.

"It seems simple to me. The Arab was found at the scene. Tobón extracted a confession from him which was then backed up with another from the grandson along with various bits of conclusive evidence. The grandfather was charged with first-degree murder and locked in a cell while Tobón interviewed the grandson. When this interview had finished and the lad charged, he was returned to the same cell as his grandfather where they found the old man dead. The pathologist was called. He diagnosed a heart attack which was confirmed after the postmortem. I'll leave Tobón to go into the detail."

"It all sounds cut and dried," said Prado.

"It's what I concluded," said Conchie. "So

immediately called your boss to begin an independent inquiry as protocol describes."

"And here I am," said Prado reaching out and touching her arm. "It's great to see you again."

Conchie grinned and slid her chair back from him. "I've given orders Inspector Tobón, and his team is to be at your disposal. I've also set aside an office for you along the corridor from me. I'll just make a quick call, then take you down to meet everyone." Conchie picked up the desk phone. "Briefing room, three minutes." She replaced the handset, left her hat on the desk, and led the way to the door where she paused and put her hand on his arm.

"Leon, I'd prefer it if we kept our history confidential," she said. "You'll extract fuller explanations if they think you are completely independent."

He patted her hand. "No problem. I'll try not to call you Conchie."

She fluttered her eyelids, blushed, and yanked open the heavy door.

9

Detective Inspector Humberto Tobón was sitting in his spacious office, tapping a report into the police central computer when his door was opened. He looked up and saw Sergeant Chavez beckoning, she didn't look happy.

"We are to report to the briefing room immediately," she said. "He's arrived."

Tobón frowned, saved his work, slipped into his jacket from a hanger on the back of the door, checked his hair in the small circular mirror hanging from the same hook, and followed her out.

"I get pissed when she summons us like naughty pupils to the headmistress's office," she mouthed as he caught up with her.

"I hear the famous Prado resembles a headmaster himself," said Tobón.

"I had a word with an old friend who worked with him on the serious crime squad in Málaga," she said.

"And?"

"He doesn't miss a thing."

"Just relax and tell it how we agreed. Remember, he's a cop investigating cops. Without our collaboration and concrete evidence, he's fucked."

"What about the grandson?"

"Stop worrying. Who will believe him?"

"You better be right. I need this job."

***

They arrived at the briefing room, which was laid out in classroom style on the ground floor. The rest of Tobón's team were already seated. The four uniformed female officers who attended the cathedral, two forensics ladies, and the pathologist. Tobón nodded at them and took a seat on his own to one side at the front. The sergeant joined the other ladies.

The room darkened. The projection screen wound down from its ceiling alcove with a quiet whirr of the electric motor and a squeak from the spindle. The photo of the dead Arab lying on the bunk in his cell appeared on the screen. The briefing room door opened, and two dark figures moved between the rows of chairs, turned, and faced Tobón's team. The two glared at the assembled group while waiting for the coughing and foot shuffling to stop. When it was silent. The comisario principal stepped forward and indicated the man on the screen with her arm.

"Detective Inspector Tobón," she said in a quiet but commanding voice. "I've invited you and your team here this afternoon to tell us about the demise of this man earlier this morning. Detective Inspector Prado from Málaga national police has been appointed as the independent officer responsible for preparing a detailed report as to why this man died in our custody. When completed, the Inspector's findings will be forwarded to the minister of the interior for analysis.

I'm confident I don't need to remind anyone, however, should any of you be found responsible in any way for this death, the consequences could have a dire effect on your employment record and pension. I advise you to give your full cooperation to Inspector Prado. I will leave you in his more than capable hands and don't forget not only your reputations are on the line here but those of everyone at this station, including mine."

Prado waited for Conchie to turn the lights back up and close the door behind her. He slipped off his jacket, pulled an empty chair forward, turned it around, sat, and leaned his arms on the backrest. He took the recorder out of his trouser pocket, held it up for all to see, and turned it on.

"Just to make sure I can hear the recordings," said Prado. "Would you move closer?"

Prado waited until everyone had followed his instructions. Tobón hadn't moved, so Prado nodded at him and watched like a hawk until he reluctantly joined the others.

"Thank you," said Prado. "I noticed most of you have filed your reports on this morning's events. As we know, the written word is carefully thought about, edited, and then reedited by our colleagues. It's often sanitized further by superiors before being signed. Officers, we all know it's bullshit, so what we are going to do is this. I will read everything uploaded but then pretend I haven't. I invite those who might wish to reconsider their narrative to resubmit a new version. In other words, until I declare this investigation is closed, I am offering amnesty to anyone who wishes to change their report at any time. Understood?"

"Extremely generous of you Inspector," said Tobón, his eyes not matching the warmth of his voice.

"However, there will be no discrepancies between the reports and the actual events. It might be how you work in Málaga but in Córdoba, we are accustomed to accuracy in everything we do at the first attempt."

"Excellent, Inspector," said Prado. "My wife will be delighted. She wasn't expecting me back home for at least a few days."

Nobody chuckled but Prado noticed a few hands being raised to mouths. "I'll read the reports tonight," said Prado. "Meanwhile, I want each of you to tell me in your own words your exact involvement in the case, your thoughts about what you observed, and any conclusions you may have drawn starting with your attendance at the crime scene in the cathedral."

"I can't allow it," said Tobón jumping to his feet. "What happened at the cathedral has no bearing on the death of this bloody Arab."

Prado didn't flinch. He returned the man's glare. "I disagree, Inspector. According to the death certificate, Ibrahim Kamal died of a heart attack brought on by natural causes. I, therefore, need to establish if this was a sudden illness or if it had been building for some time? I'm looking forward to hearing the pathologists' findings, but he only saw the man when he was already dead. All the rest of you saw him alive and supposedly well at around six am this morning. Now, who wants to start?"

"If we must then I will," said Tobón sitting back down.

"I'd prefer if we could start with those first on the scene," said Prado looking around expectantly.

The four uniforms held up their hands. Prado was astonished how similar they were in looks, all in late their twenties with curvaceous figures, beautiful classic

Latin faces with long dark glossy hair and brown eyes. Prado pointed at one and nodded.

"My name is María Cano," she said, her voice shaking. "My partner, Ellie, and I arrived first and met the dean at the courtyard entrance. He escorted us to the chapel where we saw a torchlight had been jammed in between the railings. Its battery was fading so it was extremely gloomy. The dean had locked the gate, so we switched on our torches and illuminated the scene."

"We saw a body laid out underneath a cross," said Ellie. "There was blood around it on the floor and a man sitting to the left-hand side staring relentlessly at the corpse. We asked him to stand and back away but the dean informed us he only spoke Arabic."

"How did the man seem to you?" said Prado.

"Frail," said María.

"Frail as in about to die?" said Prado. "Or just as a man of his age might appear?"

"He didn't look as if he was ill," said Ellie. "Just old and weary, like my grandfather. He's over eighty and we think it's only a question of days before he goes but we've been saying the same for years. It's amazing how resilient he is. This man reminded me of him."

"Anything else?"

"To do with the man, no," said María. "When the Inspector arrived, we were posted to guard the cathedral entrance. Other than seeing our colleague Marta escorting the man to her vehicle, we had no further involvement with him."

"Is this what's in your report?" said Prado.

"Yes, sir," said the officers in unison.

"Thank you," said Prado turning to Marta and her colleague. Are these the 'my girls' Conchie was referring to, he wondered? Or does their loyalty lie with

Tobón?

The women exchanged glances. One nodded at the other.

"I am Marta, and this is my partner Lucía. We arrived some five minutes after María and Ellie," she said. "We'd agreed on the radio we would secure the main entrance to protect the integrity of the scene. My first view of the man was when I escorted the bishop to the chapel some ten minutes after taking my post, but I wasn't close enough to reach any conclusions about his condition."

"My first view," said Lucía. "Was when I was instructed to pick him up from the chapel, escort him to the car and drive him to the comisaría. When I handcuffed him and dragged him off his feet, I realized he stank worse than the corpse, but he hardly weighed anything and after a few moments of stiffness, walked without any problems at the same speed I did. In the car, we gave him some water which he gulped down gratefully and settled down in the back seat. Within seconds, he'd nodded off."

"On arrival at the comisaría," said Marta. "We woke him up gently and handed him over to the desk sergeant for processing. We then returned to the cathedral as instructed and controlled the main entrance until the pathologist had removed the body and cleaned up the scene. Afterward, we were posted outside the chapel until requested by the Inspector to arrest the grandson from the Red Cross detention center."

"What time?" said Prado.
"At nine thirty-five," said Lucía.
"Describe what happened," said Prado.
"It was a problem, sir," said Marta.

"In what way?" said Prado.

"We had to wake him up," said Lucía. "He also smelled but not as bad as his grandfather. He didn't understand what we were saying and was initially reluctant to accompany us. He leaped out of bed and tried to dodge past us, but we were prepared and drew our weapons. We handcuffed him and he came along quietly."

"And this is what is in your report?" said Prado. Both officers nodded. "Thank you," said Prado. "All four of you may return to normal duties."

Prado noticed the visible sense of relief among the four officers as he watched them stand and leave the room. He turned back to the others.

Tobón was avoiding eye contact. The sergeant smiled at him. The forensics officers and pathologist were regarding him with curious expressions.

For a moment, Prado was tempted to question Tobón next, but tactically, he decided it would be best to hear all the evidence first and save him until last. He turned and looked at the two forensics officers now dressed in casual clothes, black pants, and short sleeve blouses. Again, he was astounded by their classic Latin looks and resemblance to the four uniformed officers. He wondered who was making the recruiting decisions, Conchie or Tobón?"

"Now we'll move on to forensics," said Prado. "Who will start?"

"Another María, I'm afraid," said the one on the left. "They refer to me as María fea, ugly María."

"I can't imagine why," said Prado.

"My nose is a millimeter longer than María guapa, pretty María," she said. "But I don't mind. I have a boyfriend, guapa doesn't."

"The joys of colleagues' humor," said Prado. "In Málaga, we have five María's. We tried using the first letter of their surname to differentiate, but when they matched too, we switched to numbers."

Prado couldn't help noticing out of the corner of his eye Tobón appeared unhappy with this frivolity. Good, he thought. He checked his recorder was still working, looked at María fea, and nodded.

"My role is to record the scene in detail as we find it," she said. "I photograph everything first then search for smaller items not so visible such as threads, hairs, etc."

"Have you prepared a list of your findings?" said Prado.

"Everything," said María fea. "It's attached to my report along with copies of all the photos.

"Including an inventory of the chapel content and their condition?"

"Yes, sir."

"And images of the Arab and the deceased?" She nodded. Prado waved his recorder. "Yes, sir," she said.

"Did you form an opinion of the Arab?"

"He impressed me, sir. He must have been squatting for hours and I know even for most fit men it is an extremely uncomfortable position for more than a few minutes. I suspected he must have practiced yoga or something because his power of concentration and ability to shut out everything while chaos was all around him was remarkable."

"So, you had no concerns about his health?"

"He was elderly and frail, but not ready for his maker."

"All done?" said Prado

"Yes, sir."

"Thank you, María," said Prado moving his eyes towards her colleague and nodding.

"Catalina, sir," she said.

"Whew," said Prado.

"My job is collecting samples and prints," she said smiling.

"Which can be gruesome?" said Prado.

"After six years, I'm accustomed," said Catalina.

"Have you had the results back from this morning's harvest?"

"Yes. We have our lab in the comisaría, sir, and are completely self-sufficient."

"What did you find?"

"I found the dead priest's blood on the hands of the elder Arab and his clothing. The younger Arab's right thumb print was on the stem of one of the candlesticks. On one edge of the top rim of the same item was the blood of the dead priest along with a few of his hairs."

"And your conclusion?" said Prado.

"The young Arab hit the priest over the back of the head with the candlestick. After he was dead, he and his grandfather strapped him to the cross and shoved him down to the floor to make it look like a suicide."

"Anything else?"

"Fabric samples from the younger Arab's clothing were found on the table where the candlesticks were, along with a few of his hair strands. Blood from the priest was found on both their clothing."

"And where is this candlestick now?"

"It's been submitted into evidence and will be locked in the evidence room."

"This all sounds convincing," said Prado. "Were there any other samples?"

"Yes, the younger Arab's thumb print was found on

the entrance gate to the chapel and on the torch jammed into the railings. Both sets of prints were found on the cross and the leather straps pinning the priest's arms to the cross."

"Were there any other prints on the straps?" said Prado. Catalina paused as if she hadn't expected this question. "Well?" said Prado.

"Father Julián, sir," she said. "His prints were all over both straps."

"Where are the straps and cross now?"

"They are still in the pathology lab," said Catalina. "The cross and statue were too large for the evidence room, and it was thought best to keep them together. However, María has taken close-up photos of the dusted prints. Copies are in the evidence box."

"Were father Julián's prints on the cross?" said Prado watching her face. She couldn't disguise a quick flash of alarm and just for a second couldn't resist glancing in Tobón 's direction. He ignored her.

"Yes," she said.

"Was there any blood spatter on the priest?" said Prado.

"No," said Catalina. "Only stains from his blood pooled around his corpse."

"Was there any blood spatter elsewhere in the chapel?"

"No, sir. Why?"

"I'm just trying to establish where the father was standing when he was hit with the candlestick. I would have thought being hit with a metal object would have caused some spray and given us an idea where he was at the time?"

"My job is just to report what I find," said Catalina.

"Did you check anywhere else in the cathedral?"

"Yes, sir," said a relieved Catalina. "The public entrance, the door into the courtyard, and the flooring between the chapel and the main entrance but I found nothing relevant to this case."

"Did anything pique your curiosity?"

"There were traces of cement dust and a strong cleaning agent, which were particularly concentrated in a spot about a meter square in size some two meters directly outside the chapel gate."

"Did you speculate how cement dust might be in that exact spot?"

"No, sir but I was informed a major construction project was only completed late the previous evening. The builders could have spilled something."

"This is fully detailed in your report?"

"Yes, sir along with copies of the evidence."

"You were in close contact with the elder Arab when using your swabs on him, how did he seem to you?"

"María said it all, sir. I have nothing to add except his feet were disgusting, I couldn't bring myself to touch them even with my gloves."

"He had walked a long distance," said Prado.

"Yes, on the excuse of a pilgrimage to the cathedral," said Catalina. "If he was a devout Muslim, he would have removed his sandals and washed his feet before entering what he considered to be a Mosque."

"Interesting observation, thank you, Catalina, both of you may now leave but I will probably need to talk to you more as I progress with the inquiry. Please do not leave the city until informed my findings are complete."

"You have no right," shouted Tobón, standing and pointing his finger at Prado. "These girls are entitled to freedom of movement while not at work."

Prado returned Tobón 's aggressive glare. "There is no need to shout, Inspector, we are all adults here with a job to do, now sit down." Prado turned to the forensics officers. "Do you have any commitments out of town for the next few days?" Both shook their heads. "Do you have any objections to my request?"

"No, sir," they said together.

"Then we don't have a problem. You may go."

Prado waited until they had departed then looked at the pathologist.

"Dr. Jaime Paloma," said the overweight scientist adjusting his thick-lensed spectacles. "Which case would you like me to start with?"

"Am I to assume, doctor, you examined the priest and the dead Arab?"

"I carried out a full postmortem on both, inspector."

"Then start in the cathedral and take me through."

"I won't repeat what has been said concerning images and samples, except something is missing from the officers' reports."

"What do you mean?" said Tobón.

"On the floor next to the marble table were several fibers, which later proved to be from a monk's sackcloth robe. I compared some DNA samples on the robe against Father Julián's. They matched."

"Preposterous," said Tobón, standing and pointing his finger at the pathologist. "My girls never miss a thing."

"Sorry, inspector, not true. They might look pretty but are not competent. If you like I can send you a long list of everything they missed at other crime scenes."

"Gentlemen," intervened Prado glaring at Tobón.

"From the outset, I've been struggling to fathom the issue of the priest's nudity. Nobody can seriously imagine he walked naked from the palace to the chapel. He must have been wearing something. The presence of the father's robe is therefore logical. The question is, why wasn't it there when the inspector's team arrived. Where the hell is it now and who took it?"

Tobón sat down. The pathologist looked smug at his little victory.

"Carry on, doctor," said Prado.

"I also have to say I am mystified by the evidence on the candlestick. I gave each a cursory examination at the scene, but could see no hairs or blood on any of them"

"Once again," shouted Tobón pointing at Paloma. "You've fucked up. You should have looked closer at it. When Catalina examined it in her lab she found the print, hair, and blood immediately."

"She may well have done, but they were not present on the candlestick at the scene. Once again, you have been tampering with the evidence."

"And you forgot your glasses again," said Tobón looking meek but sitting back in his chair shaking his head in disgust."

"Enough, inspector," said Prado. "Dr. Paloma, do you wear spectacles all the time?"

"Only for close-up work."

"Were you wearing them at the scene?"

"Er… no, I'd left them in the car, but I had my magnifying glass."

"Did you check the candlestick with it?"

"No."

"I see. What was the cause of death for Father Julián?"

"He was killed outright by a heavy blow to his head. I won't bore you with the science but something heavy cracked the back of his skull forcing several fractured bone fragments deep into his brain. There were also severe injuries to his forehead and nose, but they didn't play any role in killing him."

"Could the something heavy have been the candlestick?"

"It could have been but up until now, I hadn't considered it."

"Did you examine the candlesticks more thoroughly later?"

"I decided they were not material to the investigation and left them at the scene."

"What did you think when you heard Catalina's report?"

"As I said earlier, completely mystified. There was nothing on or around the wound to Father Julián's skull linking the candlestick to the killer blow. I would have expected some metal traces or flakes of wax but found nothing."

"Did anything in the wound indicate what object was used to strike the killer blow?"

"All I could find were timber splinters from the cross and rust from an iron bolt head."

"Tell me about this bolt head," said Prado.

"It fixed the top of the cross to the wall mounting. It was a substantial item made of forged iron some two hundred years ago, the circular head of which was about three centimeters deep and in diameter. The spindle was some twelve centimeters long and went through a hole in the timber, where it stuck out four centimeters, the end of which would have fixed it to the wall bracket. There are photos in the file."

"Is there any possibility," said Prado. "The father could have unbolted the cross, strapped himself to it, heaved it onto his back, and fell forward down onto the stone floor?"

"The father was an extremely fit and strong man in his early forties so yes, I would say it could have been possible but unlikely."

"Why?"

"There are easier methods to end one's life with a better likelihood of success. Using the cross and straps meant several things could go wrong."

"I agree," shouted Tobón. "The cross weighs over two hundred kilos. Not even an Olympic champion could have moved it."

"Thank you, Inspector," said Prado continuing to watch Paloma. "You'll have your turn later."

Paloma glared at Tobón irritated by the man. That there was no love lost between these two was obvious, thought Prado.

"Anything else you can tell us about the father?" said Prado.

"One more thing," said Paloma. "Shortly before he died, the father had been the recipient of anal sex.

"You never mentioned it to me," shouted Tobón.

"And you never read the report. As usual, inspector, you were bullying me for instant answers before I had finished my work. It was the final part of the father's body I checked after you had left the lab."

"How recent was this anal sex?" said Prado.

"A condom had been used so no sperm was present," said Paloma. "I would estimate by the condition of the condom lubricant and the dilation of the rectum, it was shortly before he died."

"Would you say it was consensual?" said Prado.

"There were no signs of restraint, so I would say he was a willing participant."

"What about the father?" said the sergeant. "Could you tell if he had also worn a condom?"

"No, he hadn't. I concluded he was a passive recipient."

"A final farewell, perhaps?" said the sergeant.

"Did you trace any DNA of his partner?" said Prado.

"None."

"No perspiration or pubic hair?" said Tobón.

"Nothing, just the condom lubricant."

"Were there any signs of his sexuality in his quarters or on his computer?" said Prado.

"Nothing," said Tobón.

"What about his contacts?" said Prado.

"We haven't found his phone," said the sergeant. "However, the dean gave us his number and we've requested a call log from his provider. They can't send it until tomorrow."

"For now, though," said Prado. "A gay lover could be a suspect. Does this change any of your conclusions concerning the Arabs, Inspector?"

"Of course not. The evidence against them is overwhelming, plus," said Tobón barely able to hold back his triumphant expression as he extracted two pieces of paper from his jacket pocket and waved them in the air. "I have these."

"Confessions?" said Prado.

"Signed and dated."

"Were they witnessed?"

"By me, sir," said the sergeant.

"Can I see a video transcript of both interviews?"

"Of course," said Tobón.

"Was an official translator present at all times?" said Prado.

"Most of the time," said Tobón. "She had to slip out to the restroom on two occasions."

"Leaving you alone with the suspects?" said Prado.

"Right, but as I can't speak Arabic, nothing was said during these pauses."

"Was the recorder turned off during her absences?" said Prado.

"Yes."

"Do you speak French, inspector?"

"No."

"Sergeant?"

"Yes, sir," said the sergeant looking down at the floor.

"I need to watch the interviews and read the transcripts before we can make any further progress," said Prado. "Dr. Paloma, tell me how the Arab died."

"My assistant and I were summoned from my lab at nine fifty-five, to attend a cell in the secure area which is below this room. A prisoner had been found dead. I took my camera and medical bag, and we went down to the cells. On arrival, I went into the security office outside the cell block and ran through the camera footage monitoring the cell doors. I didn't see anything untoward so didn't think it necessary to collect prints or samples from any doors."

"Had the camera been tampered with?"

"There were a couple of fuzzy spots, but the equipment is ancient and unreliable, so I was accustomed."

Prado mentally added the security footage to his to-do list.

"The security officer opened the door to the Arab's

cell. We entered and saw him lying on his bunk dressed in an orange overall with bare feet. I checked him over and confirmed he was dead. I took photographs and we transferred him to a body bag, after which he was wheeled to my lab where I cut off his overalls and checked him over. Other than several blisters on his feet, I found a few mild bruises on each bicep. I opened him up and it was immediately obvious he'd had a severe heart attack and died instantly."

"Any thoughts on what may have brought on the attack?"

"What concerned me was the expression on his face. It looked pained and angry, and his fists were clenched tightly. I unclenched them and found his fingernails had dug deep into his skin. I assumed he'd been enraged over something, which had caused him to hyperventilate and triggered heart seizure."

"Anything to add?"

"No. Will you need me again?" said Paloma.

"Depending on my discoveries," said Prado. "Will you be around?"

"I'm the senior brother of Hermandad de la Vera Cruz, so I'll be busy with the procession tomorrow but for the remainder of the week, I'll be at your disposal."

"Thank you, Doctor," said Prado turning to Tobón and the sergeant. "I propose we resume our conversation later after I've read the files and seen the interview tapes. Before I go, having heard the officers' reports, is there anything you'd like to comment on?"

"No," said Tobón. "Other than to say your investigation is a complete waste of time. We have no secrets here. This is just another of our many successful investigations and in this one there is no case to answer. The Arab died of natural causes. I suggest for everyone's sake you wrap it up and go home to your wife. Ronda, isn't it?"

Prado glared at Tobón, unflinching.

Tobón grinned, helped the sergeant to her feet, and left the room.

10

Have I just been warned off? Thought Prado as he left the room and headed down to the cells, his pulse thumping furiously. And why had not one single person mentioned the event on Wednesday? Conchie must know about it and maybe Tobón, but they acted as if it doesn't exist. Yet it's probably the main reason behind the father's death. And how did the Arabs become involved? Did they just happen to be there and were a convenient solution, or were they targeted? Maybe they are deliberately keeping the event from me, so I focus only on the death in custody? He shook his head to clear out the clutter swimming around and at the bottom of the steps knocked on the security office door. He rubbed his earlobe while he waited. Yet another young and beautiful female officer opened the door and looked at him.

"DI Prado," he said showing his ID. "I'm the investigating officer for the death in custody."

"Officer Elena Tobón," she said frowning. "How can I help?"

"Are you related to DI Tobón?" he said.

"His niece," she said.

"I need to see the cell block footage for three hours up to and including the removal of the deceased prisoner this morning," he said.

She opened the door and Prado went into what was a tiny cubicle. She pulled a chair from behind the door and parked it next to hers. "Please take a seat, sir. It will only take a second to set up the recording. Is high-speed OK for you?"

"Fine," said Prado.

"Have you worked here long?" said Prado while she clicked the mouse.

"I started a few months ago," she said concentrating on the screen.

"What enticed you into police work? Your uncle?"

"I suppose so, but I love technology. My degree was in computer sciences. My uncle just persuaded me to put my skills to solving crime rather than designing games or websites."

"And they started you here? Bit of a letdown?"

"To be honest, yes, but then I found trying to make this antiquated system work properly was challenging."

"So, now you know all about it?"

"Inside and out, sir. Here we go. Shall I set it running?"

"Please."

"You want me to stay? Only I fancy a smoke?"

"Just show me how to stop, start, slow, and reverse," he said grabbing the mouse. "I'll be fine."

"This is the speed and direction control," she said moving his hand holding the mouse. "Click when you want to change."

Elena picked up her bag and left closing the door behind her. He clicked start and settled back in the uncomfortable chair as the images flashed by. He ran it through which took three minutes and spotted nothing out of sorts except for two occasions when the picture went fuzzy. In the end, he looked at the total real runtime. Three hours and four minutes.

He wound it back to the start and ran it again watching the time clock. He noted the timer stopped during the patches and restarted from zero when the clear picture resumed. He timed each fuzzy patch, both lasted five seconds. He ran through again and added up the three separate sections of images. He added the patches to the sections which came to less than the runtime. Why? He thought. Perhaps Phillip can make something of it.

Prado inserted his pen drive into the security computer and copied the file. He tapped his fingers on the desk while looking through the small window in the door hoping Elena didn't return before the recording had finished. He heard voices approaching, but the copy needed a few more seconds until it was done. The door handle was pressed down, and the door started to open. He reached out and grabbed the drive but then the door paused as the voices continued chatting. He left it running watching the door like a hawk. It was done. He palmed it into his hand and sat back in the chair as Elena said goodbye to someone then came in, a faint scent of cigarette smoke wafting in after her.

"Did you see anything?" she said.

"Nothing out of the ordinary. Who else has access to this system?"

"Everyone in the station," she said looking relieved. "Why?"

"So, anybody could tamper with the footage?"

"Yes, but only a few would know how to and cover their tracks."

"You, for example?"

"Yes," she looked down. "And half a dozen others."

"How often do you pop out for a smoke?"

She looked down, ashamed. "Once an hour for ten minutes."

"So, anyone who knows your routine could pop in while you're out and you would be none the wiser?" She nodded. "Could you make a list of all officers who could manipulate this system while I have a quick peek at the grandson, can you give me his cell key, please?"

She went over to a cupboard hanging on the wall behind the door, twisted the numbers on the combination lock, and took out a key.

"Cell five," she said handing it over and glancing at the telephone.

"If you want to check with your supervisor," said Prado pocketing his pen drive. "It will be fine."

"You'll have to press the buzzer for me to let you out of the block," she said picking up the phone.

"Thanks."

Prado headed out into the corridor, opened the outer door to the block, and went along to cell number five. He unlocked the door and went in. A young, small, skinny man barely twenty years old with a sparse beard, dressed in an orange overall with bare feet scrambled up from the bunk he was lying on. He looked terrified but more significantly to Prado, he was puny like the picture he'd seen of his grandfather.

"Do you speak any Spanish?" said Prado.

"Only Arabic," said the man in badly accented Spanish, his voice trembling.

Prado pointed to himself. "Prado."

"Faraq. Faraq Kamal."

Prado checked the cell for a camera or microphone but saw nothing. He took out his phone and called his translator, Amanda.

"Leon," she said after a few rings. "How are you?"

"Fine," he said. "Yourself? Good, listen, sorry to disturb your Sunday and I know you must be busy with wedding preparations, but I need to talk with a young man in Moroccan Arabic. His name is Faraq Kamal and I'm here in his cell at Córdoba Police Station. He's been charged with murder. All I want at this stage is for you to introduce me to him and say we have been called in from Málaga to investigate the death of his grandfather. Then ask him outright if he killed the priest on his own or with his grandfather."

"He killed a priest," said Amanda. "Where?"

"In the cathedral. However, I suspect he is innocent, and he has been bullied to confess. I'll hand you over now."

Prado passed the phone over to Faraq who was unaccustomed to such devices and wasn't sure what to do. He tentatively put it to his ear. Prado watched him as he listened to Amanda speak. Slowly his expression changed from terror to hopeful to angry. He spoke quickly and animatedly for several seconds before passing the phone back to Prado.

"What did he say?" said Prado.

"Whilst he appreciates you want to help him," said Amanda. "Frankly he doesn't trust anyone and won't divulge any information."

"Has he seen or been offered a lawyer?"

"He wouldn't say. Leon, listen, until this man has been treated with some respect, he won't say a word. So far as I can make out from his rather garbled explanation, he's had no food, has been screamed at and bullied to sign something he doesn't understand because he hoped he would be fed in return. He sounds terrified of the police."

"How do you suggest I gain his confidence?"

"Bring him a meal and talk with him man-to-man."

"Difficult."

"You need my help," said Amanda. "I can leave now and arrive in about two hours."

"Are you sure?"

"Yes, it's a good excuse to escape wedding discussions."

"There is one problem."

"What?"

"It's Palm Sunday."

"Of course, processions."

"Tell you what," said Prado. "Head off as soon as you can and by the time you're about to arrive, I'll have thought of a solution."

"On my way."

"Thanks, Amanda, and say Hola to Phillip."

Prado ended the call, pocketed his phone, looked at Faraq smiled, and nodded. Then he reached out his hand slowly, patted the young man's shoulder, and let himself out. He turned at the door and smiled. Faraq nodded back, a faint look of hope in his dark brown eyes.

Elena buzzed him out and slipped him a piece of paper.

"The list of tech-savvy officers," she said.

"Thanks," said Prado and headed up the stairs.

After he'd left, Elena picked up the phone. When someone answered she said.

"He's gone."

She listened to the reply.

"Yes, I gave him the list," she said.
She listened again.
"No, your name wasn't on it."
She ended the call and shrugged.

11

Amanda returned her phone to the kitchen island at Phillip's villa and sighed.

"Something wrong?" said Phillip, shaggy blond hair in need of a trim. He loaded the dishwasher with the lunchtime dishes.

"Prado needs my urgent help in Córdoba," she said playing with her long dark hair.

"Why?"

"A Moroccan Arab is accused of murder and doesn't speak any other languages."

"Surely, they have a translator?"

"Yes, but it's more complicated. In short, Prado is in a hostile environment and doesn't have an interpreter he can trust. Do you mind if I go?"

"Of course not," he said gazing at her through his ice-blue eyes. "After a week of intense wedding arrangements, you could do with a change of scene."

"Not worried about me being swept off to a harem in Marrakesh?"

"You'll be with Leon, why would I?"

"Callous brute, you don't care about me."

Phillip stood, his tall, athletic frame towering over

her. He put his arms around her waist, lifted her onto the island, and moved between her legs.

"I love it when you're mean to me," he said gazing at her elfin face and hazel eyes. They kissed.

"You two at it again," said a young boy of nearly eight, running in through the terrace door followed by three young blond girls ranging from five to ten.

"No peace for the wicked," said Amanda jumping down. "Darling Sasha, I have to go out for the afternoon, and I was just saying farewell to your father."

"Yeh, yeh," said Sasha. A mini version of his dad. "In which case you won't mind if I go next door and play at the farm with my cousins?"

"Sure, auntie Glenda won't mind?" said Phillip.

"No," said Anna the eldest, her long blond hair flying left and right as she shook her head. "We'll be out in the fields picking the last of the strawberries."

"And eating half of them," said Amanda.

"What do you mean?" said Louisa, at seven, a smaller version of her sister. "We've just had Uncle Phillip's scrummy barbecue."

"Yes, but you only ate half the burger," said Amanda.

Tina, the youngest at five stood with her thumb in her mouth watching the banter.

"All right then," said Amanda. "But please don't wipe your hands on your t-shirts. The strawberry juice will stain them permanently."

"Don't worry, Mom," said Sasha. "They have gloves and aprons, we'll be fine."

Phillip looked at Amanda.

She glowed with pride. Mom was a new progression.

Amanda wasn't Sasha's birth mother. Unaware to Phillip, he'd been born post-divorce after Valentina; his ex had moved back to her native Russia. She'd recently brought Sasha to Spain and left him with his father before going off to a hospice to die of pancreatic cancer. She'd wanted Sasha to remember her as the joyful woman she was, and not some miserable, wasted skeleton. Amanda had readily stepped in and the two had bonded incredibly quickly. When the time came, they'd all scattered Valentina's ashes over Phillip's rose bed.

Amanda changed from her shorts and t-shirt into a long black dress covering her shoulders and arms, packed a head scarf into her handbag, and went out to her car. They each took turns kissing her goodbye and watched as she climbed into her silver-gray Prius, backed out of the drive, and headed off toward the main road down to Nerja.

The Córdoba trip was a perfect excuse to leave the house without any difficult questions. Translating for Prado wasn't the only item on her agenda. Amanda stopped by the post boxes at the entrance to the urbanization and picked up her phone. She checked which was the duty chemist in town then headed off to the one by the medical center. She parked on an empty disabled bay and jogged over to the shop where she purchased a small item. She trotted back and took off to meet Prado.

She hadn't said anything to Phillip because she wasn't sure. The pregnancy test kit should confirm one way or the other. She'd stop for a coffee at a service station and find out.

She had no reservations about being pregnant on her wedding day, at least she wouldn't be showing.

Having a baby had been her lifetime dream since she was a teenager. She'd just never had a spare moment to meet the right man being too busy working as a videographer dashing all over Spain doing daft things like running with the bulls in Pamplona with a camera mounted on her chest. If the test was positive, she'd be ecstatic and knew Phillip would treasure becoming a father even though at forty-four he was maybe a little old for babies. But she loved seeing how he was with Sasha and his nieces and was confident although a little one might bring him some disturbed nights overall; he would treasure the experience. A little person created by the love they had for each other. A tear rolled down her cheek.

"Stop it, you soppy bitch," she said out loud. "You're not pregnant yet."

She thought back to when it all began, which seemed like yesterday. Meeting Phillip had come out of nowhere. Almost a year earlier, she'd been making a documentary of the San Isidro Festival in the gardens at Nerja Caves when she inadvertently filmed an abduction. It wasn't until she ran it through her editing software back at her apartment in central Málaga, she spotted a young blond girl being forced into a van. She reported it to the police the next morning and showed her film to Prado, then went with him to the girl's apartment in Nerja where she met Phillip. He was a friend of the abducted English girl and had translated for Prado on an earlier case.

Although he was ten years her senior, she felt a connection taking root while they helped Prado find the abductors.

Phillip ran an information website about Spain with his American business partner, Richard. They started working together. Richard retired so they merged interests. Six months later they were living in her apartment during the week and his villa at the weekend. At last, the two busy but lonely souls could share their mutual interests and now each other.

"If someone is up there," she mumbled to herself as the kilometers sped by. "Thank you."

Ninety minutes later she pulled off into a service station, topped up with gas, and went into the café. She read the test instructions while enjoying a coffee then slipped into the ladies to take care of business.

The result took five minutes.

It was positive.

She did a little jig, returned to her car beaming like a Cheshire cat, and phoned Prado.

"Sorry I haven't called you," he said. "Where are you?"

"About an hour away."

"Then add the Eurostars Palace Hotel to your Satnav and stop outside reception. I'll be watching for you and will arrange to park in their underground lot. We'll have to walk to the police station and back, but we'll see the procession on the way which is an amazing sight."

"Where are you?"

"I'm visiting my parents."

"Oh, then I'll leave you to it. See you shortly."

Amanda cut the call, started the engine, and rejoined the highway.

On each side of the road, stretching as far as the eye could see, were the lush green vineyards of Morilla and Montiles, famous for their Manzanilla, an excellent alternative to the sherry wines of Jerez de la Frontera. Normally her videographer's eye would be scouring the landscape for unique perspectives but today she was dreaming about the patter of tiny feet. Never had focus, lighting, or translations for Prado been so far from her mind.

12

There was no sign of Prado as Amanda stopped outside the hotel entrance. But before she had even stopped her engine, a uniformed porter was knocking on her window. She opened it a little and looked at him with a puzzled expression.

"Señora Salisbury?" said the porter.

She nodded.

"Inspector Prado asked me to meet you, take the keys and park your car. He's waiting inside."

"Fine," she said collecting her bag and jacket. The porter opened the car door, she clambered out and handed over the keys.

"The car will be in the underground lot and the keys with the receptionist," said the porter as he climbed in.

Amanda left him to it and went through the lobby door. Prado was sitting on a sofa in the far corner with a briefcase next to him. He was on the phone and beckoned for her to join him. By the time she reached him, he'd ended the call and stood to meet her. They hugged and exchanged cheek kisses.

"You're looking radiant," he said. "Looking forward to the wedding?"

"Thank you and yes, but I'm enjoying this little break from the constant questions and decisions."

"I'm sure Phillip knows exactly what you want by now."

"I would hope so. How is Inma?

"She's picking up her outfit tomorrow, so champing at the bit."

"Have you seen it?"

"She wants to surprise me."

"And you?"

"My outfit?"

"Yes."

"Nothing new but have no fear, I'll be as dapper as always but enough banter. I want to assure you this shouldn't take long. We'll have you back home in the briefest of moments."

"No worry. Any developments since we last spoke?"

"Let's head off to the police station. I'll tell you about it on the way."

They went out the hotel door and headed for the crowds on the opposite pavement. After they'd squeezed into the boisterous throng, Prado leaned over. "Put your arm in mine then you'll be closer. I don't want to be shouting police business."

She smiled at him, slid her arm through his, and momentarily leaned her head on his shoulder. "There," he said. "Practice for Saturday with your father." She laughed. "Before you leave, remind me to hand over a pen drive with a video. It's the footage of the security camera monitoring the cell block at the police station. Could you give it to Phillip? It may have been tampered with, and I want him to apply his usual magic to see if he can reveal anything."

"Sounds intriguing?"

"Everything about this case is beguiling. I have a dead priest with an unidentifiable gay lover. A graffiti artist thought it a good idea to spray Mezquita on the cathedral wall. An elderly Arab who sat by the body for hours then died in custody. His young grandson has been charged with killing the priest. The bishop, a friend of the Minister of the Interior picked up the graffiti artist's spray can but forgot to give it to the police. A prima donna Detective Inspector who resents my intrusion. A gaggle of beautiful women police officers all with classic Latin looks, and a police chief I used to go to school with still fancies her chances. It's a mess and has me dashing all over the place."

"After a year working with you and Phillip," said Amanda, "solving a conspiracy of abusers, illegal gamblers, religious artifact thieves, and forged Picasso paintings, it sounds a cinch."

"Ojala, if only. At least, only two foreigners are involved with this one."

"Has the boy been fed?"

"No, but in my briefcase, I have a portion of my mother's homemade lamb stew, some bread, and a bottle of mineral water."

"Don't they feed prisoners here in Córdoba?"

"They have no catering facilities and expect families to take care of their own."

"To be fair, I guess most arrested are locals?"

"Probably."

"I take it you don't agree with the local Inspector as to who killed the priest?"

"I concede the evidence against the Arabs is overwhelming, but the bishop is adamant the grandfather was a kindly, God-fearing man whose only crime was to not leave the dead priest alone. He also believes the old man when he said the grandson was in bed at the Red Cross detention center."

"Have you checked the security footage at the Red Cross?"

"Not only do they have no cameras, but their security is so lax; a flock of sheep could have wandered in and out and nobody would have noticed. Detainees can come and go as they please and so long as they return at nighttime, no alarm is raised. Many abscond before their asylum applications can be processed."

"But most are sent back home before they can even apply."

"If they have no papers, can't speak the language, or feed themselves, they stand no chance of being approved. At least they know where they stand and aren't kept hanging around."

"Only to try again as soon as they get off the plane in Tangiers. Were they both earmarked for instant deportation?"

"They'd only been there less than a day. It's the weekend, they hadn't even been interviewed."

"It will be interesting what the boy has to say about life as an undocumented migrant."

"More important to me is what Inspector Tobón said to him."

"What should I ask him?"

"I need to know where he was last night and if he has an alibi. If he can't prove his whereabouts at the time of the priest's death, we're stuffed."

"What evidence is there against him?"

"He signed a confession, so the evidence is secondary. However, they have his prints on the stem of a candlestick with the priest's blood and hair on one end. Fabric samples from his clothing were found on the table where the candlesticks were, along with a few of his hair strands. Blood from the priest was found on his clothing. His prints were found on the entrance gate to the chapel and on the torch jammed into the railings. Both sets of Arabs' prints were found on the carving and the leather straps fixing the priest's arms to the cross."

"Sounds convincing."

"It does but first I need to hear the interview recordings. Then we'll go talk with the boy."

"Should I ask him if anybody had taken hair samples or if his clothing had been removed?"

"Both he and his grandfather were wearing cellblock overalls. Their clothing will be festering in the evidence room."

"So, any hairs could have come from their clothing?"

"If we are assuming all the evidence has been fabricated, then yes. I would imagine such unwashed items would contain several hairs."

"What are you trying to prove?"

"All I want is the truth," said Prado. "Despite my abhorrence of this arrogant inspector, I have no agenda."

They were forced to stop and watch a squad of armed soldiers from the Spanish Legion twirling their weapons in unison before standing to attention and singing their regimental anthem in surprisingly harmonious voices. To Amanda, such a cultural display by a ruthless team of killers seemed incongruous in the middle of a religious event. At least they could sing, she thought.

They made their way to the river where Amanda released Prado's arm and they could walk more quickly among a thinner crowd.

On arrival at the comisaría reception, Prado was handed a key and a plastic card by the desk sergeant. A burly, seasoned veteran with heavy jowls and stinking of tobacco.

"This is for your office," he said. "The passkey is to access any room in the building."

"Including the evidence room?" The sergeant nodded. "I'll also need a visitor's pass for my translator," said Prado.

"I wasn't told about her," said the sergeant.

"Well, I'm telling you now. Feel free to check with the comisario principal. I'm sure she'll be delighted to be disturbed for such a trivial matter."

The sergeant stared coldly-eyed at Prado, nodded, and picked up a pass.

"Name?" he said.

"She's American," said Prado. "Give me a pen and a scrap of paper and I'll note it down for you."

After several sighs and mutual glaring, a handwritten pass and clip were handed over and Amanda pinned it to her dress.

"Where is the evidence room?" said Prado.

"On the lower floor, next to the cellblock," said the sergeant.

Prado nodded and headed for the stairwell to the left of the reception desk. Amanda trailed after him.

They walked down the stairs and paused outside a green-painted door. All the doors were painted green. A lopsided sign stuck off-center on the upper part of the door said, 'Evidence Room'.

"Here it is," said Prado swiping his card against the

reader.

The door clicked, he pushed, and they went into a small anteroom.

"Can I help you?" said another seasoned officer from behind a sliding window in the wall opposite the door, his glasses perched on the end of his nose.

"I want the files on the two Arabs charged this morning," said Prado.

"Pass please," said the officer.

Prado handed it over. The office inserted it in a reader, looked at his screen, and passed the card back to Prado. The officer turned and walked to the back of the room between ceiling-high racks jammed with files and boxes. He stopped, perused the file numbers, bent over, and heaved a box from the middle row. He brought it back and placed it with a thump on the table then pointed to a booth to the side of the waiting area. "You can only access the file here. If you need to view any digital materials, use the laptop in the booth with headphones. Replace everything in the box exactly as you find it."

The officer slid the box through the window. Prado picked it up surprised by its weight and headed toward a booth. Amanda opened the door; they went in and closed the curtain behind them.

Inside the booth were a desk, a laptop, and two sets of headphones already plugged in. Two plastic chairs faced the bare, cream-painted wall. Prado placed the box on the desk, lifted off the lid, and leaned it against the wall. He flicked through the pile of contents wondering what was so heavy. There were sealed clear plastic envelopes containing clothing, a candlestick, photographs, samples, and printed reports. On top was an envelope containing a DVD labeled 'Interviews'. He tried lifting the candlestick with one hand but had to use two.

"This must be solid gold," he said.

Amanda picked it up and stroked the gleaming metal.

"It has to be over five kilos," she said. "And worth a fortune."

Prado replaced it in the box picked up the DVD envelope, scribbled his name on the label on the front along with time and date, and opened it.

"Is the laptop on?" said Prado.

Amanda sat down and pressed the return key. The screen lit up and requested log-in details. Prado took out his wallet and removed the comisario's codes. He logged in and brought up the Arab's files. A copy of the interviews was already online. He clicked on the grandfather's file and waited for the video to start.

"What the?" he said when presented with a fuzzy screen.

He fast-forwarded all the way through but saw nothing but blackness. He tried the grandson's file, and it was the same. Amanda inserted the DVD into the side of the laptop, two files were listed. Prado clicked on the first one, put the headphones on, and sat back in the chair. Both files were blank. He rummaged through the box.

"What are you looking for?" said Amanda.

"Typed versions of the transcripts," said Prado looking frustrated. He completed his search and looked at Amanda. "Nothing," he said.

"Can we identify who has accessed this box or any of the envelopes?" said Amanda.

Prado examined each envelope for signatures but there were none.

"What about the database?" said Amanda.

Prado browsed through each file.

Nobody had accessed the files but more worryingly the uploading had all been in the name of the comisario principal. He shook his head at Amanda.

"I don't believe Conchie would knowingly upload corrupted files or any that might have been tampered with. We've been well and truly stitched up here."

"There's still the boy," said Amanda.

"Let's go and see him," said Prado with a nasty taste in his mouth.

They packed everything back into the box, replaced the lid, returned it to the scowling evidence room officer, and went out.

Prado knocked on the door of the cellblock security office. A young male officer opened the window and raised his eyebrows.

"Key for cell five," said Prado with a sense of foreboding.

"There is nobody in the cells at the moment," said the officer shaking his head.

"What do you mean?" said Prado. "Where is the young Arab?"

"He's been transferred to the main prison," said the officer.

"I gave strict instructions he was to be held here until my return," said Prado.

"I know nothing about any instructions," said the man shrugging. "Two prison officers turned up about an hour ago, presented the correct paper for his transfer, so I collected him from his cell and handed him over."

"Can you describe these officers?" said Prado.

"Sorry, just two men in prison uniform."

"Would they be on camera?"

"They came in and went out through the rear entrance. The door camera should have them."

"Can we look at the footage on your computer?"

"Of course, hold on while I bring it up."

Prado watched him as he sat at the machine and accessed the database. He found the right camera and set it running.

"Here's the van arriving," said the officer. "I'll slow it down."

The screen went black.

"That is weird," said the officer.

"What?" said Prado.

"I'll run it again," said the officer. "There is the van then nothing for twelve minutes. When it restarts the van has gone."

"Someone deleted it?"

"Looks like it. I'll check who."

The officer switched to the log screen.

"It was deleted by the comisario principal two minutes after the van departed," he said.

"You're sure about that?"

He zoomed in on the log.

"There's her name and authorization code."

"Thank you. Do you have the transfer paper?"

"Yes," said the officer reaching behind him. He passed the single A4 slip through the window. Prado glanced through the text. He read the transfer destination.

"Centro Penitenciario in Sevilla?" he said.

"Correct, sir. Córdoba is full.

"Do you have a spare copy?"

"No, sir, but you can photograph it with your cellphone."

"Hold it up."

Prado took out his phone, lined up the lens with the paper in the officer's slightly trembling hand, and took several shots.

"Thanks," he said and handed it back.

As they left the corridor, Prado exchanged glances with Amanda.

"Stitched again," she said.

13

Going up the stairs to reception, Amanda thought Prado was about to explode. She'd never seen him so angry. Before he went searching for someone to slam into a wall, she grabbed his arm and gestured they should go outside. She led him into the car park.

"This is a deliberate attempt at obstructing my inquiry," he said, his face bright red.

"Yes," said Amanda. "But the young officer is not to blame, he's just following protocol. I suggest the best thing we can do is drive to Sevilla and interview the Arab. Hopefully, now he's away from Córdoba, he might be less frightened and more cooperative. This could work better for us?"

"Yes, but you have to be home," said Prado, his rage dissipating as quickly as it had arrived.

"Don't worry about me. Phillip will understand."

"Are you sure? Don't you have things to do for the wedding and your guide to Spain?"

"Yes, but nothing Phillip can't handle."

"Then let's go."

"Shouldn't we inform the comisario principal that somebody is using her name and authorization code?"

said Amanda.

"Probably, but we don't know if it was her or someone abusing her authority, either way, I'm unsure whether I can trust her or not. The less we tell anyone, the safer our young Arab will be."

They walked out of the police station and headed toward the hotel. The procession was still under way as the sun set over the river, but they avoided the area around the cathedral and twenty minutes later arrived at the hotel.

Prado collected his car keys from reception, and they took the elevator to the underground garage.

"Here," said Prado throwing his keys to Amanda as they approached his Mercedes. "You drive, I have calls to make."

They jumped in and headed off to Sevilla.

When they were on the A-4 motorway, Prado took out a magnetic blue light from the glove compartment, switched it on, opened his window, and placed it on the roof. He nodded at her. She pressed her foot to the floor, her pulse racing as she accelerated to over a hundred and sixty kilometers per hour. Prado watched her for a minute or two and seeing she was more than comfortable, called his boss.

"How did it go with the bishop?" said el jefe.

"There were several surprises," said Prado. "However, I'm not disturbing your Sunday evening for a complete update. We have a problem needing urgent action at higher levels."

"Go on."

"The young Arab has been charged with first-degree murder based on a signed confession and some convincing physical evidence. Someone though has tampered with the videos of his interview, so I have no way to compare his signed confession with what he said to Inspector Tobón and his translator. Therefore, it's crucial I talk with the boy face-to-face. Amanda spoke to him on the phone while I was with him in his cell, but he refused to say anything. He doesn't trust anyone, especially the police. Amanda kindly agreed to come up and help me talk with him. When she arrived, we discovered the comisaría doesn't have any catering facilities for remand prisoners, so he'd been transferred to the prison. However, Córdoba jail was full, so they sent him to Sevilla. He left about ninety minutes ago."

"Amanda's with you?"

"She's driving."

"What do you need me to do?"

"Don't speak with anyone in Córdoba, I don't want them knowing what we are up to. Can you call the prison governor in Sevilla and confirm the boy is on his way? If so, when he arrives can they delay his admission procedures until I have talked with him?"

"You're on your way?"

"We'll be arriving in about an hour."

"I'll call you back."

"Thanks."

"There's a service station coming up," said Amanda when Prado had ended his call. "I need the restroom and something to eat. Do we have time now for a ten-minute break?"

Prado looked at his watch. It was nearly nine o'clock. The sun was long gone, and a full moon was rising in the star-studded sky behind them.

"Good idea," he said. "We can spare a few minutes."

He opened the window, pulled the blue light off the roof, and switched it off.

Prado topped up the tank while Amanda used the services then bought some snacks and mineral water. Five minutes later, they were back on the motorway but left the blue light in the glove compartment. Prado had just taken his first bite of the serrano ham and brie roll when his phone rang.

"Any news?" he mumbled.

"What?" said el jefe.

"Sorry, eating," said Prado.

"Where are you?"

"About forty-five minutes from the prison."

"I've just finished speaking with the governor," said el jefe, his voice sounding even more clipped than usual. "He has some disturbing news."

"And?" said Prado.

"Earlier this afternoon, one of their transfer vans with its two officers didn't return from taking several prisoners to another jail on the other side of Sevilla. The van's onboard tracking device had been deactivated and the officers' phones were untraceable. It took a while to realize they hadn't returned so it has only just been reported. The Sevilla police have only just started looking at traffic camera recordings but so far have seen nothing. Do you have a copy of the transfer paper?"

"I took a photo."

"Email it to me. I'll forward it to the prison for their comments."

"Straight away. While I work out how to email it, something the bishop said adds more confusion to this case."

"What?"

"The bishop is close friends with the dead priest's family, he officiated at their youngest daughter Irena's wedding. It was agreed with Tobón the bishop would inform them about their son's death. During their difficult conversation, the priest's father revealed Irena was taken from her bed three nights ago and returned this morning to their doorstep in a comatose condition. She'd been drugged and remembers nothing since going to bed. The Sevilla police were informed and organized a massive search for her. Now here is where the confusion sets in. The dead priest was informed about her disappearance last Friday but never told the bishop or any work colleagues. The bishop mentioned it to Tobón who said he would contact the Sevilla police to inquire about the case. However, Tobón never said anything to me about it, and there is nothing in the reports I have so far had time to read."

"How can I help?"

"Call the comisario principal in Sevilla. Find out as much as you can about Irena's ordeal and what conversations they had with the Córdoba police about it."

"No problem. Will you still go to the prison?"

"No point but while I'm near Sevilla, I want to meet the dead priest's father and talk with the police chief."

"You want to meet them in Sevilla?"

"Preferably on the outskirts to avoid the procession traffic. Could you set up the meetings and text me through the details?"

"Does it have to be tonight?"

"Yes, I have an important meeting with the bishop at the cathedral crime scene at eight in the morning," said Prado remembering Father Julián's message about lives in danger. "And whatever happens, I mustn't miss it."

14

"Fuck," said Prado banging his fist on the dashboard. "The prison governor at Sevilla knows nothing about any remand transfers ordered by Córdoba. However, one of their vans along with two guards disappeared earlier this afternoon. Whoever collected the boy could have used this missing van and the guards' uniforms. What the hell is going on, Amanda?"

"You're being led a merry dance around Andalucía which is keeping you away from what started all this."

"The death of the priest."

"Exactly. Where is the spray can now?"

"In my briefcase."

"The prints might point you in the right direction."

"They could but I've had no time to scan them. What do you think was the point of daubing 'Mezquita' on the side of the cathedral?"

"It's an ongoing soap opera about what to call the building," said Amanda. "It's been playing for decades. I've done several articles over the years, and it still isn't resolved. Until recently, the church and most brotherhoods have ignored its Islamic past and insisted on calling it a cathedral. However, recent thinking by the church in response to the global trend to embrace diversity is to rename it a Mosque-Cathedral. However, the council is seriously divided over the issue. The business-minded and marketing people prefer to call it a Mosque-Cathedral to attract global tourism. Others, including the deputy mayor, several senior councilors, and some brotherhoods want to reduce tourism and call it a cathedral. They justify their position with the constant complaints from taxpaying residents about litter, lack of parking, and overcrowded streets. The Islamic Institute is even blunter. It was built as a Mosque. Most of the original construction still stands. It looks like a Mosque inside and out except for the relatively small area converted into a cathedral and has Islamic prayer facilities for thousands of Muslims. Ergo, it is a Mosque."

"You're saying whoever sprayed the wall might reveal which faction was responsible?" said Prado.

"Which might point to why the priest died and who was involved."

Prado nodded, reached over, and patted Amanda's shoulder. "Thank you," he said.

After five minutes of silence, Amanda glanced over and smiled. Prado had fallen asleep.

Half an hour later, Amanda spotted the lights of Sevilla twinkling brightly on the distant horizon ahead.

Prado's phone rang. He jerked awake causing it to slide from his lap to the floor. "Shit," he said groveling for it for several seconds. He found it and looked at the screen. It was el jefe.

"Comisario Principal Toboso will be waiting for you in the Guardia Civil office at Sevilla airport," said el jefe. "It's on the eastern edge of town so you'll miss the traffic. I'll text you the address. Julián's father will also be there."

"Thank you, sir, and sorry to be a nuisance on a Sunday," said Prado.

"The joys of police work," said el jefe. "I also have some news about the Arab boy."

"They've found him?"

"No, but traffic cameras traced the missing prison van and guards."

"Where?"

"Parked outside a restaurant at Rio Frio on the A-92. The guards had been drugged and their uniforms removed. They came round about half an hour ago."

"Did they say what happened?"

"They had turned off the motorway heading back to their prison and were driving along an isolated stretch of road with olive trees on either side when they were overtaken and flagged down by a Guardia Civil officer on a motorbike. They stopped on the hard standing, wound down the driver's window, and waited for the officer to approach. While they were waiting, the passenger door was yanked open, and a masked person dressed in black pointed a gun at them indicating they should get out and open the back doors. After they had complied, they had to face the back of the van and place their arms on the roof. The Guardia officer, now also masked, pulled down their pants and injected each of them in the backside. After which they remember nothing until waking up in their underwear."

"Any traces of the boy?"

"They found a copy of his signed confession with a clump of dark hair placed by it. There are also fingerprints from a right hand on the window."

"Have they compared them with what's on the

comisaría file?"

"Not yet why?"

"Good, because the computer log entry will reveal we've found the van and I don't want anybody in Córdoba to find out."

"But we need to confirm they match."

"Send them to me, I'll take care of it in the morning. Meanwhile, the confession will have to do."

"Why are you so concerned about keeping this from the comisaría?"

"Several reasons. The main ones being camera footage of the prison van arriving, and departing has been deleted. The Arab interview videos as well."

"Who by?"

"The comisario principal but it could be somebody else using her details. The point being I can't trust anybody there."

"Should I initiate a search for the Arab?"

"Could you assign another officer to investigate but on no account must they have any contact with Córdoba."

"Why can't you do it?"

"I suspect these tactics are designed to have me chasing around the country and distract me from the main event."

"Which is?"

"The death of the priest."

"Why?"

"Father Julián wiped his computer clean and emptied the cathedral office filing cabinet before sending a cryptic final email to the bishop."

"What did it say?"

"Thanks to those behind the mask, lives are at stake on Wednesday. For your safety, delete this now. God be with you."

"As you said, cryptic. What's with Wednesday?"

"There's a crucially important event in the cathedral on Wednesday morning involving the Pope and the world's religious leaders."

"Why didn't you tell me this before?"

"It's top-secret, I had to bully the bishop to tell me."

"Did anyone mention it in the comisaría?"

"Absolutely nobody, which is puzzling bearing in mind Tobón is involved with the security."

"This puts a completely different perspective on your investigation. I'll have to consult with upstairs and get back to you."

"The man in charge of security is General Quijano. I suggest we should involve him now rather than later."

"Good idea, I'll call him."

"Thanks, one more thing. Father Julián was the recipient of protected anal sex shortly before his death."

"This is turning messier by the minute."

"Can we do a full background check on the priest and DI Tobón?"

"Shooting in the dark?"

"Purely to eliminate the possibilities, and can we include their financials?"

"It will have to wait until morning."

"Fine."

"Where will you go after you've finished in Sevilla?"

"Back to the hotel in Córdoba."

"Will you mention the anal sex to the priest's father?"

"If I'm to clarify the gay sex element to this, I have to."

"I'm sure you'll be sensitive."

"I will."

Prado ended the call.

"Follow the signs to Sevilla Airport," said Prado looking at the map on his phone. "We're to meet the police chief in the Guardia office. It's complicated to access from this direction, but I'll direct you. Basically, we must go past, turn around and come back."

"Fine," said Amanda yawning. "Have they found the boy?"

"Only the vehicle and two guards. There is evidence the boy was in the van."

"So, you might still need my services?"

"Until after we find the boy, yes. Do you need to be home?"

"No, but I haven't brought any overnight things."

"I'm sure the hotel can fix you up with some basics."

"Let's see what we learn in Sevilla and then decide. Do you want me in on the meeting with the police chief?"

"Better not. It might make the priest's father feel uncomfortable."

"As you wish. Where do I turn?"

"At the roundabout in three hundred meters."

Amanda found the right road, headed back toward the airport, and pulled up on the pavement outside the Guardia Office.

"I'll stay in the car," she said.

"I shouldn't be too long and thanks for being so flexible," said Prado.

Amanda watched him walk around the side to the office door wondering where his meeting might lead them next. When he'd gone inside, she phoned Phillip and brought him up to date with the case. However, she didn't mention the baby. That was something she wanted to do safely in his arms.

15

Prado paused outside the Guardia office to marshal his questions. It was located at the rear of a tractor dealership about a kilometer from the airport terminal building. He knocked on the door and went into a small room divided in two by a partition with half-height opaque glazing. A uniformed sergeant was sitting behind a desk tapping on a keyboard. She looked up.

"DI Prado," he said.

"They're expecting you," she said nodding at the closed door to her left.

Prado opened the door and walked in.

A slender balding man in his late fifties with a goatee beard, wearing a polo shirt and blue jeans was sitting behind a timber desk. He stood and came round to greet Prado with his arm outstretched. He was about the same height as Prado. Prado grasped his hand, and they shook.

"Toboso and this is José María," he boomed in a deep baritone voice indicating the elderly gentlemen sitting in one of the visitor chairs opposite the desk. "The victim's father."

Prado went over to the frail man who was struggling to stand. He put his hand on his shoulder. "No, please remain seated."

The old man was relieved and sank back down into the plastic chair.

"Sit down," said Toboso returning to his seat. "Fire away."

"My first questions concern both of you, but if it's acceptable, I'd like a word in private with José María when we're done." They both nodded. "First of all," said Prado looking toward the old man. "May I say how sorry I am for your loss. Having talked with the bishop your son was a much-loved member of the cathedral team."

José María nodded but his eyes watered. He shook his head and returned Prado's gaze.

"Can you throw any light on your daughter Irena's disappearance?" said Prado.

"No," said José María. "She can't recall anything."

Prado switched his gaze to Toboso.

"Have the police made any progress finding her abductors?"

"It's a total mystery," said Toboso. "Nobody saw or heard a thing."

"Any sign of a break-in?"

"Yes, the back door was forced open, probably with a crowbar but there were no prints or DNA evidence."

"How about the rug?"

"Aside from the scuff marks of Irena's bare feet," said Toboso. "We found some dirt particles probably from the perpetrator's shoe. However, our soil experts tell us it's common around the Sevilla region and impossible to pinpoint."

"But it does indicate local perpetrators," said Prado.

"Rather than from Córdoba for example?"

"We're working on that presumption, yes."

"Has anyone from the Córdoba force made inquiries about her disappearance?"

"None of our officers have admitted to receiving such a request," said Toboso. "However, unofficially it's possible. There are bound to be friendly colleagues in both offices."

"Not many," said Prado.

"I'll make some calls when we're done here. Anything else for me?"

Prado shook his head.

"José María," said Toboso. "I'll wait outside then take you back home."

"Thank you, sir," said Prado. After Toboso had closed the door behind him, Prado turned back to the old man.

"This must be difficult for you," said Prado.

"Not my finest hour," said the old man.

"Do you think Irena will pull through?"

"The doctors remain confident she can go home tomorrow."

"Let's hope so. How is her husband coping?"

The old man paused before replying. "He should have been home."

"Where was he?"

"In Jerez de la Frontera. It's close enough for him to have made it home."

"What was he doing in Jerez?"

"He's in the wine business and was attending a new product launch."

"Could he have been drinking and didn't want to drive?"

"Probably, but he knows how Irena hates being left

alone."

"Is he away often?"

"No, usually, on these business occasions he makes it back."

"How often would you say he stays away overnight?"

"Twice, maybe three times a year."

"Do you think it's a coincidence he was away the night she was taken?"

"I don't know."

"Do they have a good marriage?"

"Not particularly. He's the controlling type."

"Is he in a brotherhood?"

"Yes, he's in tonight's procession."

"With Irena's blessing?"

"She has no say in the matter."

"Were you in a brotherhood?"

"Never. None of my side of the family is devoted."

"Only your son?"

The old man's face softened. "I have no idea how. He showed no interest in the church until he went to university. After he'd graduated with engineering, he announced he was staying on to study theology. I tried to persuade him otherwise, but he was committed and happy about it, so I gave him my full support. Over the years, he's never had any doubts about his decision and relished his work as Sacristan. He particularly enjoyed his responsibilities for cathedral maintenance so at least we had something in common."

"Why?"

"I was the city engineer for decades."

"Which is how you know the police chief?"

"His father worked for me."

Prado paused and looked at the old man who

regarded him.

"Anything else, Inspector?"

"One more thing and it's a question I've been dreading since I heard about it from the pathologist who carried out the postmortem."

"What?" said the old man looking concerned.

"What can you tell me about your son's sexuality?"

"Sorry, I don't know what you mean."

"There is evidence your son was a passive participant in anal sex shortly before he died."

José María slumped into his chair. Prado jumped up thinking he'd had a heart attack.

"I'm alright," snapped the old man when Prado knelt and touched his shoulder. "Just shocked. It goes against everything my son believed in."

"Are you up to explaining?"

"Of course. Please don't think I'm playing the role of indignant and ignorant parent, Inspector but I would seriously reconsider the pathologist's report. My son would never willingly participate in sex of any sort. He'd been open about his lack of interest since he was a teenager and never showed a desire for either girls or boys beyond friendship. We never heard of or met any potential partners and there were never any rumors. After he joined the Church, that was it. He told us he had committed himself to a celibate life in the service of his beloved God and we had no reason to believe or doubt him. He was a disciplined and committed person. If he indulged in anal sex, it was not with his consent."

"Thank you, José María," said Prado. "I'm sorry to have to bring this up."

"You're doing your job," said the old man looking perkier. "Which in circumstances like this must be extremely stressful."

Prado reached out, took the man's hand, and squeezed it. "Yes, it is more than stressful but for some weird reason, I relish the challenge. Please be assured I will do everything possible to find the reason for your son's death."

The old man smiled at him with tears in his eyes, "Yes, inspector. I have every confidence."

"I understand you are good friends with the bishop?"

"He's more like family to us but more importantly, there is something special about him. You can trust his perception and judgment without hesitation. He's a good ally to have on your side."

16

Prado said his farewells and returned to the car. Amanda saw him coming and started the engine.

"Hotel?" she said as he climbed in.

"Yes, we're done for tonight."

"What about your mother's stew?"

"I've had my bellyful, so I'll bin it back at the hotel, shame, it's delicious."

"How did it go?"

"José María is convinced Julián was not gay, and I believe him."

"He could have been raped or been held down and had something inserted."

"Another attempt to put us off the scent?"

"To have you chasing around Andalucía hunting for a missing Arab and a mystery gay murderer would keep most detectives on their toes."

"Yes, but most detectives don't have your razor-sharp mind to share their case details with."

"True," said Amanda trying to look innocent.

"Will you go home tonight?" said Prado.

"Phillip said he would be most cross if I did," said Amanda. "He will feel happier if I drive back tomorrow after a good night's rest. If you don't object, I took the liberty of calling the hotel and booking a room. If I may, I'd like to visit the crime scene with you in the morning. Assuming there is no sign of the Arab boy, I'll head back after."

"Did you tell him about the case?"

"And the event on Wednesday. Do you mind?"

"No. Excuse me, I have to update el jefe."

Prado swiped his phone and waited for his boss to answer.

"How did it go?" said el jefe.

"Did Toboso call?"

"Yes, he was most impressed. Thought you handled the old man extremely well."

"I didn't know they were old friends."

"Neither did I but it explains why he is giving the old man such a personal service."

"Can we add his daughter Irena and his son-in-law Javi to our background checks? Javi was away the night she was abducted, and he is a member of a Sevilla brotherhood. It would help to establish which one and if they have an association with any in Córdoba."

"What did the old man have to say about his son's sexuality?"

"Swears blind he is celibate, and I believed him."

"You think it is another attempt to mislead you?"

"Possibly, it certainly tempted me out of Córdoba, but I couldn't dismiss it. The church's sexual abuse reputation is running low. If this case turned out to be yet another scandal and I ignored it, then I'd have failed miserably at my job."

"You'll talk to the bishop about it tomorrow?"

"Delicately. Any progress on decrypting the father's message?"

"Nothing concrete, but one idea is based on the father looking downward when he died, perhaps he's pointing us to something underneath the chapel."

"Assuming he killed himself," said Prado. "Which I think unlikely, he was a strong and happy man, unlikely to be suicidal."

"But maybe he was secretly gay, and someone had confronted him about it which was driving him crazy."

"Possible but it goes against everything his close friends and family have said about him."

"Accepted, but with builders crawling all over the cathedral for the last year or so, they could have installed something under the chapel floor."

"I think it's grasping at straws."

"You're probably right but there was a thorough builder's clean in a small area in front of the chapel sometime late yesterday. Have a close look tomorrow."

"I will. In the meantime, we need more information about the builders," said Prado. "And a list of their staff working on site."

"Do you have a name?"

"Construcción Artesanos SL. They are a Córdoba firm specializing in restoration work. They also bring in experts when necessary. I believe one was an underpinning company using the latest technology to stop old buildings sinking or sliding down hills. They were working on the foundations at the southern end of the cathedral and the roof above. I can't understand why they were cleaning at the north end."

"Ask them."

"I'll discuss them with the bishop tomorrow. By the way, I'll be adding a room to the bill for Amanda at the hotel tonight. She's heading back to Nerja tomorrow."

"Fair enough. I've spoken with my boss, and he has

agreed for me to contact General Quijano. If there's any response, I'll keep you informed, otherwise, I think we can call it a night. Let me know how it goes with the bishop and please contact your old girlfriend as soon as possible. Despite your concerns about her trustworthiness, she is the boss and is entitled to a progress report."

"The morning will have to do, goodnight, sir."

"Goodnight, Leon."

It was just after midnight when they approached the hotel.

"No need to park the car," said Prado. "The porter will take care of it."

Before she'd even stopped outside the main entrance a young man was waiting for them and opened her door. She climbed out, handed over the keys, and waited by the entrance for Prado to join her. He was yawning.

"You must be tired," said Amanda as they approached the reception. "No need to wait with me. I'll see you for breakfast at six-thirty."

"You sure?"

"No problem."

Amanda checked in, collected her key card, and was heading for the elevator when a thought struck her. She'd left the pregnancy test in her car and wanted to take another look at her result. She would make an appointment with her doctor in Málaga for a full examination but for now, it would give her comfort to lie in bed with her little secret and imagine what words she would use tomorrow to tell Phillip.

She went to reception, collected her car keys, and headed to the elevator. She went in and pressed parking. The door slid open to a fire lobby which other than the light from the elevator car was pitch black. Why hadn't she noticed this before when with Prado? She edged out and was startled when a bright light came on. She laughed when realizing it was sensor-operated. She needed her key card to open the heavy fire door into the car park. She pushed hard and went through. Again, the light came on automatically. She pressed her vehicle's remote control, heard her central locking release, and saw her emergency lights blink around the corner.

She opened the driver's door and was bending to reach the glove compartment when a leather-clad hand clamped over her mouth and held her in a vice-like grip. She screamed, wriggled, and kicked out but to no avail. Someone else yanked down the top of her pants and underwear. She felt a prick in her backside. Seconds later, nothing.

17

In the quiet hotel restaurant, Prado was enjoying his second cup of coffee and nibbling on a toasted bread roll drizzled with olive oil when he realized Amanda hadn't joined him for breakfast. He checked his phone. It was six forty and no messages. He shrugged; it was unlike her to be late but there was still plenty of time before their appointment with the bishop at the cathedral.

Ten minutes later, and still no sign of her. He called her on WhatsApp but there was no reply. He wiped his mouth on his serviette, pushed back his chair, and headed for the lobby.

"Is Señora Salisbury still in her room?" he said to the receptionist.

The young, uniformed lady checked the register on her computer, picked up the desk phone, and dialed Amanda's room.

After a few rings, she shook her head.

"I'll just check her key card movements," she said tapping her keyboard. "She never went to her room but went straight from here to the car park via the elevator. I have her leaving the car park exit barrier at ten minutes after midnight."

"Oh," said Prado. "Perhaps she changed her mind and went home."

"Let me ask the room maids to check her room," said the receptionist picking up the phone again, pressing some buttons, and issuing her instructions. "It'll only take a minute."

"Is the car park exit on CCTV?" said Prado.

"Just a minute, sir. I'll call the manager."

She went through the door to the side of reception and returned with a harassed Señor Marin.

While Prado explained his concerns to the manager, the reception phone rang. The receptionist answered, listened, and interrupted. "The room is empty and there is no sign of occupation last night."

"Let's go to the security office and check the camera footage," said Marin leading Prado out of the lobby and through a door marked, 'Staff Only'.

"Is the car park entrance locked?" said Prado as he followed along a corridor with office doors to the left and right.

"No, it's controlled by a security barrier. It can only be operated by a room key card or by a four-digit code issued by reception."

"So, you can't just arrive and drive in?"

"No or drive out. All visitors must communicate with reception first."

"How often is the code changed?"

"Once a week."

They arrived at a door labeled 'Security' and went into a small room with a bank of six black and white TV monitors. A laptop was on top of a table.

"Our security manager must be on his rounds," said Marin sitting in the only chair. "But we can look at the footage."

He pulled the laptop toward him, moved the mouse, set the car park footage to run from ten p.m. the previous evening, sat back, and watched.

"Will this take long?" said Prado.

"The camera only runs when a moving vehicle activates the sensor," said Marin.

"What about people? Do they set it off?"

"No, only vehicles."

"Is the car park accessible on foot?"

"Yes, we leave the shutters up all the time. Otherwise, the noise annoys the guests in the rooms above. Here is the recording."

Prado watched the evening's comings and goings over Marin's shoulder. The final image was of Amanda's Prius stopping at the exit barrier, an arm reached out and a gloved hand tapped the key card on the reader. The barrier went up and the vehicle drove through. The car park ceiling lights reflected on the car windows making visibility difficult but by the shape of the driver's silhouette, it was a woman with long hair.

"Is it her?" said Marin.

"Almost certainly," said Prado. "However, it's most unlike her not to have checked out first and not to have informed me."

"When are you due to meet her next?"

"Eight a.m. at the cathedral but if she's gone home, she won't be there. I'd like to look at the car park if I may," said Prado. "Just to put my mind at rest."

"We can access it from this corridor," said Marin. "I'll show you."

Prado followed Marin to the far end of the short corridor, through a fire door and down a flight of steps. Another fire door provided access to the exit barrier from where they walked into the depths of the garage. They passed his car, turned a corner, and stopped where Amanda's car had been parked. There were no marks on the floor but when Prado bent over and looked underneath the Ford parked in the adjacent space, he saw a small object halfway under the chassis, but it was in deep shadow and unrecognizable. It was just out of his reach. Marin couldn't bend over low enough to even see it.

"I'll call the porter to bring a broom," he said.

Minutes later a young man had rescued the object and showed it to Prado. It was a phone with a cracked screen. Prado dug out his phone and called Amanda's number. It started buzzing. Prado took the phone from the porter wanting to check the call log, but it needed her fingerprint. He placed it in his pocket and called Phillip.

"Is Amanda with you?" said Prado when Phillip answered.

"I assumed she was with you, but I've been trying to reach her," said Phillip. "Is anything wrong?"

"When did you last speak to her?" said Prado.

"Last night while you were at the airport. I insisted she stay in Córdoba rather than drive back, afterward, I went to bed. We agreed to speak at six a.m. for when she would set her alarm, but I heard nothing, and she doesn't answer. I'm worried, Leon."

"She was seen, or at least someone resembling her, driving her car out of the hotel car park around midnight. I've just found her phone underneath the vehicle next to where she was parked. For some reason, before going up to her room, she came down to the car and either drove off somewhere or she's been taken."

"For fuck's sake Leon, who by?"

"I have no idea, but it's probably something to do with the case she was helping me with."

"Probably, you're a policeman for Christ's sake, you must know something more definite."

"Yes, but not enough to pinpoint who has taken her, why, or where."

"She has a vehicle tracker app on her phone."

"Good, but I can't access it, I need her password."

"I don't know her password. She uses her index finger; we both do but decided to have a copy of each in case of an accident."

"You don't know her password?" said Prado.

"No, do you know Inma's?"

"Fair point, can you email the fingerprint?"

"No, it's on an adhesive film. We tested it and it worked fine but I'll have to bring it to you?"

"Would you mind?"

"Try and stop me. Where shall I meet you?"

"At the hotel."

"Fine, I'll be there before eleven."

"Call me when you're half an hour away. Meanwhile, I'll put out an all-points bulletin with her photo and car details. Phillip, I know you're upset, so am I, but try not to worry too much. I don't think she's in mortal danger."

"Why not?"

"Whoever took her, is trying to distract me from investigating the death of the priest. If they meant harm to Amanda, they would have killed her in the car park not run the risk of abduction. They also probably want to find out from her what I am up to so they can stay ahead of me."

"You better be right; I'll pack a few things, take

Sasha to my sister's, and leave shortly."

Prado ended the call.

"Amanda's fiancée, Phillip Armitage," said Prado turning back to Marin. "Will be arriving around eleven. Give him Amanda's room."

"Will you be sending a forensics team?" said Marin.

"No," said Prado. "You saw the gloved hand on the footage; these people know what they are doing. Thanks for your help. I'll see you later."

Prado was a few steps away when something jumped into his head.

"Can you change the sensor settings on the garage cameras?"

"Yes, what do you suggest?"

"Whoever took Amanda came in by foot. It might be shutting the door after the horse had bolted but can you make sure everything and everyone coming in and out of the garage entrance is recorded?"

"I'll attend to it personally, inspector," said Marin.

"Thanks," said Prado. "I'll make my way back to my room."

Back upstairs, Prado opened the safe took out his scanner turned it on and walked around the room. It and his devices were clean.

Opening the back of Amanda's phone proved impossible, so he placed it in the safe. The spray can was next. He lifted two sets of prints. One on the rim which was probably the bishops. The others were on the nozzle and body of the can. He opened his laptop, plugged in the scanner, and searched the database. While the search was running, he called el jefe. He drummed his fingers in the dresser, thinking through his strategy, while he waited for his boss to pick up.

"You're early," said el jefe.

"Amanda has been abducted," said Prado.

"Oh no," said el jefe. "What do you want me to do?"

"Two things. Put out a nationwide search for Amanda's Prius and her photo, you have the details on her consultant's file. Check all the traffic cameras in and around the city from midnight onwards, not just for her car but any vehicles remotely near the hotel around the time."

"No problem," said el jefe. "You said two things?"

"I've never asked for anything like this before, but exceptional circumstances need special action, and what I'm about to propose breaks all conventions. For it to be approved we are going to need some help from the bishop, his minister friend, and support from the general."

"Go on."

"There is no doubt in my mind Inspector Tobón is disrupting my investigations. Maybe with the support of the comisario principal, his sergeant, and some of his glamorous team. Either way, I cannot trust anyone and need to prevent them from interfering. The only way I can think of is to send a small team to take over the comisaría in Córdoba. Preferably, senior detectives from Málaga with a few armed officers. I need people I know and trust to work with. At the moment, I have no idea who is on my side. You'll need a warrant signed by the interior minister with the irrefutable authority to arrest Inspector Tobón and Sergeant Chavez, lock them up and search their homes. Everyone else is to be suspended, should hand over their phones, and stay at home under threat of immediate termination of employment and pension rights. The replacement team will then change all passwords and deal with any urgent issues arising."

"What about the comisario principal?"

"I don't believe she's involved but before I can take her into my confidence, I need to know she is clean. She'll probably hate me for it, but I'll have to live with it."

"It's a tall order," said el jefe. "What are your grounds for such drastic action?"

"Therein lies the problem," said Prado. "The only facts are that crucial evidence has been deleted from the police database. The rest is pure assumptions, but I can think of no other explanation. Nobody else could stay one jump ahead of me in everything I'm doing. Nobody else could have manipulated or disposed of evidence so thoroughly or quickly. Tobón must think I'm stupid to believe the Arabs confessed especially with such massive holes in his proof."

"You mean the candlestick?"

"Yes. It is seriously doubtful the candlestick was used to kill the priest. It's far too heavy to use quickly, especially by a puny boy or his grandfather."

"So how was he killed?"

"When the father was crushed under the carving, the bolthead fixing it to the wall penetrated his skull. What I don't know is, did the father kill himself to tell us something, or was he killed because he'd discovered something."

"I'll be interested to learn what the bishop thinks?"

"I'll ask him. We're meeting shortly at the crime scene."

"Will you mention your proposed takeover of the comisaría?"

"I have no choice. The bishop has a huge personal stake in Wednesday's event and is terrified of anything going wrong. He has a much greater chance of persuading the minister to let us take over Córdoba than we do. However, we should not give up on the general. We need him to be badgering the minister as well. A two-pronged attack is more likely to result in a quick decision."

"I agree but if our proposal is rejected what then?"

"It will leave Tobón, and his cohorts out on the streets and free from any restrictions. If they do intend to disrupt the signing, nothing will be in their way. And I don't need to remind you Julián's message indicated lives are in danger and that includes the Pope, the Archbishop of Canterbury, and senior Muslims. If anything happens to them on our soil on Wednesday, it will mean war."

"Dramatic but possible. Do you think Tobón abducted Amanda?"

"I think he arranged it as another diversion. Locking him up and removing his means of communication will unsettle him and whoever he instructed to take Amanda."

"Agreed," said el jefe, "I'll try my best from this end but it's up to you to convince the bishop."

"I'll call you when I've finished with the bishop. Interrupt me with any developments about Amanda."

"Fine," said el jefe.

Prado checked his laptop.

The fingerprint search had finished. There was no match on the criminal database.

"Sorry, one more thing," said Prado. "I've just run a fingerprint check on the graffiti artist with no results. Can you request a national identity register search?"

"Just Spanish nationals?"

"No, include all foreign residents."

"Fine. Have you informed Phillip about Amanda? He must be worried sick and probably furious."

"He is. He'll be here in a few hours."

18

Amanda opened her eyes. Above her head was a dim light source but the room was gloomy and difficult to see detail. She'd been trying to stir herself on and off for what seemed like hours, but her mind was too foggy to register her surroundings and every time she attempted to lift her lids, a heavy weight bore down and closed them again. She tensed her body, testing her extremities. Everything seemed to be working except there was a soreness in her neck and her backside felt tender. She was lying on a hard surface, wrapped in what felt like a woolen blanket, at least it smelled clean. She had no idea what time it was but was dying for a pee and her stomach rumbled with hunger.

She fumbled around her. Behind her head and to the right was a vertical surface with a pattern of regular indentations, but the areas in between were cold and crumbly. To the left, she felt an edge with a similar cold roughness. She threw off the blanket, swung her legs around, dangled them over the edge and a light came on. She blinked and looked around her.

Dungeon was her first impression. The tiny rectangular room was built with crumbling sandstone blocks. A large cross hung on the inner wall below a small skylight covered in thick dust. Opposite was a wide rusty iron door with a barred opening. A breath of stale air wafted through it. Below the opening was a narrow slot with a shelf projecting out evenly on both sides of the hole. For food trays she assumed. In the opposite corner were a toilet and sink. They seemed relatively new, and she recognized the well-known logo of its Spanish manufacturer. There was even soap, a plastic cup, and a small clean towel. She drank some water which tasted fine. Out of curiosity, she tried the door.

Nobody was more shocked when it squeaked open. She went out into a poorly lit corridor with more iron doors on both sides. She looked left and right, saw a distant light to the right, and set off toward it. As she progressed, lights came on to illuminate the way forward, while those behind went out. They must also be on sensors, she surmised. The end of the corridor was blocked by another iron door again with a small, barred opening at head height. She peered through and nearly jumped out of her skin when an elderly woman's face appeared right in front of her.

She smiled at Amanda and gestured she should stand back. Amanda heard a bolt being slid open and the door pushed toward her. When it was completely open the woman reappeared from behind the door, smiled at her, put her finger to her mouth, and shook her head. She was dressed in white nun's clothing.

"Don't you talk?" said Amanda.

The nun shook her head and indicated Amanda should follow.

At least I won't have to make polite conversation, she thought to herself and almost giggled out loud with a sense of relief she didn't seem to be in any immediate danger.

Amanda walked behind the nun who zipped along with a spritely stride for her age. They were in a much wider space more hallway than corridor, with a pointed roof supported by timber beams. Timber doors led off to the right and left but all were closed. More crosses and lanterns hung from the walls and high up in the roof were large skylights. Rays of bright sunlight illuminated their path. Must be early, she thought looking at the length of shadows. I wonder how old this place is, sixteenth century?

Double-width timber doors loomed ahead. They stopped. The nun peeked through the glazed aperture and knocked twice. The left-hand door was opened from inside. They went through and into a large rectangular refectory with a similar roof to the hallway. Floor-to-ceiling metal barred windows to one side provided stunning views over lush green lawns. Squat, widespread mature olive trees formed a dense barrier at the end. A few fluffy white clouds were dotted in clusters in an otherwise clear blue sky.

In the center of the room was a row of eight wooden well-used tables. On each side was a matching bench that could seat five people. Only three benches had an empty slot. They were a complete mix of humanity. Young, old, male, female, smart, scruffy, beautiful, and ugly but all dressed in blue overalls and work boots. Many had one thing in common, the haunted look of the addicted. At the head of each table was a nun carefully observing her charges in between spoonsful of something with milk.

The elderly nun indicated Amanda should follow her ageless colleague who was short and rotund with round dark-framed glasses. The nun led her to the stainless-steel servery, where she was invited to pick up a tray from the rack and help herself to a choice of cereals, fresh fruit, bread roll, and a selection of juices from a row of various containers. She piled fruit into a bowl, poured a glass of orange juice, and was led over to a free space at the end of one of the middle tables.

She wondered what to do with the tray but saw her fellow diners had simply placed theirs on the table and eaten directly from it. She sat next to a young girl with streaked purple hair, dressed in a gothic outfit with piercings to her nose and ears with tattoos all around her neck and cheek. She was heavily pregnant.

Amanda smiled but the girl stared straight ahead and took an occasional sip of her juice. Amanda regarded her fellow diners. Nobody returned her gaze and they seemed to be wrapped in their little worlds.

Tranquilized? She thought. They scared her. Is this what's in store for me?

She lifted the spoon and nibbled a slice of apple. It tasted delicious, the juice as well.

She finished her fruit and looked around to see if it was permissible to help herself to another bowl full. She caught the eye of the middle-aged stern-looking nun at the end of her table, held up her bowl, and looked inquiringly hoping it was the required etiquette. The nun nodded.

Amanda stood, replenished her bowl, topped it with what resembled homemade yogurt, and returned to her seat. Nobody noticed. She ate quickly and as soon as she'd finished the last mouthful, a bell rang. Just a short burst but enough to stir the room into action.

Everybody stood, picked up their trays formed an orderly queue, and loaded them back into the rack under the watchful eye of another sullen elderly nun.

Amanda had no idea what to do next so turned to the smartly dressed teenage man behind her. "Where do we go now?"

The responding 'ssh' was deafening.

The man nodded toward the same door Amanda had entered.

As she approached the exit, the young man tapped her on the shoulder. She turned to him, and he nodded at the two nuns standing by the door watching their flock with hawk-like eyes. Was he trying to warn her of something? When it was Amanda's turn to go through the door, the nun who she had first met in the hallway beckoned to Amanda with her finger. She turned and strode off. Amanda almost trotted to keep up with her.

The nun led her over to a timber door in the corner of the dining hall, opened it, and gestured for Amanda to follow her into what appeared to be an ante room to the dining hall. It had no windows, only skylights. A long table covered with a crisp white tablecloth was at the end near the far wall. A large cross was mounted in the center. Twelve empty chairs were positioned between the wall and the table facing her. A brilliant ray of sunlight shone down through a skylight onto a spot about two meters in front of the table. The nun stopped and pointed to a tiny cross on the stone floor directly under the sunlight. Stand there, she gestured with the palm of her hand.

Satisfied Amanda had complied and wasn't about to flee in terror. The nun left through the same door they entered.

Amanda waited. With each passing minute, the full realization of her predicament started to nag at her confidence. She'd been drugged, abducted, and was being held in an old convent somewhere. She took a deep breath wishing that Phillip would magically appear and whisk her away. What did they want with her?

She was on the verge of weeping when a door in the far corner opened, and persons filed in. They were dressed in white tunics, white cloaks, and tall white conical hats with facemasks down. Some were tall, others short, most had rounded stomachs and hairy hands. They sat down facing her.

"Don't be afraid, Amanda," said a male voice seated in the center. "Our appearance may be alarming, but we mean you no harm. We are deeply religious, and providing our simple rules are adhered to nothing here should worry you. I understand from the gentleman who had you committed, you are suffering from only a mild addiction to opiates. As you are pregnant, we will not be treating you in any way, just monitoring your behavior. If we are satisfied you can cope back out in the real world, you will be returned to your home in Nerja after Wednesday. If all goes well, your wedding should be able to proceed as planned."

"May I inform my fiancée I am still alive?"

"Sorry,"

"My fiancée?"

"Do you mean Señor Phillip Armitage?"

"Yes."

"Forgive my confusion. He knows you're alive. It was him who committed you."

19

Prado was surprised by how early the procession spectators had begun setting up shop behind the barriers around the cathedral. He was in good time for his meeting with the bishop so popped into the café opposite the courtyard entrance for a decent coffee. He relished the treat. After the hotel stewed and filtered offering, it was so much better. There wasn't a seat available, but the bar service seemed rapid. Within minutes, he'd ordered, been served, and paid. He took his cup outside, put his briefcase on the floor, stood by the door, and relished the bitter café solo sip by sip as he prayed Amanda was well and would be tracked down quickly.

He spotted the bishop crossing the road. Prado finished his drink, picked up his case, and returned the cup to the bar. The barman nodded his appreciation. Prado smiled, sorted out the chronology of his questions, and headed over to the cathedral. The bishop was standing by the public entrance chatting with two burly uniformed security guards.

"Good morning, bishop," said Prado.

"Good morning, inspector," said the bishop then

turned back to the guards. "Gentlemen, this is detective inspector Prado I was telling you about. Inspector, this is my chief of security Guillermo Rojas, and David Bustillo, one of his assistants. The inspector and any colleagues he may bring are to be allowed access to all parts of the building whenever he wishes, but for his safety, one of you must always accompany him."

"Not necessary," said Prado.

"I know but believe me there are old stairways and badly lit tunnels crumbling in places. Our insurance company insists on it."

"Fair enough," said Prado. "Can we start at the chapel?"

"Follow me," said the bishop.

"Let me guess," said Prado to Guillermo as they walked side by side. "Military Police?"

"Is that a guess?" said Guillermo.

"Hardly," said Prado. "Military bearing and expressionless appraisal. Where were you stationed?"

"Rota," said Guillermo. "It's near…"

"I know where it is," said Prado. "Would it surprise you to know the military police is where I started?"

"I'd concluded you were probably a teacher before joining the police."

"Many make the same conclusion."

"Where were you stationed?"

"With the legion in Ronda. How was it sharing the base with Americans?"

"If you spoke English, fine, but it wasn't exciting. Most of my time was spent coaxing drunken sailors and airmen out of the Cádiz city center bars before they wrecked the place."

"Is English speaking the reason you were offered

this job?"

"No, but it helped, all our staff speak English. It's the main form of communication with tourists."

"Sign of the times, I guess. You a Córdoba boy?"

"No, Almeria."

Prado nodded; grateful he'd found an ally in what was currently an alien hometown wanting rid of him. They arrived at the chapel. Prado walked around looking at the floor in front of it but could see nothing out of the ordinary where the builders had cleaned. Guillermo unlocked the chapel gate and held it open. Prado and the bishop went in. It was spotless with a faint odor of bleach. Prado wandered around looking at the sturdy wall mounting brackets and the painting of Jerusalem.

"What value?" said Prado.

"About 12,000 Euros," said the bishop, "but the candlesticks are a lot more."

Prado picked one up, it was the same weight as the one in the evidence room. "Solid gold?" he said.

"Twenty-four carats," said the bishop. "Each worth over 300,000 Euros."

"They are far too heavy for either of the Arabs to use as a murder weapon."

"That was my thinking, too. I heard you met José María last night."

"Yes. He called you?"

"He did and mentioned your concerns about his son's celibacy."

"And what are your thoughts, bishop?"

"As I am sure you are aware, the Catholic Church is not having a comfortable time with accusations of abuse. In all my postings, it has been my focus to stamp out even the mildest hints at impropriety. I've uncovered a few lost sheep on my journey and have acted ruthlessly when necessary. Consequently, my reputation is usually enough to deter any of the clergy or staff members from any form of sexual or psychological abuse. My churches are happy and safe places. The result of a lifetime of looking out for potential abusers means I can spot one almost immediately. I can assure you Father Julián was not only completely celibate but was asexual. He didn't need to distract himself from choir boys with angelic complexions because the only thing mattering to him was their welfare and singing voice. What I'm saying inspector is whatever the pathologist discovered with his corpse had nothing to do with the father himself."

"Thank you, bishop. I had reached the same conclusion. All we need to do now is identify how he died and who interfered with him."

"Any ideas?"

"As yet, none. I'm hoping my visit here this morning may open a few pointers."

"How can I help?"

"What can you tell me about Irena's husband?"

"Javi is a macho racist," said the bishop. "He's an excellent provider and an attentive husband but in the traditional sense. She does all the work while he lords it over the house."

"Is he the controlling sort?"

"He dominates her every moment. Who she meets, what she wears even how she eats."

"Is he violent?"

"Physically, no but he bullies her with deeds. For example, she became friends with a neighbor who lived in the next-door apartment. She was a documented immigrant from Syria, a doctor. The two girls went shopping together and chatted regularly over the apartment balcony. Javi went ballistic, ranting on about how Spain should be cleansed of all foreign scum."

"Did you see this?"

"No, but both José María and Julián informed me. I told them from my experiences of domestic abuse, and I see many, he was likely to become progressively worse and they should watch over their daughter carefully. Javi's response was to move to a villa on the outskirts of the city. In preparation for a family, he said."

"Could Javi's brotherhood in Sevilla be affiliated with any in Córdoba?"

"Possibly, but I'm not sure."

"Do you know the brotherhoods in Córdoba?"

"Of course, I've met all the senior brothers except for one."

"Why haven't you met them?"

"They exclude women."

"Good heavens, I thought we'd rid ourselves of such absurdity. What are they called?"

"Hermandad de Corpus Puro."

"Pure body brotherhood?"

"Correct."

"Do they participate in the Córdoba procession?"

"My first task as bishop was to give them an ultimatum. Open their arms to women or be banned from any association with the church. They declined and so for the first time in decades will not be in our procession."

20

Amanda slumped into a heap on the floor, head in hands, weeping. The sun's rays continued to shine down on her from the skylight above. Her long black raven hair sparkled as her body shuddered.
She didn't notice the twelve filing out silently.

Two nuns approached from behind. One stooped and tapped her gently on the shoulder. She ignored them, too distraught to think of any rational behavior.

They left her for a few minutes, then each grabbed an arm, lifted her to her feet, and frogged marched her out of the room, back along the hallway to its far end, and into what resembled a library.

The nuns let her go watched her carefully, concerned expressions on both their faces. Amanda pulled herself together and dried her eyes. She nodded at them to indicate she was under control. They seemed satisfied and left her alone.

She leaned on the bookshelf nearest the door and looked around the spacious room. More bookshelves lined each of three walls. A large window almost filled the other views over a huge walled garden. The central open area was covered in rugs and furnished with armchairs, sofas, and occasional tables. On the wall above a huge walk-in fireplace hung a painting of a person dressed in a white tunic and purple cloak. It was a frail elderly man with sparse hair and a lined face. A sign at the bottom described him as 'Jesús Blanco. El Fundador del Hermandad de Corpus Puro,' founder of the pure body brotherhood.

Her fellow diners from breakfast were sitting or standing around preoccupied with themselves. Some were browsing the massive range of books. A few were talking, albeit quietly in various-sized groups. It seemed tranquil and could be described as normal except gothic girl wasn't the only pregnant female. Nearly all the women of childbearing age were pregnant to varying degrees but there were no children. Why? She wondered.

She moved tentatively toward the window to join the most animated gathering. They made room for her.

"This is the only place we're allowed to talk," said the young man who had stood behind her in the breakfast room.

"You just been admitted?" said gothic girl.

"Last night," said Amanda. "I think."

"Don't drink the milk at suppertime," said the young man. "It's a sleeping draught."

"Where can one phone?" said Amanda.

"Only the brothers have phones," said a long-haired hippy man in his forties. "Have you read their pamphlet?"

"Not seen one," said Amanda.

"You'll find a pile on the table by the door. I suggest you take one and read their rules. Failure to comply is rewarded with a few weeks in solitary with only bread and water."

"What is this place?" said Amanda.

"It's the Monasterio de Corpus Puro," said an older woman who looked to be in her sixties, but it was difficult to tell.

"I thought it was a convent with all the nuns," said Amanda.

"No, it's always been a monastery," said the older woman. "But because it was so isolated, they couldn't attract new members. As the aging monks died off, it gradually emptied and lay rotting for over a hundred years. The man in the painting was gifted it during the Civil War."

"Who was he?" said Amanda.

"One of Franco's right-hand men," said older woman. "The one responsible for driving the religious fanaticism of his dictatorship."

"Blanco believed in a pure world," said gothic girl. "Where everyone went to church and behaved like saints. He founded a brotherhood named after the monastery and started recruiting members. Many of them racist thugs from Franco's regime. In the early days, members subscribed willingly to their creed but after Franco died and the next generation took over some of their children refused to toe the line preferring to indulge in the pleasures of the modern world. So, what did they do with these black sheep? Hello, it's us. They locked us up in here and attempted to recondition us. For example, they weaned me off heroin."

"Me from alcohol," said the older woman.

"Me from sex," said the young man leering at Amanda.

"You're joking?" said Amanda.

"Sadly not," said the young man shaking his head,

embarrassed.

"How does this place survive?" said Amanda.

"Fees for weaning services," said the older woman. "My daughter paid them to dry me out and continues paying them to keep me here because she doesn't want me at home. Most of their income though is donated by brotherhood members."

"What are they known as?" said Amanda.

"Hermandad de Corpus Puro," said Hippy.

"Never heard of them," said Amanda.

"You will," said the young man.

"Why?" said Amanda.

"They are the most racist organization in Spain," said gothic girl. "Before members are accepted, they are obliged to prove their purity as a Spaniard undiluted by Moorish blood or any other nationality. Furthermore, they must have a useful profession, skill, or qualification. Once accepted, they dedicate their lives to the expansion of the brotherhood's power by applying for the highest positions in public service and industry so they can influence policy and decisions. They block anything to do with modernization, globalization, improving women's rights, or liberalizing immigration."

"That's outrageous," said Amanda. "How long have you been here?"

"Five years, I think," said gothic girl. "We never know what day it is let alone year but at Easter, they give us a special dinner. I've had five."

"Three," said sex addict.

"Four," said older woman.

"We represent a fraction of the patients here," said Hippy. "Our rooms are on the same level as this, but below, there are two floors full of dissidents or anyone who refuses to accept their rules."

"Plus, the odd criminal they can't persuade the courts to convict," said older woman.

"How did you find out?" said Amanda.

"We take it in turns to deliver their meals," said sex addict. "The prisoners often ask us to contact lawyers or relatives. Occasionally, the brothers reward a change in attitude. See the old man by the bookshelves talking to himself. They let him join us last week. He's been on the lowest floor for over twenty years."

"Doesn't anyone escape?" said Amanda.

"Some have tried," said the older woman. "But we are in the middle of nowhere surrounded by millions of olive trees. Escapees are soon recovered."

"Is Córdoba the nearest city?" said Amanda.

"Yes," said gothic girl. "Most of our families live there, occasionally they visit."

"You must look forward to seeing them," said Amanda.

"Regretfully no. They only come to see if we've changed our attitude," said sex addict. "And are willing to rejoin the family concentration camp."

"Sorry?" said Amanda.

"There is little difference to living here or at home," said gothic girl. "It's all rules, obligations, and expectations."

"At home, they expect us to be top of the class," said sex addict.

"And spend all our leisure time revising," said gothic girl.

"No dancing, alcohol, and approved partners only," said older woman. "We're like robots in their service."

"My fiancée had me committed," said Amanda. "Yet I know he is not a member of the brotherhood and was at home in Nerja when I was brought here. They said they would let me go in a few days if I behave."

"First of all," said hippy. "I guarantee it wasn't your fiancée who brought you here. What was the last thing you were doing?"

"Translating for the police who were investigating the death of a priest in Córdoba cathedral."

"Then it's likely you were too close for comfort," said older woman. "It's their way. Rather than confront the problem, remove it."

"Will they kill me?" said Amanda.

"They are deeply religious," said hippy. "It's unlikely. Premature deaths do occur but only in rare circumstances."

"Don't believe them about you only being here for a few days," said older woman. "Nobody is released, ever."

"They dare not," said gothic girl. "Look at me, see the other pregnant women. They use us to produce the brotherhood's next-generation against our will. If the truth were made public, they would be exposed as rapists and bullies. They are too afraid to face those consequences."

21

"Banning Hermandad de Corpus Puro from participating in the procession," said Prado. "Must have infuriated them."

"Probably but I have my standards and won't be bullied by anyone," said the bishop. "However, I wasn't surprised when anonymous messages started arriving."

"Did you inform the police?"

"Yes, but nothing came from it?"

"Were they threatening?"

"Just insults to start with."

"How were they delivered?"

"By post. The messages were made of letters or words cut out from a local magazine. To date, I've ignored them as they refer to an argument dating back decades about how to describe this building."

"Amanda, my translator has written several articles about the Mosque or Cathedral debate," said Prado.

"I won't bore you further," said the bishop. "Other than to say it's about to be permanently resolved. One clause of Wednesday's agreement is the name must change to Mosque-Cathedral, it will be announced shortly after and guaranteed to cause an uproar."

"Can the council vote not to accept it?"

"No. It's complicated, but the Bishopric of Córdoba has legally owned the cathedral since 2006. The council has no mandate over the building at all. We can do what we like but out of a sense of civic duty we would prefer to have the council's support."

"Do you personally support the name change?"

"Wholeheartedly. Why do you ask?"

"You were angry at the graffiti artist."

"He was desecrating our beautiful building and it triggered a bottled-up reaction to an event shortly before the father's death."

"What?"

"The last anonymous message received was a death threat."

"Do you still have it?"

"In my office."

"Have you informed the police?"

"No, frankly with the death of Julián, it has slipped my mind."

"What did it say?"

"Change the name and die. It's a cathedral."

"Was the message aimed at you, or could it have meant any of your staff?"

"It was addressed to the staff. I'd always assumed they meant me, but I suppose it could have been Julián or any of my staff. What a selfish fool I've been. I could have warned everyone to be on their guard, instead I kept it to myself."

"Don't blame yourself, bishop, we're dealing with warped minds here. Nobody can forecast how they think or what they might do next but clearly, it confirms they are extremely dangerous and should be taken seriously."

"Could the graffiti also be linked to Father Julián's death?" said the bishop.

"Possibly. Hopefully, the prints on the can might give us a lead but until then I must concentrate on what we have. Can you confirm Father Julián's responsibilities were the sacristy, the building restoration, and the easter processions?"

"Correct."

"Anything else he may have been involved with?"

"Impossible. He hardly had enough hours in the day to cope as it was."

"If we rule out anything to do with the anonymous messages or a gay lover, could his death be linked to any sphere of his operations? These candlesticks, for example, are worth a fortune even melted down. Is it likely he'd uncovered an illicit trade or forgeries among the antiquities?"

"It's possible but highly unlikely. All our items are chipped and invisibly sprayed with ID numbers. The inventory is checked every evening, and nothing has been reported as out of the ordinary."

"Could it be something to do with the processions?"

"They are under his control from a logistical viewpoint but once all the arrangements have been agreed with the brotherhoods, Father Julián's job was just to maintain contact and ensure everything went smoothly."

"Perhaps it's the building project. Was anyone else from your staff working with him in managing the project?"

"No, he worked alone with the engineers and contractors."

"And all the paperwork has disappeared from his filing cabinet?"

"Yes, and his email correspondence."

"I'll need a list of his contacts for the project," said Prado.

"Regretfully, all I received from him were the brotherhood contact details. There was nothing about the restoration team but the project manager on site is a man named Cristiano Da Rosa."

"Is he employed by the builders?" said Prado. "Or freelance?"

"You'll have to speak to the builders."

"Construcción Artesanos SL?"

"As I said."

"Based in Córdoba?"

"Yes."

"Did you meet any of their directors?"

"Yes, but only as a matter of courtesy. I can't recall names."

"Would you mind speaking with their chief executive and asking him to provide you with a contact list of all workers here on-site in addition to Da Rosa, for example, the professional advisers and any external contractors involved in the project?"

"Of course. I'll call them from my office."

"Do you have time?"

"No, but this is too important to ignore."

"Meanwhile, I'd like to take a look at the building works."

"Are you sure, it means low, dusty, narrow passages?"

"All part of the service, bishop."

"Guillermo will show you the way. Join me in my office when you're done."

The bishop turned and strode out of the chapel entrance.

As Prado reflected on the death threat, Guillermo appeared at the chapel gate.

"I understand you want to see the building works," he said.

"Problem?"

"Not at all, but we'll need hardhats and overalls. I'll lock up here then we'll go to the builder's site office."

They walked the length of the building side-by-side passing through the cathedral on the way. The cleaners were just finishing up, someone was practicing on the organ and a few priests were chatting in front of the altar. One spotted them and came over."

He held out his hand as he approached.

"Father Demetrio," he said. "Dean of the cathedral."

"Detective Inspector Prado."

"I'm escorting the inspector to the builders' office for a tour of inspection," said Guillermo.

"Do you understand what modern underpinning is?" said Prado.

"Sorry, inspector," said the dean. "My job is just making sure the builders leave everything tidy and don't interfere with our religious calendar. Father Julián was our restoration expert."

"Did the bishop speak to you about the chapel of the Souls of Purgatory?" said Prado.

"Concerning any link to the father's demise?" said the dean.

"Yes," said Prado. "Were you able to throw any light on it?"

"Regretfully not. It was named by El Inca, the original owner in 1612 and was probably personal to him."

"Did El Inca have anything in common with the father?"

The dean stroked his chin for a few moments and said, "The only thing I can think of is they both served as Sacristan to this cathedral."

"What about you, Guillermo?"

"I know nothing about chapel names but can explain the basics of the underpinning technology," said Guillermo. "But don't ask me anything too detailed."

"I'll try my best not to," said Prado shaking hands with the dean. "Nice to meet you father."

They continued their walk toward the sacristy. As they entered Prado admired the incredible collection of artifacts.

"I understand these were the responsibility of Father Julián," said Prado as they passed display cabinets of golden staffs, bishops' hats, chalices, and incense holders.

"Correct," said Guillermo. "It's my job to check the inventory every day after closing and report my findings to him."

"Everything in order?"

"Believe me, this place is theftproof. If the alarm goes off, sliding doors crash down from the ceiling blocking both sacristy exits in less than a second."

"So as chief of security, you feel confident Father Julián's death had nothing to do with the cathedral's antiquities."

"Completely," said Guillermo as they continued through.

"How many of these objects were here during El Inca's time as Sacristan?"

"Only a fraction," said Guillermo.

"Is there a list?"

"I have a master list of all objects, the source, dates of manufacture, and donation."

"Could you email it to me?"

"As soon as we're done."

"Thanks. What are those?" said Prado pointing to do a vertical display of objects as they exited the sacristy.

"Stonemasons' marks from the Middle Ages," said Guillermo. "As each stone was laid, the mason identified his work with his sign or letter. Stonemasons were paid according to how many items they had laid. These marks ensured they weren't ripped off."

"Not much changes," said Prado.

Guillermo grimaced. "Here," he said as they approached a broad passageway between two chapels. "This leads to the external door where the builders' materials and machines were brought into the cathedral."

They walked along the short passage to the metal-lined door. To the side was another wide timber door. Guillermo unlocked it and led Prado inside a spacious rectangular room with no windows.

"This area was used as the builder's office," said Guillermo pressing a bank of switches just inside the door. The room brightened as ceiling lights flickered on revealing ladders, buckets, trowels, mops, and other ancillary building equipment. "At the far end is the stairwell leading down to the basement underneath the sacristy and mihrab, and up to the roof. They had to carry everything by hand. It was dusty and hot with poor ventilation. Exhausting work but these guys were paid incredibly well."

Just before the top of the stairs, was a row of metal lockers. Hanging on hooks mounted on the wall next to the lockers were orange Hi-Viz jackets and matching hard hats, with integral spotlights and clear plastic drop-down facemasks. Guillermo took off his uniform coat, hung it on a hook, slipped into a builder's jacket, selected a hat, put it on, and dropped the mask. Prado followed suit. Within seconds he was perspiring.

They went into the stairwell, descended two flights of wide stairs but the third was narrow and both had to stoop.

"We are now under street level," said Guillermo as they reached the bottom where he unlocked a heavy steel door. They went through into a long rectangular room some fifty meters long. All along its center, vertical iron girders five meters apart supported the ceiling. It was musty and airless. Prado found it difficult to catch his breath.

"These are the original foundations and base of the outer south-facing wall," said Guillermo. "To give you some context, the VIP platform is outside. If you look at the ceiling, you can see where the cracks have been filled in. The iron girders are to reinforce the support to the upper floors."

Prado glanced up.

"Ye gods," he said. "The cracks were enormous. Are you sure they are safe?"

"The builders assured me they are and have issued a twenty-five-year guarantee. They reinforced the foundations to stop the cracks from growing larger and installed gauges every few meters to measure any further slippage. The gauges are hardwired to a unique WiFi system. If any crack expands beyond defined tolerances. An alarm goes off in the general office, the duty security officers' cell phone but more importantly at the builders' alarm station. They send a team immediately to examine the cause of movement and carry out additional reinforcement as required."

"How?"

"You see what appear to be short spigots sticking out of the wall and the floor. Each has a pressure gauge attached to it."

"What are they for?"

"Each spigot represents the end of a spider's web of flexible tubes inserted deep into the walls and the original foundations. Permanent liquid cement is pumped into these tubes via these spigots to the required pressure. It inflates the tube which prevents further slippage of the foundations. Similar technology was used on the Leaning Tower of Pisa, under various palaces in Venice, and in London to prop up the old buildings when they started building the Crossrail tunnels underneath. If there is more slippage, they increase the pressure in the tubes by pumping in more grout."

"Impressive."

"What I like about it is once the tube network was installed any further work is relatively quick, clean, and inexpensive. It should extend the life of the original cathedral by centuries."

"How are the spigots closed to make sure the liquid cement doesn't leak?"

"Each has a valve which can be connected directly to the grout pump. They are sealed with a yellow tag which can be quickly released to pump in more grout. Afterward, they are resealed."

"Sounds brilliant but how do you prevent a terrorist from removing the caps?"

"The pressure gauges are connected to the monitoring system. Any release of grout sets off the alarm and the huge door we entered through slams shut and locks solid."

"What would happen to the building if this technology failed, and the cement leaked out?"

"We have been assured by the contractors even a serious earthquake won't affect the underpinning, so we don't worry about it."

"Humor me for a minute. Someone knowledgeable about the technology and its monitoring system would know how to undo all these safety precautions without setting off the alarm. It might be difficult, but it could be done. If so, what would be the outcome?"

"This end of the building would slowly collapse."

"How slow?"

"Difficult to say, inspector but it wouldn't be instant. The grout would take several hours to leak out as it's almost solid. Even when it's out, it would be impossible to forecast when the structure would weaken."

"What if there were a large crowd standing directly over this area?"

"Impossible. We are below the sacristy, mihrab, and chapels. Any crowd would not be directly above here but in the body of the cathedral."

"What kind of warnings could we expect if the grout did leak out?"

"Even if they managed to override security on the spigots, the crack monitoring equipment would signal any building movement giving plenty of time to evacuate."

"Except," said Prado. "If the grout has been substituted for explosive."

22

"Hopefully, you understood some of that," said Guillermo as Prado changed into his jacket.

"You explained it well," said Prado. "We'll need to check the tubes for explosives but assuming they are clear I doubt the underpinning could be used as an effective weapon."

"I agree," said Guillermo. "When will they send sniffer dogs?"

"Soon as I can stir up enough panic among my superiors," said Prado.

"Good luck with that."

They shook hands and Prado headed toward the cathedral door. Outside, he threaded his way through the narrow gap in the barricade and crossed the road to the bishop's palace. The coffee and toast still wafted over the gathering crowd. He breathed in deeply wondering how much to tell his boss of the latest developments. He took out his phone and swiped el jefe.

"How was the bishop?" answered his superior.

"Under a lot of stress," said Prado. "And just to make matters worse he's received a death threat."

"In what respect," said el jefe.

"Someone is determined the cathedral name should not be changed to Mosque-Cathedral."

"Any idea who?"

"The police haven't reported any progress, but purely based on previous discussions, the bishop thinks it could be conservative members of the council or a brotherhood."

"Any particular brotherhood?"

"Hermandad de Corpus Puro. Can you run a check on them?"

"Do they have a location?"

"No, I only have an email address and a warehouse in Córdoba where they keep their throne. I'll email the details when we're done. Any progress with Amanda?"

"Yes and no," said el jefe. "We've been trailing through the traffic cameras and think we might have something."

"Tell me."

"We tracked Amanda's car after it drove away from the hotel, it went south and crossed the bridge over the river Guadalquivir but disappeared between two cameras. The only available turnings off were two dead ends, one into an urbanization, the other an industrial estate. We checked every vehicle for an hour before and an hour after and ran the plates of those which also disappeared between the two cameras and think we struck lucky. A gray Seat saloon car with fake plates followed Amanda's car. It re-emerged ten minutes later, drove back over the river, and headed out of town on the CO-3405 going north."

"Any indication of where it stopped."

"There are few cameras on what is a rarely used country lane. The last camera is at a roundabout on the fringe of the city. The next is in the village of Villaviciosa de Córdoba fifty kilometers north of Córdoba. The Seat never appeared there meaning it stopped somewhere between the edge of the city and the village."

"Any side roads turning off?"

"No roads, only farm tracks. We're scouring maps of the area now to identify possible buildings but there are over two hundred and fifty square kilometers of olive groves and almond trees. There's a military base about twenty kilometers away just off the nearest A432a main road. They have agreed to send a helicopter which should be starting its search pattern later this morning, but we need to give them some pointers where to look."

"Can you give me the name and number of their commanding officer?"

"On its way."

"Thanks. Did you tell them not to mention it to the Córdoba city police?"

"Their flight plan is registered with the aviation authorities. It has nothing to do with Córdoba."

"Excellent. How about the fingerprints?"

"I have a reply from the registry but until we can take over the comisaría, there isn't much we can do about it."

"Why?"

"The prints belong to a French citizen who is a resident in Córdoba. He's a member of the Islamic Institute and has a record of protesting about the cathedral's name. However, there is nothing serious against him and he's considered harmless. Perhaps the bishop has heard of him?"

"What's his name?"

"Farook Slimani."

"Algerian origins?"

"We think so. Will you tell the bishop?"

"I'm on my way to talk with him now. I've just been to the scene of the crime and had a look at the completed building works."

"All in order?"

"Even if the works fail, there will be plenty of warning and the cathedral is unlikely to collapse quickly enough to kill anyone."

"But it still sounds a possibility," said el jefe. "And the works should be searched for any signs of interference."

"A job for General Quijano," said Prado.

"I'll mention it to him. Will you discuss taking over the comisaría to the bishop?"

"Yes. Have you assembled a team to take over?"

"Almost."

Prado ended the call, arrived at the palace gate, and rang the bell. Father Ildefonso wearing a black cassock over his suit opened, led him silently to the bishop's office, and closed the door on his way out. The bishop dressed in his day clothes waved him to the visitor chair in front of his desk.

"Did you speak to your boss?" said the bishop.

"Yes, he's extremely concerned about Wednesday and will discuss it with General Quijano. The spray can prints have yielded some results. Does the name Farook Slimani sound familiar?"

"It does but he's harmless."

"Maybe, but he does have a police record and his arresting officer was Tobón. He may have been paid to add to the chaos."

"But I saw Slimani before the police arrived at the

cathedral and well before I called the minister."

"Which indicates a coordinated plan."

"With what objective?"

"Wednesday," said Prado. "The father's death and everything else points to distracting us away from Wednesday."

"What do you mean by everything?"

"Both my translator Amanda and the Arab boy who I now consider to be a key witness to Tobón's actions have been abducted."

"Oh no. Any idea by who?"

"I don't have evidence, but I suspect Tobón, or his boss arranged it."

"Why them?"

"The boy was collected from his cell by imposters and evidence has been tampered with or gone missing. Only senior officers in the comisaría could have managed that."

"Why aren't I surprised? Any progress on finding Amanda and the boy?"

"A car, assuming to be carrying Amanda, was seen heading north toward Villaviciosa de Córdoba but didn't reach the village, we think it stopped somewhere en route. As far as the boy is concerned, there is evidence indicating he was in an abandoned stolen prison van discovered at Rio Frio."

"The fish farm village on the way to Granada? But surely, it's in the opposite direction."

"Again, more distraction. As was taking Father Julián's sister. It tempted me away to Sevilla. I think it's part of their plan to have me running around looking at the wrong things. The abductions however demonstrate a higher level of risk and desperation. I believe it could be their first mistake."

"Tobón can't be doing this alone," said the bishop.

"I agree," said Prado. "I believe he is part of an organization with plenty of resources, connections everywhere, and enough balls to take extreme risks."

"Such as a passionate brotherhood with warped objectives."

"Hermandad de Corpus Puro, for example."

"Exactly. Where might they keep Amanda and this boy without fear of detection?"

"A headquarters, perhaps?" said Prado.

"Maybe deep among the olive groves between the city and this village you mentioned."

"Could be. We have a military helicopter about to begin searching the area, but they need some pointers where to look."

"Shall we try Google Earth?"

"I'll do it later, bishop. The most important issue now is to remove Tobón and his boss from the scene. Otherwise, all we are likely to find are more distractions."

"Never heard of anything so drastic before. Wouldn't permission be required from the highest levels?"

"Exactly, bishop."

"Oh, I see. You want me to have a word with the Interior Minister?"

"I need permission to take over the comisaría," said Prado. "Lock, stock, and barrel because we don't know how many officers Tobón and his boss have working with them. The only way to stop their continued interference is to take them all off the street, remove their communications and stop them from accessing the police computer. In effect, we shut them down. Then we have a chance to concentrate on flushing out what they have in mind for Wednesday."

"You have a trustworthy team?"

"Málaga's finest. My boss is preparing them now."

"What you propose is mind-boggling, Inspector. Our own people ousting their own police force. It's bad as life under Dictator Franco."

"I agree, bishop. However, don't forget what is at stake. A chance to wrench humanity back from the brink of moral bankruptcy. Whatever it takes, your event must be allowed to proceed, and I can't think of another way to prevent whatever they might be planning," said Prado checking his watch. "And, we only have forty-eight hours."

"You're right, Inspector," said the bishop picking up the desk phone and dialing. "I'll call the minister."

23

Amanda picked up a leaflet from the table by the door and looked around for an available armchair to sit and absorb the philosophy and rules of Hermandad de Corpus Puro. If she did escape, Prado would welcome the information. She glanced at the front page. The title read, Enlightenment through Purity of Body and Soul.

Adolf Hitler's, Arbeit macht frei, work makes free, sprang into her mind.

A bell rang.

Everybody was instantly silent, stood, and faced the door. Two nuns appeared and led the way outside. Everyone followed in single file. Amanda stuffed the leaflet into her pants pocket and tagged onto the end just behind the hippy.

"Gardening," he mouthed back at her.

The column turned left out of the door and walked to the end of the hallway where one of the nuns unbolted the double timber doors and pushed them open. They stood one to either side as the inmates filed out down several brick steps. At the bottom, each picked up a garden tool and a basket from a rack and headed off along gravel pathways to their allocated patch.

Amanda paused at the rack unsure where to go.

One of the nuns came down the steps, indicated a basket and trowel, before pointing to weeds among the paths. Amanda tucked the basket into the crook of her arm, grabbed the weeding weapon in her right hand, and headed off to the far corner. The nuns watched her go for a few seconds, returned inside, and locked the doors behind them.

There weren't many weeds, but it was still backbreaking work. What she liked though was the freedom to move around the garden. She estimated it to be three hundred meters long by two hundred across surrounded by one wing of the brick-built monastery and a three-meter-high wall. Vines grew up the south-facing walls. In the late spring sunshine at such a high altitude, grape buds were beginning to form. In the individual raised beds were fruits and vegetables of all sorts.

Amanda stopped by gothic girl who was weeding in between the early shoots of sweet potatoes. She bent over and jabbed the trowel into a patch of thistles.

"They have everything here," whispered Amanda.

"Completely self-sufficient," gothic girl whispered back. "With water well, solar energy, wind power, battery, and backup generator. Sometimes we care for the animals. They are in a huge barn on the other side of the house."

"Not vegans, then?"

"No but everything they eat is natural. The meat tastes delicious, one of the few advantages of living here is three squares a day of excellent nutritious food."

"I'll make a permanent reservation," said Amanda.

Gothic girl looked at her. "Sex addict wasn't

joking," she said. "This is it. Say hello to the rest of your life."

"What about escape?"

"Easy," said gothic girl. "Just slip behind the orange trees at the far end slipping your pants down as if you are going for a pee. Behind the trees is a compost heap with a drainage channel at its far end. It goes under the wall. The channel is about three meters long and large enough to wriggle through. You must bash the wire netting outwards at the far end but it's rusty and won't take a minute. Then scramble down a small cliff into a dry riverbed. It leads into the olive groves. The downside is you'll stink like hell."

"How far away is the main road?"

"We're kilometers from any highway, village, or telephone. The dogs and jeeps will find you within thirty minutes. Then it's solitary for a week and down to the lower levels until you've proved yourself a good girl for long enough."

"If I go now, when will they know I'm missing?"

"Not until lunchtime, in just over two hours."

"How do you know all this?"

"I learned the hard way. You'll need water, it's hot and dusty as hell."

"Is that why they don't supervise the outdoor activities?"

"Yes, but also, they expect new arrivals to escape. It's a test to see what you're made of, and they love hunting you down. To them, it's a sport."

"The nuns?"

"No, the brothers. The creeps you met with the hoods. Oh, and when they eventually catch you, they will gang rape you, lock you up and feed you on bread and water."

"You learned from the experience?"

Gothic girl nodded. Amanda heard her sniffing.

"Is it why you are pregnant?"

"Not this time. I've already delivered two babies. The first from the rape, the others as part of their future generation program."

"Who is the father?"

"It could be any one of the brothers. Once a woman is declared ready for the next child, they take it in turns to visit your cell until tested positive."

"Why didn't you resist them?"

"I did initially but four hold you down. It's pointless so you get it over with as quickly as possible."

"Will they do the same to me?"

"No, you aren't pure bred like me and the brothers, but they are sadists and will still have their fun with you."

"What happens to the children?"

"They are taken at birth; mothers aren't allowed to see them let alone hug or feed them. All we do is express our milk."

"Where are they?"

"Some are adopted by brotherhood members, but many are kept here in the nursery. The nuns look after them and educate them into their twisted doctrine. When they are old enough, they are sent to university and when qualified fed into the machinery of state. Córdoba is completely controlled by them."

"What about other cities?"

"They are spreading around the country but only recently. There aren't enough to make much of an impact but in ten to fifteen years it will change. They'll be everywhere."

"Where is the nursery?"

"In the staff accommodation block where the brothers, nuns, and kitchen staff live. It's opposite the kitchen and across the car park."

"Then I have no choice but to escape. What direction is the nearest village?"

"There are no villages. All the land around here is owned by the brotherhood with isolated cottages and farms every two or three kilometers which belong to members or loyal tenant farmers. You can't trust them. The only route out is east toward the main A432 road which links Córdoba with Espiel, but you'll need to avoid the rivers and a lake."

"How far is the A432?"

"Around eight kilometers but it's slow going, lots of hills and loose soil."

"What about farm tracks?"

"The first place they'll check. Remember, they've been hunting escapees for decades. They know all the tricks."

"Is there a better plan?"

"I would go around midnight."

"I thought the door to the cell corridor was locked?"

"It is but with your skinny arms, you'll be able to reach through the bars and unbolt it. Forget about the cross-country route, it's too slow and dangerous. If I was going again, I'd head for the kitchen. Someone as tiny as you could squeeze out through the pantry window and into the staff car park. They don't lock the vehicles and leave the keys in a cupboard in the lobby of the staff accommodation block."

"Won't the engine wake them up?"

"Probably but you don't need to start it. The car park is at the top of a hill and slopes downward. Push the jeep to the exit and let it run. Start it when you're out of earshot."

"You've thought all this through, why don't you come with me?"

She looked up and Amanda knew straight away. Gothic girl shook her head. "If I wasn't pregnant," she said. "I would but I'd only slow you down. Anyway, life here is no worse than it was at home. Better in many ways as I'm under no pressure and have no responsibilities."

"Then why are you telling me all this?"

"Because you're not like me. I can see it in your eyes. If anyone can escape from here, it's you, and every single one of us will be rooting for you."

"Thanks, I'll give it some thought. Why don't they lock the cell doors?"

"They do on the lower floors but on ours, they are happy if we intermingle."

"What if one of the men comes to your cell?"

"Some do, but only if you are already pregnant. Any other time both parties will be condemned to the lower floors and believe me, nobody wants to be down there. It's full of evil people. Remember, if you do decide to go, tell no one."

"Of course not."

Amanda heard a distant noise. She looked up but couldn't see anything in the glare of the sun. It was faint but seemed to be less so with each passing second and it faded away as quickly as it came. She looked at gothic girl who was also looking upwards.

"Helicopter, extremely high," said gothic girl. "Perhaps, they are looking for you?"

Amanda regarded her while her mind churned with confusion. Were they coming for her? Should she stay or go?

Gothic girl stared back but said nothing.

Amanda reached out and gripped her shoulder firmly.

She would leave tonight.

24

Prado listened carefully as the bishop explained the situation to his minister friend. He could only hear one side of the conversation and it was frustrating, the bishop was overcomplicating matters with too many what-ifs. With each passing sentence, he sensed the bishop's growing frustration as he failed to press the minister's button.

"Excuse me, bishop," said Prado grabbing the phone.

"Sorry to interrupt, minister. I'm DI Prado sent to investigate the death in custody at the comisaría in Córdoba."

"Raul Cantarero," said the minister. "Just tell me one thing the prime minister will immediately understand and be able to approve your requested take over."

"Minister, it is my firm belief if we do nothing, something deadly will happen to your distinguished guests on Wednesday morning. No matter how much security is in place they will be helpless to prevent a well-organized operation. It would prove embarrassing to me, you, and our country's international reputation."

"I'm aware, Inspector, but you have no proof to

substantiate your assumptions."

"Proof of individual involvement no, but evidence has been tampered with by a senior officer, and a key witness not to mention my translator have been abducted. To me, it demonstrates panic and desperation. These people will stop at nothing to prevent the signing. Should their plans turn out to be harmless, no damage has been done. Just a few cops with their noses out of joint and I creep away with my tail between my legs. It doesn't concern me, but what if their plans are a danger to the Pope what if they mean to kill the Islamic clerics? It would mean war. Are you and the prime minister prepared to stand by and do nothing?"

"A blunt way of putting it, Inspector."

"Minister, I'm here on the front line. Making these judgments has been my job for over thirty years. Never have I uncovered what I suspect to be the worst potential terrorist threat ever. What's even harder to bear is these terrorists are Spanish nationals and include unidentified prominent citizens in the local police, brotherhoods, and Town Hall."

"That is my problem, Inspector. It's highly unlikely."

"Easy to say when skulking in your ivory towers in Madrid minister, but here in Córdoba, we live with the largest Islamic icon outside of the Arab World. We've been squabbling what to call it for decades. Emotions about the issue are at fever pitch and if we do nothing, Wednesday morning will be a bloodbath and responsibility will lie clearly in your hands. I'll pass you back to the bishop. Good day."

The bishop took the phone. Before speaking into it, he regarded Prado with a look of respect.

"The Inspector cuts straight to the chase," said the bishop.

"Certainly convincing," said the minister. "However, this is above my pay grade. I'll have to seek approval from the prime minister."

"Time is running short, Raul," said the bishop. "And the longer we leave it the more likely our intentions will be uncovered and the less likely we can stop those involved."

"I know, Salvador. I'll speak to him now and call you back."

"I should be cross with you," said the bishop glaring at Prado as he replaced the receiver. "I don't think Raul has ever been spoken to so forthrightly."

"I don't care who is mad at me, bishop," said Prado. "I said what was needed. Now it's out of my hands and I can't do anymore."

"I'll pray your words are enough," said the bishop.

25

Prado left the bishop in his office and headed toward the hotel. The procession crowds had visibly swollen and there was a carefree buzz of conversation as old friends renewed acquaintanceships. He checked his messages as he passed the bustling café. Phillip was due in twenty minutes.

In the reflection of the glazing, as Prado was approaching the hotel lobby, he saw Phillip's BMW cabriolet turn into the hotel entrance. The porter rushed out. "It's Ok," said Prado. "He's with me and we'll be here for only a few minutes." The porter nodded and returned inside.

Prado turned and went to the curb. Phillip wound down the window. His ice-blue eyes tired and strained thought Prado.

Phillip climbed out and stretched. His tall athletic frame towering over Prado, shaggy blond hair fluttering in the gentle breeze.

They shook hands.

"How are you?" said Prado.

"Desperately worried," said Phillip. "Any developments?"

"No news," said Prado. "However, it's not all doom and gloom."

Phillip looked hopeful for a second.

"We think she was transferred from her car into a gray Seat. We tracked it until it disappeared between cameras in a remote countryside area to the north of the city. A search helicopter is over the area now, but we need to give them more specific parameters."

"Do you have a large TV in your room?"

"Yes."

"Let's plug my laptop into it and look on Google Earth."

They went up to Prado's room, set up the computer, and were soon zooming in on the road to CO-3405 going north toward the village of Villaviciosa de Córdoba.

They made a list of buildings large enough to hide vehicles and a prisoner. There weren't many. As they progressed further north, even fewer.

"Wait," said Phillip. "What's this?"

"I don't see anything," said Prado. "Just blurry trees."

"Exactly," said Phillip. "It's the map provider's method of disguising secret establishments such as a military base, research or monitoring facility, or an estate owner with powerful friends. Either way, it's been redacted."

"Any idea of the size?"

"No but warn the pilot it might be a no-fly zone. They should climb high and zoom in with the camera."

"I'll add it to their search list."

They continued further north and noted down a few more properties.

While Prado texted the commanding officer of the

helicopter with the coordinates of the redacted area and several buildings worthy of closer examination, Phillip logged into the land registry but came up with no results.

"What does it signify?" said Prado.

"No entries in the land registry usually imply nothing is there. We'll have to wait for the helicopter to find out. What about locating Amanda's vehicle?"

"Do you have her fingerprint film?"

"In my wallet."

Prado opened the room safe, dug out Amanda's phone, and gave it to Phillip. He turned on the phone and laid the film on the screen. The home screen appeared instantly, and Phillip flicked through her icons. He opened her tracker app and seconds later, the location of her car appeared. It was on the industrial estate.

"At least it confirms she was in the gray Seat," said Prado. "Shall we go?"

Ten minutes later, they pulled up outside a small warehouse in the middle of a row of identical units on the industrial estate. There was no sign and no response to their banging on the door. However, their noise attracted the attention of a neighbor.

"It's empty, mate," said the scruffy man in a dirty blue overall, lighting up a cigarette. "Been empty for months."

"Do you know who the landlord is?" said Prado flashing his ID.

"No idea," said the man. "And the back window was broken over the weekend."

"How do we get around to the back?" said Phillip.

"Tell you what," said the man stubbing out his cigarette. "Follow me through our unit. It'll be quicker.

This way."

They followed the man through what was a small engineering shop making washers, nuts, and bolts of unusual dimensions. Three men in similar overalls were working at lathes and machines. It stank of cutting oil but seemed well organized. At the back was a room. The man led them inside to what was a small kitchen with a microwave on one wall and a small rectangular dining table in the middle of the floor. A row of metal lockers lined the other wall. He opened a glazed door which opened onto waste ground. A concrete pathway covered the length of the units providing access to each. They walked next door and spotted the broken window. The door was locked but Prado reached through the jagged glass and pressed down the handle. It opened and they entered an identical room, but it was unused and there were moldy cups in the sink.

Prado opened the inner door, and they went into a completely dark, empty, and musty space. The only illumination was from the broken window behind them. In the middle of the floor was Amanda's car. Phillip looked relieved.

"We should leave this for forensics," said Prado. "But you take a quick look, and I'll scan for prints."

Phillip switched on the flashlight from his phone and directed the beam around the Prius interior. Other than keys in the ignition and some printed cardboard wrapping on the floor, he could see nothing. He opened the door using his jacket sleeve. The interior light came on. He bent over and picked up the remnants of a box. Pregnancy Test, he read. His heart raced. Was this Amanda's? He opened the glove compartment but saw nothing out of the ordinary. He backed out and showed the box to Prado.

"Is this Amanda's?" he said.

"Your guess is as good as mine," said Prado. "She hasn't mentioned anything to me. Would you mind?"

"Of course not, I'm just desperate to find her whatever condition she is in."

Prado turned on his fingerprint scanner and checked the steering wheel and driver's door handle, but everything had been wiped clean.

"Nothing," he said shaking his head.

Prado's phone rang. He glanced at it. It was el jefe.

"Where are you?" said el jefe.

"With Phillip. We've just located Amanda's car."

"Found anything?"

"Not relevant to the case and no prints but forensics might find something."

"I agree but not the locals. We'll have to wait until we have confirmation from the prime minister," said el jefe. "Then send in our team."

"I'm aware," said Prado.

"I've also heard from Sevilla," said el jefe.

"And?"

"They've arrested Javi, Irena's husband."

"What for?"

"Abducting his wife."

"Why am I not surprised? How did they work it out?" said Prado.

"She called the emergency services."

"Had he attacked her?"

"No, he's the one needing attention. The ambulance had just dropped her off but because she hadn't been home for four days, the groceries were low. Despite her frailty, he demanded she go to the supermarket. On her return, when removing the shopping bags, she found the remaining opiates plus used and unused hypodermic syringes tucked under the mat in the trunk of their Volvo. She didn't say a word just threw them at him as he was watching the TV, then smashed him over the head with a frying pan."

"Will he survive?"

"Who cares? Will you want to talk to him?"

"Yes, but I have no time. Can you ask Toboso? Javi wouldn't have risked his marriage without instructions from someone that has control over him. The question is, who?"

"Must be someone in his brotherhood," said el jefe. "It's the only connection."

"Let's hope you're right."

"Sorry," said el jefe.

"About what," said Prado.

"Wait," said el jefe. "Another call."

Prado overheard mumbling, a click, and silence.

He ended the call.

"What now?" said Phillip.

"We wait," said Prado.

"Then tell me everything from last night onward," said Phillip. "Amanda is missing but I have no idea as to why."

"It only seems like five minutes ago I was telling Amanda the same story," said Prado. "The funny thing is, I don't have any more evidence, but I think I know where it's going. On Wednesday morning the world's religious leaders, including the Pope, are meeting at the bishop's palace to sign an accord uniting them in peace. It will be followed by a new form of universal service in the Mosque-Cathedral which will be filmed, and the subsequent documentary will be broadcast globally to educate worshippers of all religions on how to participate in the new order of things. To cut a long story short, some right-wing radicals are desperate to stop the event. I don't know who, although I suspect it is members of Hermandad de Corpus Puro. A misogynistic brotherhood based in or near Córdoba determined to keep Spain free of anything other than pure bred Spaniards and a traditional chauvinistic catholic church. I believe these are the people who have taken Amanda along with a key witness, an Arab boy who Amanda came up here to translate for. Ever since I arrived, I've been led a merry dance. I believe this was a deliberate ploy to keep me away from investigating the death in the cathedral because they fear I might unravel their plans. This can only have been arranged by officers in the comisaría and probably led by Inspector Humberto Tobón and or the comisario principal. I've proposed a team from Málaga take over the comisaría and lock up Tobón and his team until Wednesday is over or they can verify their innocence."

"Won't you need approval from higher up," said Phillip.

"It's on the prime minister's desk as we speak," said Prado. "I pray he understands the urgency."

Prado's phone rang.

"It's on," said el jefe. "The prime minister has granted permission and has sent us the necessary authorizations. Our team is leaving in ten minutes for the airport. You're to meet us at the comisaría in about an hour. Can you invent a plausible reason to have a chat with the comisario principal and keep her busy until we arrive?"

"No. but I'll think of something," said Prado.

26

Prado looked at Phillip a mixture of fear and excitement in his eyes. "It's on," he said. "I'll drive Amanda's car, you follow me.

"Where?"

"Our team are due at the comisaría within the hour. We're going to have a chat with the comisario principal and keep her busy until el jefe arrives.

To avoid the procession crowds, Prado led them south out of town onto the motorway. They drove to the eastern junction and approached the city from the opposite end to the cathedral. Prado used his pass to access the comisaría, both cars drove through and parked next to an unmarked Mercedes. "It's her car," said Prado. "Fingers crossed she's in her office."

They went in the front door and asked the female desk sergeant to see the comisario principal.

Prado glanced at his watch. Twenty-five minutes had passed since he spoke with el jefe. Thirty-five remaining until all hell let loose at the comisaría but still he had no idea how to keep Conchie distracted.

The desk sergeant called through and after a brief conversation waved them to go ahead.

They jogged upstairs. Prado knocked on Conchie's door and went straight in.

Conchie was already moving toward him, her face lit up by a bright smile.

"Leon, I was beginning to think," she said then stopped when Phillip trailed in after Prado.

"Sorry, ma'am," said Prado. "May I introduce you to Phillip Armitage. He's one of my translators."

Conchie stepped toward Phillip, hand outstretched. Phillip grasped her hand firmly.

"To what do I owe this pleasure?" said Conchie, her face puzzled.

"We were wondering if you might help us," said Prado. "Phillip is here for one reason and one reason only."

"Inspector, what is this?" said Conchie.

"Phillip is getting married this coming Saturday," said Prado. "But he has a minor problem we were hoping you could help resolve."

"Congratulations, Phillip, but how could I possibly assist?"

"Well, you see ma'am," said Prado. "As we speak, it's a tad difficult for the wedding to proceed."

"Please stop playing games with me," said Conchie.

"His fiancée is Amanda Salisbury," said Prado watching her reactions like a hawk.

"And?" said Conchie, face a complete blank.

"Can I take it you've never heard of her?" said Prado.

"Only vaguely," said Conchie. "But I can't remember the significance of the name?"

"Amanda is not just Phillip's fiancée; she is also my Arabic translator. She arrived here yesterday afternoon to help me talk with the Arab boy. Not only was he missing from his cell, but Amanda was filmed by the hotel security camera being abducted last night. The bride is missing."

"I knew nothing about this. Why didn't you tell me?"

"Wait, ma'am. You knew nothing about the Arab boy going missing from your cells yesterday afternoon?"

"Nothing at all."

"Then I suggest you request Inspector Tobón to make his report immediately."

"I will," said Conchie turning back to behind her desk, picking up the phone and speaking quietly into it before replacing the handset. "While he is on his way, perhaps you can tell me what this is about?"

"If only I could, comisario principal," said Prado. "Sadly, there isn't much to say. You see, ever since I started this investigation, I've been led on a merry dance around Andalucía chasing ghosts instead of focusing on the real crime scene."

"Which is where?"

"In the cathedral. Why didn't you tell me about Wednesday?"

"It's top-secret," said Conchie. "And had nothing to do with the death in custody which is why I requested an independent officer to come in the first place."

"Don't say another word," shouted Tobón bursting through the door in his shirt-sleeves, his face red with rage, pistol strapped into his shoulder holster.

Prado turned and faced him, stood completely still, and glared at Tobón.

Phillip edged to the left so Tobón couldn't see them both at the same time.

Phillip inched closer to Tobón.

Prado glanced at Phillip and shook his head.

"Who is this?" said Tobón indicating Phillip.

"Shall we sit down," said Conchie. "And discuss this calmly?"

"Great idea, ma'am," said Prado walking over to the side of the office, picking up two more visitor chairs and placing them next to the one already opposite the desk.

He and Phillip took a seat at either end leaving the middle chair vacant.

They watched Conchie as she gestured forcefully for Tobón to join them.

He reluctantly sat in the middle chair looking left and right at Prado and Phillip.

"Do you usually address your superior in such a manner?" said Prado.

Tobón mumbled.

"Speak up man," said Prado.

"Sorry, ma'am," said Tobón. "I was concerned you might be revealing confidential elements of the case against the Arab boy."

"Where is he, inspector?" said Conchie.

"What do you mean," said Tobón. "He's downstairs in cell number five where he's been since yesterday."

"Shall we go and have a chat with him?" said Prado.

"Good idea," said Tobón standing.

Tobón led the way downstairs and into the cell block. His niece gave him the key and exchanged concerned glances with him. Tobón ignored them.

They went into the passageway and Tobón opened the door to cell five.

It was empty.

"I don't understand," said Tobón. "Last time I was here, so was he."

"When?" sad Prado happy the time was passing so quickly on this wild goose chase and impressed by Tobón's acting skills."

"After I charged him, yesterday afternoon."

"I find it highly improbable you weren't aware two officers from Sevilla prison came to collect him late yesterday afternoon?"

"Why would I?" said Tobón. "He'd confessed, been charged and the evidence sent to the evidence room. As far as I was concerned the case was closed. I've moved onto another one."

Prado checked his watch.

Fifteen minutes to drag out this farce.

"The boy is not here," said Prado. "Shall we return to the office and continue our discussion?"

They trooped back upstairs and sat down as before.

Another five minutes wasted.

"Would it be possible for some water?" said Prado.

"Of course," said Conchie standing and walking over to her sideboard. By the time glasses had been found and bottles circulated, more time had edged by.

"May I enquire who this gentleman is?" said Tobón after taking a sip.

"His name is Phillip Armitage," said Prado. "He's an official consultant and translator to the Málaga police. You can check his file if you like."

"Could you have a look, ma'am," said Tobón.

Conchie scowled but sat down behind her desk and tapped the keyboard. She shook her head and tapped again looking frustrated.

Prado's phone vibrated. It was the signal from el jefe confirming the comisaría communications had been blocked and they were only minutes away.

"I can't log in," said Conchie.

Tobón looked alarmed, his hand edging toward his pistol.

"Señor Armitage," said Prado staring at Tobón. "Is also the fiancée of another of my translators, Amanda Salisbury.

Phillip stared at Tobón while Prado said Amanda's name.

Tobón looked furious and moved a hand nearer his pistol.

"Amanda was with me yesterday when we went to speak with the Arab boy," said Prado. "Regretfully, he'd departed about an hour beforehand. Later, after we'd driven to Sevilla and back, Amanda was abducted from her hotel and hasn't been seen since. We found her car which is now parked outside but have no idea where she has been taken or by whom. I understand you solve most of your cases, inspector, perhaps you'd be so gracious as to help us track her down?"

"I'd be delighted," said Tobón his red flush fading slightly. "Assuming my boss has no objections."

Something crashed loudly behind them.

"Hands, where we can see them, shouted a voice."

Tobón went for his pistol, but Phillip was ready for him and twisted his right arm behind his back before he could unstrap his holster.

"What is this?" said Conchie, her face puce with rage.

El jefe stepped forward dressed in combat uniform with bullet proof vest. His pistol pointing at Tobón. Three armed officers similarly dressed stood to his side aiming their automatic weapons at Tobón and Conchie. El jefe presented Conchie with his authority which she read through quickly and turned as white as a sheet.

She glared at Tobón.

"You damn fool," she said. "What have you done?"

27

The armed officers hauled Conchie and Tobón off to the cells. El jefe holstered his pistol and sat down behind Conchie's desk. "It went surprisingly smoothly," he said removing his body armor and laying it on the floor by the wall. "I do believe we've grasped the initiative."

"Have you collected mobile phones," said Prado. "And locked up staff to prevent communications with anyone?"

"Already done," said el jefe. "We thought it best to do that first to prevent anybody warning the senior officers. What next?"

"Who else did you bring?"

"Eduardo our technician, and forensics officer Dr. Ana Galvez," said el jefe. "Plus, three armed officers, and five detectives. The general has dispatched a secret service team to join us, they should be here within the hour."

"Great," said Prado. He reached into his wallet, took out a slip of paper, and handed it to el jefe. "These are Conchie's log-in details. Eduardo needs to change all passwords and limit access to our team. Have the detectives interview the staff. We need to verify who we can trust and return them to duty with fresh orders."

"What about those out on the street?" said el jefe.

"If they call the station, they should be told to stay on duty until their shift changes. By then we should have enough trustworthy bodies to replace them. Can I leave you to organize all that, Sir? Phillip can help."

"Before I do," said Phillip. "Any news from the helicopter search?"

"They agreed to call as soon as they landed," said Prado looking at his watch. "In about an hour. Meanwhile, I'll talk to Conchie then Tobón's team. If anything transpires from our chats which might make us rethink, I'll let you know."

"Let's make a start," said el jefe.

Prado nodded and they headed off to the interview rooms on the ground floor.

Prado took a seat and waited for an officer to bring Conchie. Seconds later the door burst open, and she was pushed into the room wearing handcuffs. The burly officer behind her ignored her squeals of protest. "Leave me alone, damn you," she screamed. "Don't you know who I am?"

Then she saw Prado and sat down opposite glaring at him.

The officer removed the cuffs, served her with a bottle of water, and placed her handbag on the table in front of her. He glanced at Prado who nodded. The officer left and closed the door behind him.

"You knew this was coming?" said Conchie.

"I instigated it," said Prado.

"Is this being recorded?"

"Not yet."

"I thought we had an understanding?"

Prado looked at her and said nothing.

"You're not even embarrassed," said Conchie after a few moments. "Bastard."

"Conchie," said Prado. "I need to know where you stand. If you can satisfy me where your priorities lie, you can join us and help solve this mess."

"What do you want to know?"

"Tell me about the plot to kill the world's religious leaders on Wednesday?"

"Are you out of your mind?"

"Never been more serious."

"I have no information about any such wild idea."

"Let's start again," said Prado. "What can you tell me about Hermandad de Corpus Puro?"

Conchie burst into tears and buried her head in her hands.

Prado let her sob but moved around the table, positioned his chair next to hers, and put his arm around her shoulder. Eventually, she lifted her head and rested it on his chest, sobs slowly subsiding.

She smells nice, thought Prado.

He stroked her hair.

"The brotherhood has been the bane of my life," she said. "Before he died, my father used to be the senior brother and my brother is moving up the ranks. Thanks to their support, I have this job."

"What kind of support?"

"I told you when my sister was raped, the police blamed it on her for being drunk. At my request through my dad, the brotherhood intervened with a friendly judge. It ensured Dani Lopez had some sort of punishment even though it was only a few months behind bars."

"Did they ask for anything in return?"

Conchie nodded and sat up but remained leaning against him.

"What?" he said still stroking her hair.

"They insisted I join the police and be one of their insiders."

"You went along with it?"

"Initially, no but when they offered to remove Dani Lopez permanently from society, I agreed."

"They killed him?"

"Of course not, but when he was released from prison, they arranged for a fake social worker to meet him. She told him about a job as a gardener on an estate out of town. He jumped at it, she drove him, and as far as I know, he has been there since."

"And they've used this favor to keep you under their thumb?"

"They have and regularly remind me of my obligations by showing me photos of him working in a garden. About five years later, when they showed me the same photo again, I expressed doubts about him being alive, they took me to see him. He was furious which I liked."

"Is Lopez still alive?"

"Probably, I don't know."

"Where did they take you to see him?"

"They blindfolded me until we arrived, but we went north to what must have been a huge old monastery. The journey took about an hour along a windy road and up a steep hill."

"When?"

"Twenty-odd years ago. After the visit, I stopped asking about Lopez, he could never escape from there."

"And carried on working on the brotherhood's behalf. Conchie, it's treasonable."

"Do you think I don't know? It tears me apart."

"What do they make you do?"

"Not much to start with but as I climbed the ladder, I was asked to drop charges against brotherhood members and invent plausible excuses as to why."

"What charges?"

"Parking tickets, drunk driving, embezzlement, theft, domestic abuse, and more."

"And with each act of help, you dug yourself deeper into their pit. Would you say they have complete control over you?"

"More or less."

"Who gives you your instructions?"

"On police matters, it's Tobón. Anything else, my brother."

"At least it confirms Tobón is a brotherhood member."

"I'm convinced he's one of their top people."

"Were you aware he uses your name as authority to tamper with and delete evidence or was that you?"

"I am aware of what he does in my name."

"Including the transfer of the Arab boy?"

Conchie nodded.

"And the deletion of the Arab interviews?"

"Yes, I had no choice but to go along, it was part of my deal with the brotherhood, but I swear I knew nothing about Amanda's abduction."

"Do I get the feeling you have become disenchanted at being a puppet for the brotherhood?"

"I hate them and everything they stand for."

"Do they know your feelings?"

"I never say anything not even to my brother. I just

do as I am told."

"If you turned against them, would they be surprised?"

"After twenty-odd years of loyal service, I should hope so."

"Would you?"

"I'd need a good reason to take such a risk. It would mean losing my job and being ostracized by friends and potential employers, plus I have my pension and an aging mother to think of," said Conchie.

"Conchie, let me make this crystal clear. There is little to no chance you will keep your job. However, if you cooperate with us, you might at least remain on the force but in a considerably reduced capacity. Understand?"

She nodded and sniffed.

"You have my word, Leon. I'll do whatever you need," she said. "Are you certain about this attack? I could never imagine the brotherhood wanting to kill the Pope, they are staunch Catholics."

"The Pope is not their main concern. They aim to stop the religions from uniting together whatever the cost. All the leaders are their target, his holiness would be collateral damage. Listen, Conchie, this is pure speculation, frankly, I'm not certain about anything. But given the lengths the antagonists have been to over the last couple of days to distract me from investigating, there must be something extremely serious afoot. I can't think of any reason why they would want to interfere with the Easter celebrations, and nothing else is going on in Córdoba so it must be Wednesday's event. The world's religious leaders rarely come together, if ever. Given they are, I can only assume whoever is distracting me is highly unlikely to invite them for tea and cake."

"Why didn't you discuss it with me?"

"Because I suspected the distractions were being driven from within your comisaría. I had no idea who to trust including you. Whose side are you on Conchie?"

She stood up and paced around the room wiping her mascara smudged eyes.

She stopped and stared at Prado directly in the eye.

"Will you help me stop them?" he said.

She took a deep breath and nodded.

"Sure?" he asked.

"Definitely," she said looking relieved. "How?"

"Identify who amongst your staff we can trust and help me locate this monastery."

28

Prado sent a text for el jefe to join him in the cell with Conchie. Meanwhile, Conchie opened her bag, repaired her face, and tidied her hair. When el jefe joined them, she was back to her alluring self. They sat around the table. El jefe raised his eyebrows at Prado.

"Conchie has admitted everything and has committed to helping us," said Prado. "She knows nothing about any plans to interfere with Wednesday's event and struggles to believe the brotherhood intends to kill the Pope. Before her father died, he was the senior brother of Hermandad de Corpus Puro. Her brother and Tobón are current senior members meaning she is familiar with their philosophy but is vehemently against it. However, she was blackmailed to collaborate."

"In her position, she should have reported them," said el jefe.

"She should but the price was too high to pay, and she has an aging mother to consider. Now she wants to make amends. She told me there is a monastery to the north of the city. Conchie visited it some twenty years ago and believes it might be the brotherhood headquarters. She has agreed to help us locate it."

"You sure about releasing her?" said el jefe. "We don't want her warning anyone."

"Jefe superior," snapped Conchie. "I understand your reticence but please accept my assurances of loyalty to the crown and the force. I may have been under their thumb all these years but hated everything they made me do. I realize my career is over but before I go, give me one final chance to right my wrongs. Please?"

"May I suggest," said Prado. "Conchie works with the detectives interviewing her officers to verify their loyalty so we can return them to their duties. She knows them better than we do and if she's seen to be working willingly with us it will help them relax and be more forthcoming."

El jefe nodded, stood, opened the door, and invited Conchie to leave in front of him. She followed him and as she approached the door, turned, and glanced at Prado. "Thank you," she mouthed.

"Bring Sergeant Chavez, please," said Prado to the armed guard outside the door.

Minutes later, the sergeant appeared at the open door. The guard removed her cuffs, nudged her inside, and closed the door. Prado smiled and indicated she should sit.

"Water?" he said.

"Please."

Prado placed a bottle in front of her. She opened it and gulped it down.

Prado sat opposite, leaned forward, placed his hands on the table, and stared directly into her eyes.

She looked down and seemed unsure of herself.

"Tell me about your relationship with Detective

Inspector Tobón," he said.

She stared back at him, calmer now.

"He's my boss, I respect and enjoy working with him."

"Would you say he is a good detective?"

"Best I've ever worked with but at times he sails too close to the wind."

"He breaks protocol?"

"Yes."

"Tampers with evidence?"

"Occasionally."

"What has he tampered with in the case of the dead priest?"

The sergeant paled, chewed her nails, and said nothing.

"Sergeant, this is a matter of national security, normal rules do not apply. Our conversation is not being recorded and a solicitor is not available. I'm sure you realize your career is on the line here and the only way you can save it is to tell me the truth. What evidence has your boss tampered with?"

"I dare not say," said the sergeant.

"Are you more afraid of what he might do to you than me?"

She bit her nails harder and nodded, her eyes welling up.

"Are you concerned for your safety?"

She nodded again, tears flowing down her cheeks.

"I'm sorry to put you in this position but lives are at stake here including the Pope."

"What?" she snapped opening her bag, extracting a packet of tissues, and wiping her eyes.

"Are you aware of the event on Wednesday?"

"I know something big is due in the cathedral but

not the details."

"But Tobón does?"

"Yes, he's involved in the security but said it was hush-hush and we weren't to know or talk about it with anyone."

"If I were to tell you Tobón will not be returning to his duties and will be locked up behind bars for the remainder of his days, would you feel more inclined to be open with me?"

"No," she said.

"Why not?"

"The brotherhood. You might succeed in putting Tobón away but there are hundreds more of them and they are everywhere. The courts, security services, the council even the church."

"Do you mean the cathedral?"

"I don't know exactly, my point is you might cut off one, even ten tentacles, but it won't kill the beast."

"Are you involved with the brotherhood?"

"No way. I'm a mere woman."

"Why do you so revere Tobón?"

"He's handsome, manly, and surprisingly tender although at times his temper can turn him evil."

"Have you had an affair with him?"

She nodded.

"Are you still having an affair with him?"

"Yes," she said. "But we're more friends with benefits."

"Is he having affairs with other coworkers?"

"Yes."

"Who?"

"You've met them?"

"At the initial interview?"

"Yes."

"All of them?"

"Well, not the pathologist or those in a relationship."

"Any others?"

"His niece."

"You're joking."

She looked up and directly into his eyes.

"Sir," she said. "Please don't judge us. We are career women but for some reason, men are deterred by our looks and the fact we are police officers. Even if they were brave enough to ask, we have so little time for relationships, but still have itches and need them scratched occasionally. Tobón has beautifully manicured nails if you follow my meaning."

"I take it he's unmarried."

"No wife, plus he's an excellent cook with a cool apartment."

"Now I understand your reluctance to give evidence against him, but it still changes nothing. Unless we can discover their plot, on Wednesday morning the brotherhood is likely to kill the world's religious leaders. The consequences for the citizens of Córdoba are terrifying. I'm going to send you back to a cell and let you reflect on our discussion. Should you wish to cooperate with me just tell one of my officers.

"Guard," shouted Prado.

The guard opened the door.

"Cuff her and put her in a cell by herself. Then bring me Tobón's niece.

29

Prado popped out of the interview room for a restroom break and a cup of execrable coffee from the machine. At least it is wet and warm he thought as he stood alone in the vending area. He finished his coffee, purchased a chocolate bar, and as he paced around chewing on it wondered how to approach the niece. Should he exploit the incestuous side of her relationship with Tobón or ignore it. "I'll decide when I see her," he muttered.

He returned to the interview room to find the niece sitting at the table. She'd been crying.

Prado sat opposite her, but she wouldn't look him in the eye.

"It's Elena, right?"

She nodded.

"Do you know what the brotherhood intends to do on Wednesday?"

She shook her head.

"Are any of your other relatives' members of the brotherhood?"

"No, only my uncle," said Elena looking shyly at Prado. "As far as I know. It's impossible to tell who is, or who is not, a member. They are extremely secretive."

"You never overheard him say anything about Wednesday or saw any messages?"

"Never."

"Weren't you curious to know more about the event?"

"Yes, but too scared to inquire," said Elena. "People who ask awkward questions have a habit of losing their jobs and being ostracized by their friends and potential employers."

"What do you know about the event?"

"There is a religious gathering," said Elena. "The inspector has something to do with security."

"Were you ordered to be part of the security team?"

"No, but some colleagues in the station have to report to the airport," said Elena. "The list is on the database."

"Concerning the death of Father Julián or the Arab," said Prado. "What do you know about tampering with evidence or false reporting."

"I erased some footage on the cell block video," said Elena. "But I was only following my uncle's orders."

"You used the authority of the head of this station?"

"Yes."

"What did you erase?"

"The interviews between my uncle, the interpreter, and both Arabs."

"What was said to the elder that upset him so?"

"Unless he signed a statement, his grandson would disappear into the hands of sexual predators."

"Did he sign?"

"Reluctantly, yes," said Elena. "Afterward, he tried

to attack my uncle. When he realized the hopelessness of his efforts, he slumped back into his chair, looked pale, and had difficulty breathing."

"Was a doctor summoned?"

"No, my uncle heaved him up and took him back to his cell. The man could hardly walk."

"Can you recover the footage?"

"No, I permanently deleted anything to do with both Arabs."

"What about the transcripts?"

"I burned them," said Elena.

"How did the blood, hair, and fingerprint appear on the candlestick?"

"My uncle fabricated everything," said Elena. "I helped him."

"Would you be prepared to sign a statement confirming your role?"

"Will it save my job?"

"No, but it will demonstrate a willingness to cooperate which could bode well for references."

Elena paused, her eyes flittering all over the place.

"It's a difficult decision," said Prado. "Family or future?"

"I'll sign," said Elena. "He would in my place."

"Given the priest wasn't killed by the Arabs. What conclusions did your uncle come to about how he died?"

"He was convinced it was suicide," said Elena.

"Did he have any ideas what happened to the father's clothing or why he chose that particular chapel?"

"He never mentioned anything to me."

"What were the Inspector's justifications for fabricating the evidence against the Arabs?"

"To protect the father's family from the shame of suicide," said Elena.

"And you went along with it?"

"Yes, but I had no choice. I love my uncle deeply but am terrified of his temper. What he said was what I did."

"I noticed most of your uncle's team are attractive women," said Prado. "Why?"

"He's handsome, masculine, and an amazing lover," said Elena.

"You had no problem sharing him?"

"None at all."

"Why?"

"His secretive ways and brotherhood membership had elevated him to a mysterious godlike figure with total control over me and my colleagues. I knew he was never going to be mine and I didn't want him as such. It was just good sex."

"Did you discuss these er matters with his other lovers?"

"Occasionally. Women do you know."

"Amazing. Nobody was jealous?"

"Grateful, sir. We were grateful."

Prado looked at Elena mulling over her last words. "Was the comisario principal on his list of conquests?"

"No. She's just a puppet," said Elena. "Too short and fat. Most of us ignore her, and when she does interfere, we tell the inspector, and he deals with her."

"Thank you, Elena," said Prado. "I'm happy you've been truthful with me. Do you have anything to add?"

"No, sir," she said.

"You'll have to stay in a cell until after Wednesday lunchtime," said Prado. "And you will probably be joined by some of your colleagues so it might become a little uncomfortable, but we have no other space available. Later this morning the comisario principal will take your statements and deal with the termination of your employment. Goodbye."

Prado stood up, escorted her to the door, and handed her over to the guard.

"Bring Detective Inspector Tobón," he said.

30

Detective Inspector Humberto Tobón seemed relaxed when the guard escorted him into the room and removed his cuffs. He didn't wait to be invited to sit, just went ahead, and looked at Prado expressionless while rubbing his wrists.

Prado sat down and returned his gaze.

Tobón sneered at him, leaned back in his chair, and lifted his feet on the table. The epitome of Mr. Cool rockstar in his designer outfit.

"You think you are untouchable?" said Prado.

"Not just me, inspector, you have no idea who we are or what we are planning. And no matter what you think I've done, you don't have a shred of evidence, otherwise, you would have charged me. However, before you ask any questions, I demand a lawyer."

"This isn't an interview," said Prado glaring at him. "It's a chat between colleagues. As you say, you are innocent of any crime, so why would you need a lawyer? Anyway, as I'm not going to ask any questions you won't need one. What I am going to do is paint a picture. Then you can decide how to proceed."

"Is this how you do things in Málaga?" said Tobón.

"Play word games? Evidence, Inspector, what you need is evidence."

"Humor me for a few minutes?" said Prado leaning forward.

Tobón regarded him, uncertainty clouding his face. He put his feet down and sat forward in his chair with his elbows on the table but after a few seconds looked down.

Prado had disarmed him. A small victory at least.

"You're incorrect in one respect," said Prado. "I have enough witnesses to confirm your tampering with evidence and have you locked up for years but for the moment those charges can wait. What concerns me more is how your brotherhood intends to stop the signing on Wednesday morning. I don't know how or when, and after the event, it probably won't be clear who was culpable. Yet I will know you were the main perpetrator. No matter who else you are working with, you will be held personally accountable, and the prime minister will ensure that you are permanently removed from society. This has consequences you need to consider carefully. You are a man who relishes his luxuries along with a doting harem of attractive women available at the click of a finger. A week behind bars will destroy you. In six months, you will attempt to kill yourself because half the prison will be lusting after your pretty boy butt, while the remainder will want to carve up the man who had them committed."

"Whatever happens to me is of no concern," said Tobón. "My job is done. Everything is in place and nothing you do can stop it."

Prado looked at him, stood, turned, and left the room.

"Lock him up," he said to the guard as he passed

him. "In the most crowded cell possible.

The guard cuffed Tobón and led him down to the cells.

31

Prado went outside for some fresh air and paced around the car park pondering over Tobón's disturbing parting words. The sun was setting, a kaleidoscope of red, pink, orange, and yellow lit up the scanty clouds on the western skyline. The trumpets of a distant band signaled the start of another brotherhood setting out on its laborious journey around the city's narrow streets. Was Tobón bluffing? Was their plot unstoppable? Prado had thirty-six hours to find out before the world's religious leaders descended on the bishop's palace. Cancellation was no option; the event would proceed no matter what. Too much time had been invested, so much was at stake.

What next? Thought Prado. Sniffer dogs in the cathedral, or find this monastery? It must be both at the same time if so, where should I be? I must concentrate on the who which means the monastery. El jefe and the general's men can manage the searching of the cathedral.

Feeling more positive, he went back inside and found el jefe behind the desk in Conchie's office. He was on the phone and didn't look happy. Phillip was sitting opposite. Prado sat next to Phillip leaned forward and said, "What's happening?"

"The general's men have been delayed," said Phillip. "Their vehicle broke down."

"Then we must move forward without them. Do you recall the blurred trees we saw on Google Earth earlier?"

Phillip nodded.

"I think it's an old monastery and probably where they have taken Amanda and the Arab boy. Hopefully, Conchie should recognize it. Have we heard back from the helicopter search?"

"Not yet."

El jefe ended his call. "They'll be another two hours at least," he said. "They have to wait for a replacement vehicle."

"Sir," said Prado. "We may have located the brotherhood headquarters."

"Where?"

"I need to call the military first," said Prado taking out his phone. "I asked them to check out some coordinates and take photos."

"What coordinates?"

"Just off the road where the car disappeared with Amanda," said Phillip. "Is a redacted area on Google Earth. We think it might be there."

"Hello," said Prado turning on the speaker. "Captain Carranco?"

"Yes, inspector," said a crisp female voice.

"Did you take any photographs this afternoon?"

"Hundreds and I think we've found what you're searching for."

"Tell me?" said Prado.

"To be honest, we're mystified," said Carranco. "I'll

email you the images, but we can't see anything on military maps, old or new. In theory, there should just be millions of olive and almond trees but right in the middle is a huge building. We were told not to fly lower so we're unsure, but it resembles an old monastery."

"Did you see a command center or any sentries?"

"No. Adjacent to the building was a giant barn with a dung heap outside which suggests they keep animals but no evidence of guards, or security equipment. There was also a huge walled vegetable garden with some eighty people working in it. We couldn't see any pylons so are assuming the building is not connected to mains electricity but there was a mast for TV, mobile phones, and internet which means they do have power and communications. Counting the number of solar panels and wind turbines among the trees, I suspect they are completely self-sufficient. We couldn't trace any ownership details on the land register, but we haven't checked with the local town hall."

"Please don't," said Prado. "We don't know who we can trust there, and any inquiries may trigger a warning we are interested. What about access?"

"They are perched on top of a hill some four kilometers off the main CO-3405 and three hundred meters higher. Access is by a narrow, steep, and dusty track leading up to the main entrance which is a massive doorway under an arch at the front of the building. The doors were open and there were several vehicles parked inside a courtyard. Three jeeps, two seven-seater vans, and a gray saloon car which matched the description you gave us. We couldn't read the plates. Why are you interested in this place?"

"We suspect it is the headquarters of an extreme right-wing brotherhood with plans to disrupt a major event in Córdoba cathedral on Wednesday morning. We believe they are holding two of our people, a female translator, and an Arab boy. There may well also be some prisoners being kept against their will. Captain, we need to catch them by surprise. Could you help us?"

"Yes, but I require orders."

"I have all the authority you need Captain. I'll email it to you."

"Assuming, it checks out," said Carranco. "What do you need?"

"It's crucial we access their membership database before they can wipe everything. Driving up a steep road will need headlights and time so they will know we are coming. I'm thinking of a parachute drop at dawn with enough armed soldiers to lock everything down instantly. When all is secure, we'll drive up and meet you there."

"Our helicopter can drop up to ten soldiers from a height out of earshot. Is that enough?"

"I don't anticipate armed resistance. This is a religious brotherhood. Do you have anything to block cloud storage access and phone signals?"

"Yes," said the captain. "A surveillance drone we're dying to test under live conditions. It can stay in place for hours giving us eyes on, day and night. We'll be able to locate where everybody is, except for those underground. We could position it overhead within half an hour if you wish?"

"Fantastic," said Prado. "Go ahead."

"Do you want us to block their communications?"

"Not until just before the raid, otherwise we might alert them to our intentions but is it possible to record their transactions and calls?"

"Of course."

"Could you let us know if any warrant urgent action?"

"Certainly. How many of you will there be?"

"Two plus a team of five detectives, a doctor, and medics with an ambulance. We'll be waiting for your signal on the main road."

"We'll have the helicopter drop a flare. Anything else?"

"I'll text you if I think of something. See you in the morning, captain."

"Goodnight, inspector."

Prado's phone immediately started buzzing.

He checked what was happening.

"It's the monastery photos," said Prado.

"You should show them to Conchie," said el jefe. "While you still have time to cancel your dawn raid."

"How many monasteries can there be?" said Prado. "But I'll take them to her now. Where is she?"

"Interviewing her staff in the briefing room," said el jefe.

"How's it going?" said Prado.

"Not as bad as we thought," said Phillip. "So far three have admitted brotherhood membership but there are still nine officers out on patrol."

"Can't we summon them to base?" said Prado.

"Leave it to me," said el jefe. "You have enough on your plate. Go and see Conchie."

Prado found her alone in the briefing room, deep in thought.

She looked up as Prado entered and smiled.

"Phillip tells me you've identified three brotherhood members," said Prado.

"Not as many as I expected," said Conchie.

"So, what's depressing you?"

"Their attitude toward me and my rank. Even the most junior has no respect."

"Try not to take it personally. The problem is their conditioning, not you. They have no respect for women full stop. Anyway, sorry but it's not why I'm here."

"The monastery?"

"Yes," said Prado pulling up the first image on his phone and showing it to her. Is this it?"

Conchie took his phone flicked through them and looked at him with an expression of hope.

"Yes," she said. "Where is it?"

"On the CO-3405 heading north but it doesn't appear on any maps or at the land registry."

"Why am I not surprised," said Conchie handing back his phone.

"We're raiding it at dawn," said Prado. "Care to join us? You can make peace with Dani Lopez."

Conchie looked at him, then laughed.

32

After a substantial supper, Amanda went to bed with a heavy heart. Doubts about her decision racked her brain. I don't know whether to stay, she thought, hopefully for my baby's safety, or put as much distance as possible between me and this freak show. If I do stay though, can I trust them? I'm not pure bred and heaven knows what they will do to me or my child. No, I'll go.

The idea was to sleep until the early hours but the turmoil in her mind weighed heavily. She tossed and turned constantly hearing voices murmuring and passageway lights going on and off as fellow prisoners visited each other. Every hour or so, she went to the door and listened. Her cell light activated every time she did but went out if she stood still for a few minutes. Each time she checked, there was still someone talking or walking along the passageway.

Gradually, it quietened.

She waited for what she thought was about two hours. Surely everyone was asleep by now, she thought.

She swung her legs over the side of the bed. The light snapped on. She took a long drink of water, splashed her face, had a pee, and slipped into the rough blue overalls and workmen's boots all the patients wore. At least they were warm. She pinned her hair back, tied her black headscarf, so it covered her mouth and nose, and headed quickly up the passageway. She reached the door to the hallway and paused waiting for the light to go out before trying to open the door. When it switched off, she reached through the bars and fumbled for the bolt, but it was further than she thought. She hung onto a bar with one hand and heaved herself up. Now she had a better purchase she could just touch the bolt and after several attempts managed to slide it open.

She cheered silently, so far so good, opened the door slowly, and went through closing it delicately behind her. The dining room to the left was the route to the kitchen and pantry. She walked as gently as possible in the clumsy boots, made her way into the kitchen, and closed the door behind her. A row of electric hobs lay in front of her along with several racks of pots and pans. There were windows to the left with dull moonlight shining through reflecting off several parked vehicles outside. On the off chance, she tried the outer door, but it was locked. She made her way along the inside of the windows lined with sinks and draining boards and arrived at another door. She pressed the handle down and pushed. It opened smoothly. A rush of food smells hit her. Fresh vegetables and fruit lay in baskets on shelves on both sides. Ahead was the tiny window and it was open. She rushed over and tried to put her hands on the sill to jump out only to find her way blocked by a fine plastic mesh.

"Fuck," she muttered and went back into the

kitchen to search for a paring knife. Several drawers later she had what she needed, returned to the pantry, and cut away the mesh.

She popped her head out and peered into the moonlit gloom.

She could see the vehicles clearly and could make out the entrance to what looked like an accommodation block where gothic girl said the keys were meant to be.

She heaved herself up and squeezed through the window.

The baggy overalls jammed on the sill, so she edged back, arched her torso, and tried again.

She slipped through and hand-walked down the wall. When she touched the concrete, she dragged her legs out of the window slid them down the wall and stood up. She was out and did a little jig to celebrate.

She tried the nearest jeep door. It was open. She left it ajar and headed toward the accommodation block. She opened the door and a light snapped on.

She froze, too terrified to move, her heart in her mouth.

She waited but no one stirred.

She was in a stairwell. To the left was a glazed door. To the right was a staircase. Hanging on the wall at the bottom of the stairs was a cupboard. She opened it. There were rows of keys on hooks, neatly tagged.

She picked out three labeled, jeep, took them all, and returned to the one with the open door. The light in the accommodation block went out as she climbed in and tested the keys. The second slipped in and turned. She fastened her seatbelt, released the handbrake and the vehicle started moving slowly and silently toward the open gate. Her pulse raced as the gate drew nearer and nearer. She steered through but found the wheel almost impossible to turn without its power steering.

The road turned sharp left and became substantially steeper. She needed lights and power if she were to negotiate the approaching bend. She turned the key and started the engine. It roared into life. Now she was in control, and she set off gingerly unaccustomed to such a large, heavy vehicle.

She crawled down the slope, the sandy track hard and dusty. Pine and almond trees lined both sides.

Her progress was laboriously slow, but she dared not speed up staying in first gear. She was unsure if the four-wheel-drive was functioning and was too frightened to take her eyes off the track to look for the controls. She hung onto the steering wheel tightly as the jeep bumped downwards round bend after bend after bend.

How far to the main road, she wondered?

Something bright lit up behind her. She glanced in the mirror and was immediately dazzled. She looked forward but her vision was impaired. The lights came closer at phenomenal speed. She pressed the accelerator and immediately had to slam on the brakes for a hairpin bend. The vehicle behind slammed into the rear of the jeep which shoved her violently toward the edge of the track, but she managed to wrench it back on course and skid around the sharp curve.

The vehicle behind backed off.

But only temporarily.

It nudged her rear bumper along the next straight.

But she managed to stay on course.

Several sharp bends later, both vehicles were hurtling down the hill at breakneck speeds. Trees on both sides were interspersed with open sides topping a vertical cliff. Amanda was terrified as the headlights illuminated a dark open space with nothing below. Thankfully, as the lights turned the track came into view and pressed her foot to the floor resolved to reach the main road.

She raced toward the mother of all hair pins and jammed on the brake at the last second.

This time her chaser accelerated just as she was about to turn and smashed harder than ever into her rear. Her jeep missed the turning, went straight on, and crashed into a huge tree. It stopped dead.

She heard a bang, felt a pain in her chest and everything went black.

33

Phillip and Prado arrived first at the rendezvous point at the bottom of the track up to the monastery. They had both been up late checking on Conchie's staff verifications and dealing with those officers returning from patrol. Two more brotherhood members had been identified.

They had a few hours of tortuous sleep, but now they were within striking distance of their objective, the adrenalin kicked in. They were alert and raring to go waiting for the flare.

Phillip tried not to think about Amanda, but it proved impossible. If he closed his eyes, she appeared in a haze rubbing her tummy. If he stared too long at a bush, it took the shape of her face. He analyzed his thoughts about how he would react to being face to face with her jailers. But any clarity disappeared in a red mist of rage. He checked his watch. It was six forty-five. The eastern horizon was beginning to lighten. The silhouettes of treetops and hills began emerging from the gloom, but the monastery couldn't be seen from the road. It was beyond the first line of hills.

The others started pulling into the track entrance a

few minutes later.

First was the ambulance with a doctor and two medics in green overalls. They exchanged numbers.

Two unmarked vans followed shortly after. One with seven special forces from the general's team, the other with five detectives from Málaga and Conchie.

Everyone climbed out, stretched limbs, had a pee, and chatted quietly.

Phillip checked again.

It was almost seven, time for the drop.

Everyone stared up in the direction of the monastery. They could see nothing but millions of stars.

The captain had estimated it would take ten to fifteen minutes to secure the monastery. At precisely eight minutes past seven, a distant flare brightened the sky. They didn't wait until it extinguished but jumped in their respective vehicles and headed up the track. Prado led the convoy in his Mercedes. The ambulance brought up the rear.

Just over halfway they approached a particularly sharp hairpin bend and saw a jeep smashed into a tree. The front bumper and engine compartment had been shoved back almost as far as the windscreen but there was no steam, and the driver's door was open. Prado stopped, Phillip leaped out and ran over and touched the twisted hood. It wasn't hot but neither was it cold. He turned on his phone flashlight and peered inside. The airbags had burst but there was no sign of blood or passengers, just a long black headscarf curled on the floor in front of the driver's seat. He picked it up put it to his nose and breathed deep.

It was Amanda's.

He ran back to the Mercedes, jumped in, and

slammed the door. Prado hit the accelerator. The rear wheels span on the sand and they continued their way up the steep slope.

"Looks like my dearest fiancée attempted to escape a few hours ago," he said. "This is her scarf."

"Do you think she survived the crash?" said Prado.

"I think the airbags saved her. There was no sign of blood, but she must have been unconscious."

"Why?"

"She would never leave her scarf behind."

"Let's hope somebody has been treating her."

"Can we ask the soldiers to look for her as soon as we arrive?"

"Of course," said Prado. "And try not to worry. It'll be the first order I give?"

"Thanks," said Phillip chewing his knuckle. "But I won't stop panicking until I know she's OK."

They arrived at the monastery entrance and stopped outside. One soldier approached; weapon aimed at them. Prado opened the window and showed his ID.

"Park outside, please," said the soldier. "We're clearing the courtyard for the chopper to land."

Prado squeezed the Mercedes between a jeep and van with a damaged front on a verge next to the huge monastery wall. They climbed out and went in.

"Inspector Prado?" said another soldier as they went through the huge timber gate.

Prado showed his ID once more.

"This way, please. Captain Carranco has something she wants you to see."

They followed the soldier into the accommodation block, through the glazed door on the lower floor and along a passageway with doors off each side to the end. The soldier opened a door and ushered them in. It was a spacious room sparsely furnished with a giant flat-screen TV on the wall opposite a comfortable armchair with a coffee table by the side. Next to the coffee table was a desk and office chair. Opposite was a sideboard covered with family photos. A door to the left led into a bedroom with an unmade bed. To the right were a small kitchen – diner and a bathroom.

The captain, a tall thin woman in full combat gear with pinned back mousy hair had stashed her helmet next to a desktop computer. She was leaning over the desk and tapping the keyboard.

"Inspector Prado, sir," said the soldier.

"Ah Prado," said the captain. "These are the quarters of the senior brother. This is the master computer on their network, and I believe this is their membership list. Care to look?"

Prado went and stood beside her.

"Before we start digging into their database," said Phillip. "Have you found a petite American woman with long dark hair?"

"Not as far as I know," said Carranco. "Is she your fiancée?"

"Yes," said Phillip. "We found her headscarf in a crashed jeep halfway up the track. She must be here."

"Garcia," said Carranco.

"Sir," said the soldier standing alert at the doorway.

"Ask the security man where she is. What's her name?"

"Amanda Salisbury," said Phillip.

"Report back with your findings," said Carranco.

"Sir," said Garcia and trotted off.

"Did they have much security?" said Prado.

"Just one guy," said Carranco. "He's a hell of a specimen. More brawn than brain though and unarmed, he wasn't a problem."

"He'll know where Phillip's fiancée is," said Prado. "Someone strong must have carried her out of the jeep and brought her back. It had to be him."

"I thought the membership list was your priority," said Carranco.

"It is," said Prado. "But Phillip here will be able to make sense of it more enthusiastically if he feels comfortable about Amanda."

"I understand," said the captain replacing her helmet. "I'll go and see to it personally."

"Thank you, Captain," said Phillip turning toward the computer and taking a seat in front of it. He closed the file and searched the machine for the latest transactions.

There was one item of concern.

A draft email in Spanish and English addressed to the national and local Spanish media informing them of tomorrow's event at the cathedral. If it had been sent, it would ruin everything. He checked the sent folder, but it was empty. While the inkling of an idea germinated in his mind, he went back to the membership list and opened it up. Prado leaned on his shoulder and looked with him as he scrolled through.

Against each member was a bounty of personal information. Contact details, family connections, job, history of tasks done for the brotherhood, financial status, money donated. There were over seven hundred members. They included three judges, seven civil guards, five national police, fourteen local police, the deputy mayor, seven councilors, two politicians, and many successful businessmen.

"Conchie needs to see this," said Prado. "She will know most of them."

"But will she know which ones are involved in the plot for Wednesday?" said Phillip.

"We need to speak with the senior brother," said Prado. "He might be cooperative. Is there anything on the machine about Wednesday?"

"One thing only," said Phillip.

"Show me."

Phillip brought up the draft press release.

"This," he said.

Prado skimmed through it. "Fuck," he said. "Has it been sent?"

"Not from this machine."

"What email address are they using?"

"Info@corpuspuro.org. Thankfully, it can only be controlled from this computer."

"That's a relief but it raises the issue. What if a journalist happens to be passing the palace in the morning as the buses arrive and spots the Pope? They could blow the lid off the whole event and might even disrupt it to the extent the delegates walk away."

"I have an idea," said Phillip.

"Go on."

"We change the content of the email to something along the lines of, 'Police and military raided the headquarters building of Hermandad de Corpus Puro this morning without a warrant and arrested the senior brothers on a series of trumped-up charges. The brothers are being interviewed without a lawyer present and held against their will. The sixteenth-century monastery was gifted by dictator Franco to the brotherhood's founder Jesús Blanco in 1939. It's located halfway up the CO-3405 going north. Please see attachment for coordinates."

"Brilliant," said Prado. "They'll charge up here by

the thousand and it will keep them away from the cathedral. However, don't send it until we are ready, otherwise, the roads will be jammed."

"Leave it with me."

"I'll find Conchie and tell her about this. If she handles it well it may save her job. Then I'll go talk with the brothers."

An almighty row outside interrupted their conversation.

The helicopter landed then switched off.

Ten minutes later, Phillip was satisfied with the email text. All he had to do was press send. He returned to the membership list dug deeper and found Cristiano Da Rosa, the project manager for the works at the cathedral.

The next person of interest was David Bustillo, an assistant security guard at the cathedral.

"We need to interview these two as fast as possible," he muttered. "They must be aware of what the plans are. He sent a message off to Prado and el jefe with their address and telephone details."

"Mr. Armitage, sir," said a voice at the door.

Phillip turned and saw Garcia.

"Have you found her?"

"You're to come with me, sir."

Phillip left the machine on and followed Garcia out of the accommodation block. They skirted around the massive helicopter and through a door into a kitchen but other than a soldier guarding the gate he saw no one.

"Where is everybody?" he said.

"The patients are in their cells, the brothers are in the library with the inspector, the nuns, and other staff in the dining room. Our team and the general's men are minding the relevant doors, the detectives and the comisario principal are talking to prisoners on the lower levels, my CO is checking for other computers. Through here, please."

They went into the dining room.

Some twenty nuns dressed in white, some feeding tiny babies from bottles were seated on benches next to dining room tables. It reminded Phillip of his boarding school dining hall. Twenty or so children from three to thirteen sat on the floor in a corner, some crying quietly. Three women and five men, one a huge brute of a man sat at another table. One alert soldier stood guard, rifle at the ready.

"Security man?" said Phillip as they walked through.

"Yes, he's been most cooperative and told us where your fiancée was straight away. He even hoped she was OK."

Phillip perked up. Perhaps she is all right, he thought.

Everyone peered curiously at yet another new face as they headed for the door opposite. The guard and Garcia exchanged nods as they passed.

They went into a hallway and stopped at a door on the right. Garcia opened it and they went along a passageway and into a cell about halfway along. Amanda lay on the bed, the doctor, a slender man in his early thirties with short dark hair was examining her chest with a stethoscope.

Amanda looked up as Phillip came in.

She smiled wanly but didn't move.

"How is she?" said Phillip.

"Having seen the jeep on the way up, surprisingly well," said the doctor. "Severely bruised ribs, a dislocated shoulder, and whiplash. However, she needs x-rays to double-check there is nothing more serious inside. If you could make it quick, please, I want to knock her out for the journey to the hospital and we should go as soon as you've finished. We'll give you some privacy but please no more than a few minutes."

The doctor and medics squeezed past Phillip into the passageway.

He looked down at Amanda, his heart swelling with emotion. He kneeled, gingerly bent over, and kissed her.

"I'm not so terribly injured," she said. "You can hug me if you want."

He reached his arm over and rubbed her belly.

"Anything you want to tell me?" he said.

"Don't be too hopeful," she said sniffing. "The crash may have done something. It feels fine but I'm keeping my fingers crossed an ultrasound scan will confirm it. You saw the test packaging?"

"We found your car, it's at the comisaría. Ultimately, it led us to this place."

"What now?"

"Don't you worry about it? Just concentrate on recovery and our baby. What do you prefer?"

"A fully working model, I don't care if it's a boy or girl."

There was a sound in the passageway outside then some heated whispered argument.

The doctor came in and said, "The inspector is outside with a young Arab boy. He insists you talk with him. I've forbidden it, the last thing you need now is stress but if you feel up to it, I'll allow them in."

"Please," said Amanda. "I'll be fine."

The doctor went out to be replaced by Prado and a young puny boy.

"Sorry," said Prado bending over, kissing her forehead, and stroking her hair. "Conchie brought Faraq to me from the lower levels. I need to know everything he can tell us. Can you manage?"

"I'll try," said Amanda.

"Hi, Faraq," she said in Arabic. "We spoke on the phone. How are you?"

"Better than you, I think," said Faraq. "But I have no idea what's going on, where I am, or what will happen to me?"

"Let me ask the inspector."

"He wants to know his immediate future," she said.

"Once he's told me about his interview with Tobón, he'll be deported. He should be back home with his parents sometime this week."

Amanda explained.

The boy's face lit up.

Prado turned on his recorder and nodded to Amanda.

"Where do you want me to start?" said Faraq.

"From when you were arrested," said Amanda grimacing as she tried to move her head.

"I was asleep at the Red Cross center when I was woken by the manager indicating I should follow him. I was still exhausted by the walk from Nerja and tried to go back to sleep but the manager kept tapping my shoulder and pointing at my grandfather's bed. I noticed he wasn't there and wondered why. Worrying about him stirred me into action. I was still fully dressed so stood up and followed the manager to the lobby where two female police officers put me in handcuffs and escorted me to their car. I didn't understand what they were saying but assumed it was part of the immigration process so wasn't too concerned. They took me to the police station and put me in a cell with my grandfather. I was so pleased to see him, but he was extremely angry. He told me he'd been praying for a dead priest in the cathedral and had been arrested and didn't know why. He assumed they thought he killed him, but he was already dead. About half an hour later, the cell door opened, a woman came in and spoke to us in bad Arabic, but we understood the gist of what she was saying. We had both been arrested under suspicion of the first-degree murder of this priest. They took my grandfather away to be interviewed and brought him back about an hour later. He was in a terrible state muttering and swearing and finding it hard to breathe. I'd never seen him so distressed before and was panicking. Don't sign anything, he told me and collapsed on the bed. Then they took me. I complained to the woman my grandfather needed attention. I was desperately concerned for him. She said they would call a doctor.

"I was questioned for ages by a trendy man with long hair. I thought he was a musician, but the translator assured me he was a senior policeman. Was I part of a terrorist group, who were they, what were they planning? They carried on in this vein until I screamed, I knew nothing and demanded something to eat. They went out and came back some fifteen minutes later with a piece of paper. They gave it to me to read but it was in Spanish. The translator told me it was a statement confirming what I had told them."

"Which was?" said Amanda.

"I had never been to the cathedral or seen any priest. If I signed it, they would release me and return me to the Red Cross detention center to complete the immigration procedures. Naturally, I signed. They took me back to my cell where I found my grandfather dead in his bed. I screamed and they put me in another cell which is where your inspector found me several hours later, and I spoke to you on the phone thing."

"Later that afternoon," said Amanda. "You were taken out to a van. Tell me about it."

"Two men in uniform," said Faraq. "One large, the other as small as I cuffed my wrists and dragged me to a black van parked outside. I assumed they were taking me to the Red Cross. They fastened me to a seat, and we departed. It was only when we were under way, I noticed the bare feet of two people sticking out from behind the seats on the floor at the front, I became concerned. I had no idea what to do but worried they were going to kill me. I decided to leave evidence behind that I had been in the van so my mother would be informed. I put the copy of my statement on the floor under the seat, yanked out a clump of hair, put it by the statement, and left clear fingerprints on the window. Eventually, we arrived here, and I was put in a cell below where at last I had some excellent food."

Amanda translated.

"When our detectives have finished here," said Prado switching off his device. "They can take him to the comisaría and arrange for his deportation."

Amanda explained.

Faraq nodded looking pleased.

Phillip," said Prado. "Are you going to the hospital with Amanda?"

"Of course," he said, taking Amanda's hand in his.

"No, my love," said Amanda. "I'll be fine. You're needed here and we simply must discover what is planned at the cathedral. Otherwise, all this has been for nothing."

"You sure?"

"I'll text you."

"Please, I'll be worried sick," said Phillip turning to Prado. "I'll stay"

"Thanks," said Prado looking relieved. "When you're done here could you meet me in the library. The guard will show you where it is. There's something I need you to see."

Prado took Faraq out. Phillip bent over and hugged Amanda until the doctor intervened with an embarrassed cough. "We need to go now," he said, needle poised ominously in hand.

Phillip stood and watched the doctor inject his beloved.

Within seconds she was out.

The medics transferred her to a stretcher. He followed them outside where he took hold of Amanda's hand and walked along by her side. He shed a tear as they strapped her into the ambulance.

"She'll be fine," said the doctor patting him on the shoulder before clambering into the back and taking a seat next to her.

The medics closed the rear doors, climbed in the front, and drove off.

As they turned through the monastery gate, Phillip watched with a heavy heart.

He went to find Prado never having felt so lonely and full of despair in his life.

A soldier guarding the cell block entrance directed him to the library. He entered and found a group of men in pajamas and dressing gowns sitting in various armchairs and sofas. Another guard watched over them intently, but Phillip thought he needn't have been so diligent. They were mostly in their early sixties and by their physical appearances had led a sedentary life. Was this the leadership of the brotherhood? He wondered.

He spotted Prado taking a photo of the painting on the wall and went over to join him.

"What did you want me to see?" said Phillip as he approached.

"This painting," said Prado. "It's Jesús Blanco, founder of Hermandad de Corpus Puro."

"I thought they wore white tunics and cloaks."

"All members except the president."

"Who is the current president?" said Phillip.

"The brothers declined to say but look at the face, it looks familiar, but I can't fathom why."

"Perhaps he resembles someone you've seen during your inquiries, a relative or son perhaps?"

"They'd be too old, a grandson possibly?" said Prado.

"Have the brothers admitted anything about Wednesday?"

"They deny all knowledge of everything, rarely leave the monastery, and never had sex with those women. I'm assuming it must have been divine intervention."

"What about the prisoners in the lower cells?"

"They were legally committed here by relatives and all the correct paperwork is in their files proving it. It will need paternity tests and hours of painstaking police work collecting statements. Afterward, all hundred and sixty or so prisoners will need interviewing to identify how they came to be here and who was responsible for falsely imprisoning them. It's a huge investigation."

"It sounds exhausting, but is it the best use of your time? Can you not delegate it while we return to Córdoba?"

"You're right, I'm done here. If Conchie can keep the press busy for a day and sort out this mess, she will do more than enough to redeem herself. I'll leave her with two detectives, the rest of us will return to the comisaría and start rounding up brotherhood members. Did you notice anybody with the title president in the membership list?"

"No, but I've sent you and el jefe a copy. It needs to be studied in more detail because I've only had time to identify two people of interest. One is Da Rosa, the project manager of the cathedral building works, and Bustillo, a security guard at the cathedral. They must know what the plans are, and I suggest an immediate arrest."

Prado regarded him and nodded.

He checked the photos of the painting he'd taken were legible and called el jefe.

"Did you see Phillip's email?" said Prado when el jefe answered?"

"I did," said el jefe. "But first tell him how pleased and relieved I am Amanda is safe then I'll bring you up to date with what's happening here."

"El jefe is happy Amanda is Ok," said Prado.

"Please thank him for his kind thoughts," said Phillip.

"He says thanks."

"Warrants have been issued for the arrests of Da Rosa and Bustillo and we're analyzing each member to decide which are the important ones to talk to first."

"Have the general's men started searching the cathedral?"

"Around four hours ago with dogs and tracers for electronic signals. They've found nothing yet but don't worry, if there are explosives or devices, they'll sniff them out. Anything else of interest at the monastery?"

"Yes, but nothing to help us move forward quickly. Phillip and I are returning to the comisaría to talk to Bustillo and Da Rosa. We'll bring three detectives with us to help interview the other members but we're leaving Conchie here with two men to finish off the laborious tasks of taking statements from the patients and prisoners to identify which brothers have committed what crimes. They need some help with social workers and medics to deal with the children, the psychologically disturbed and addicted."

"Can't the nuns help?" said el jefe.

"They could but we don't know which ones may have been involved in assisting with the rapes."

"I agree Conchie should lead," said el jefe. "But she will need back up. I'll see what can be done. See you back here in an hour or so. We should have Da Rosa and Bustillo by then."

Prado and Phillip found Captain Carranco in the accommodation block checking all the other computers.

"We're off," said Prado. "Many thanks for you and your team's excellent performance in rescuing our captives. Amanda should make a full recovery."

"All in a day's work," she said. "Did you find anything useful in the membership list?"

"We did indeed," said Phillip. "Arrests are being made."

"And now you're abandoning us to deal with the leftovers?"

"I would hardly call over two hundred and forty people desperate for help as leftovers," said Prado. "We're leaving the comisario principal, two detectives, and the general's men to help out."

"Most generous, inspector."

"Our boss is arranging for social workers and medical staff to attend as soon as possible. Meanwhile, there's plenty of food and the water from the tap is superb."

"We'll have a party."

"Regretfully, that might prove difficult."

"Are you serious?"

"An army of journalists will be swarming this way sometime this afternoon. The comisario principal has been briefed exactly how to deal with them but I'm sure she'd appreciate any help. Try and keep them here as long as you can."

"Can you tell me why," she said.

"Not now but after Wednesday morning, you'll find out."

"I love a good mystery," she said and went back to studying the screen in front of her.

Phillip popped into the senior brother's room, brought up the email, and pressed send. He then deleted it and wiped the whole machine.

34

Phillip and Prado walked into the interview room and sat down opposite Cristiano Da Rosa. He was in his early forties, medium height, short brown hair, blue eyes, and chubby physique dressed in blue jeans, polo shirt with a leather jacket. They looked him up and down and stared into his eyes. The man couldn't return either gaze, just peered myopically at the table. Phillip could smell his fear.

"We found your name on the membership list of the Hermandad de Corpus Puro," said Prado. "You've been a member for sixteen years and have donated over fourteen thousand Euros. You've carried the throne during Holy Week on four occasions and have had charges for domestic violence withdrawn four times. Do you still beat your wife, Señor Da Rosa?"

"No comment," said Da Rosa.

"According to the files, Detective Inspector Tobón intervened on each charge against you. Was it out of the kindness of his heart or because he is also a fellow member?"

"My wife withdrew the charges."

"Under what pressure, I wonder," said Prado.

"How long have you been working at the cathedral as project manager?" said Phillip.

"Since the project began some eighteen months ago but I have worked there on previous occasions."

"You know the building well?" said Prado.

"It's why the company asked me to run this project."

"You've been underpinning the foundations, right?" said Phillip.

"And reinforcing the roof," said Da Rosa.

"When was the project finished?" said Prado.

"Around ten pm on Saturday night."

"Just in time," said Phillip. "What time did you leave?"

Da Rosa rubbed his eyes.

"Again, what time did you leave," said Prado.

"Look, I'm entitled to a lawyer," said Da Rosa.

"Why do you need one?" said Prado. "Have you something to hide?"

"I'm entitled."

"What was the last thing you did before leaving the cathedral?" said Phillip.

"I, er."

"You murdered Father Julián," said Prado.

"I did not."

"So, you didn't see him?" said Phillip.

"Yes, I saw him."

"When?" said Prado.

"Just before eleven."

"Where was he?" said Phillip.

"He was coming toward me. I'd just finished cleaning up some cement spillage in front of the chapel. My men must have missed it."

"What was he wearing?" said Phillip.

"A monk's robe and sandals."

"Did he say anything?" said Prado.

"Goodnight, before opening the chapel with a key and going inside. I left straight after."

"Where did you go?" said Phillip.

"Home."

"What time did you arrive?"

"I er it must have been er around eleven-thirty."

"Was your wife awake?"

"Yes. She served me with a snack, and we went to bed."

"Excuse me a minute," said Prado who stood and went outside. "I'm going to call your wife."

Phillip regarded Da Rosa. The man was sweating, looked pale and his eyes were all over the place.

Prado returned a couple of minutes later pocketing his phone. His expression was grim.

"I've just spoken with your wife," said Prado. "There seems to be some discrepancy between your story and hers."

"She's lying," he said. "Bitch."

"I doubt it," said Prado. "Why did you forget to mention the blood on your shirt and jacket sleeves?"

"What blood, I never saw any?"

"You don't do the laundry," said Prado. "But your wife found faint traces and decided not to wash them. She kept them hoping she might be able to use them against you. An officer will be collecting them from her shortly. I expect we'll discover the blood was Father Julián's."

Da Rosa slumped onto the desk.

"When you're ready, tell us what you know," said Prado.

"I didn't kill him," said Da Rosa looking up with

tears in his eyes. "It was el Fundador, he forced him to jump."

"Who?" said Prado.

"El Fundador? He's the president of our brotherhood."

"Why such a grand name?"

"Each president carries the title. It's tradition. Normally nobody sees him, but on this occasion, he was there in person."

"Who is he?" said Phillip.

"I don't know his identity, none of the members do but it's rumored that he is related to the founder Jesús Blanco. He wears a mask and whispers."

"Is he tall, fat, or thin?" said Prado

"I would say not tall, bony, he stoops and walks with a slight limp."

"What was he wearing?" said Phillip.

"A black suit, purple cloak, conical hat, and mask."

"How did he kill the father?" said Phillip.

"It's not that clear cut," said Da Rosa. "I was heading for the exit with my toolbox when I heard my name. I turned and it was el Fundador, he was standing by the chapel entrance. He beckoned me to him."

"How did you know it was him?" said Phillip.

"All members know he wears the purple cloak," said Da Rosa. "I put my toolbox down by the gate and joined him. We entered the chapel to find the father standing on the table. He'd unbolted the carving from the wall and was fiddling with some straps. It wasn't obvious what he was up to. El Fundador took a pistol from his pocket and whispered 'father.' The father turned and raised his hands, but he wasn't frightened, just angry. What do you want? He said. Take off your clothes, said el Fundador. Give them to Da Rosa. The father stripped and I had to pile them in the corner by the table. Then I was ordered to join the father on the table and strap him to the cross."

"What happened next?" said Prado.

"This is the confusing bit," said Da Rosa. "As soon as I had fastened the final strap, the father didn't wait for any more instructions from el Fundador. He heaved the cross onto his back, grunting and straining at its weight, shuffled forward, and fell onto the floor. He smashed face down onto the stonework and lay completely still. Then blood started flowing slowly from his head and pooling around his body. It was terrible. I jumped down from the table, rushed outside, and puked my guts up."

"Did el Fundador ask you to do anything else?" said Phillip.

"Yes, but it was more of an afterthought."

"Meaning?" said Phillip.

"He asked me if I had a screwdriver handle. I fetched one from my toolbox. He took a contraceptive from his trouser pocket, unwrapped it, and gave it to me. He told me to slip it over the end of the handle and ram it up the father's backside a few times. It must have been when I touched his blood, but I didn't notice at the time."

"Didn't you ask why?" said Prado.

"I wanted to but, with el Fundador one only speaks when asked but he was furious."

"How could you tell?" said Phillip.

"By his actions," said Da Rosa. "He rammed the pistol into his pocket, waved his fist up and down aggressively, and was breathing heavily."

"Why do you think he was angry?" said Prado.

"Because by jumping the father had taken the

initiative and not followed el Fundador's instructions."

"He sounds more like a dictator than the leader of caring brotherhood," said Phillip. "Yet still you obey him even to help in a criminal act? What else did he make you do?"

"I had to clean up my vomit."

"With what?" said Prado.

"The father's robes. Then I fetched the cleaning gear from the builder's office and mopped everything with a liter of bleach. I put the robes in the bucket and threw everything in a rubbish skip on the way to the car park."

"Anything else?" said Phillip.

"Delivery," said Da Rosa. "I accepted a delivery of eight cases and hid them in my locker."

"What was inside?" said Phillip.

"I don't know. El Fundador sent me a WhatsApp message instructing me to sign for them from the driver, stash them in my locker and leave it unlocked. Next morning, they were gone."

"When was this?" said Prado.

"About four months ago."

"Describe the cases," said Prado.

"They were heavy, not bulky, and smelled of oil."

"What did you think they were?" said Phillip.

"Not sure, but by their weight, it was something metallic, and the way the box moved when I lifted it was a number of items, not one solid lump."

"Did you see any signs of unusual works the next day?" said Prado. "Or something out of place or unexpected?"

"Nothing."

"Do you know any other members of the brotherhood?" said Phillip.

"A few."

"Any in the church or cathedral?" said Prado.

"Bustillo is the only one I know of in the church but a couple of the workers from Construcciones Artesanos were working on the project."

"Their names?" said Prado. "And any specializations."

"Gomez was a general laborer, Moyano an electrician."

"Did you ever see them working where they shouldn't be?"

"I don't recall, but in a complicated project of this nature, there are major tasks we all work on together and hundreds of minor tasks done by individuals at whatever time suits them. Sometimes they work at night or weekends to keep the program rolling forward on schedule."

"Had either of these two worked at night alone?" said Prado.

"Yes, on several occasions but I always knew what they were working on."

"But they could have done other things?" said Prado.

"Possibly but I never saw any sign."

"Is that it?" said Prado.

"Yes," said Da Rosa, relieved.

"What do you know about Wednesday?" said Prado.

"Pardon me?" said Da Rosa shaking his head with a puzzled expression.

"Wednesday. What's happening in the cathedral on Wednesday?" said Prado.

"Sorry, inspector, I have no idea."

"Thank you for your cooperation," said Prado. "I'm

going to hand you over to my colleagues now. They will charge you with accessory to first-degree murder and this time there will be no police friends available to persuade me to let you go."

Phillip and Prado stood up.

Prado opened the door and said to the guard.

"Take him up to the charge room, have them take his statement, and after he's been locked up bring us, Bustillo."

As Da Rosa was passing him, he added "You're to make a statement confirming everything you told us. If there is even one tiny discrepancy, the charges will be increased. Understand?"

Da Rosa nodded meekly as the guard cuffed him and led him away.

35

"Finally, some of the truth emerges," said Prado after Da Rosa had gone. "However, we are still no nearer to knowing what is planned for Wednesday, but it does seem more likely the father jumped before he was pushed because he was trying to tell us something. Since the beginning of this case, I've been puzzling over why he picked that chapel instead of one of the many others? Does it hold some theological significance we're missing? Was the carving purely an instrument of death or did taking it down signify something. What do you make of it?"

"Maybe it's not so complicated," said Phillip. "He killed himself because his death was the only way his sister could be saved, so he decided to give us a clue at the same time."

"Makes sense," said Prado. "Perhaps the bishop can help clarify matters. Meanwhile, let's see what Bustillo can tell us."

The guard returned with Bustillo, uncuffed him, and closed the door. Bustillo was a completely different character to Da Rosa; late thirties, short but with a stocky build, a hard face, and cropped dark hair wearing baggy trousers and a sleeveless t-shirt revealing huge muscular hairy arms. He moved like a cat when Prado invited him to take a seat and appeared relaxed.

"The membership database has you down as bilingual in Spanish and English," said Prado. "Correct?"

Bustillo nodded.

"Where did you learn English?" said Phillip in his mother tongue.

"In Newcastle. It's in the north of England," said Bustillo in a pure Geordie accent.

"Yes, I am familiar with Newcastle," said Phillip. "What were you doing there?"

"My parents are from Jerez de la Frontera. They couldn't find work so when I was three, they took a job as cleaners in a pub in Newcastle city center. They both spoke enough English having learned it from English neighbors who worked in a sherry bodega when they were kids. After several years, they took over the tenancy. I went to the local school. We returned to Spain when I was seventeen and I joined the Spanish Legion and served in Melilla. When I left two years ago, I was married with two sons. As my wife's family are from Córdoba, we settled here. I looked for a job in security needing both languages and started work at the cathedral."

Phillip looked at Prado and nodded.

"Why did you join the brotherhood?" said Prado.

"I was told it was the only way to climb the ladder," said Bustillo switching back to Spanish. "The best positions in most jobs were given to brotherhood members."

"Who told you?" said Prado.

"Nobody, in particular, just general chat among

friends and colleagues."

"Why Corpus Puro?"

"It was the only one with no waiting list, and I met the bloodline criteria."

"Are you religious?" said Phillip.

"Yes, as are my parents."

"What was the most important lesson you had to learn when you were initiated?" said Prado.

"To obey the brotherhood leaders, no matter what tasks I was given."

"After your service in the Legion, did you feel at home?" said Phillip.

"I have no problem following orders providing I trust those in command."

"And do you?" said Prado.

"Completely."

"Are you involved in the security for Wednesday?" said Phillip.

"Yes."

"What are your duties?" said Phillip.

"To liaise with the security team leaders of the Orthodox church from when they arrive on the bus at the cathedral. I stay with them and escort their group to the palace for the signing. Afterward to the cathedral for the service then back to the bus."

"Will you be armed?" said Prado.

"Yes, with a pistol and a baton."

"Where do the leaders come from?" said Phillip.

"Istanbul, Athens, Cyprus, and three from various parts of Georgia and Russia. Six in total."

"Will English be the common language?" said Phillip.

"Yes."

"What time are they due at the palace?" said Prado.

"The six buses arrive from ten am. The signing is at ten thirty, the service at eleven thirty and they depart at twelve-thirty."

"They're not hanging around," said Phillip.

"Deliberately so, to minimize any risks of attack."

"Who organized the security?" said Prado.

"General Quijano and his staff in liaison with the comisario principal and Detective Inspector Tobón."

"Tell me the breakdown of the security team," said Prado.

"Each group is bringing their own. They will accompany their delegates to provide personal protection. The airport, buses, and the route to the cathedral will be discreetly secured by a mix of armed forces, special forces, and national police from the local comisaría. In and around the cathedral is the responsibility of my boss, Guillermo Rojas."

"If you were a terrorist, how would you attack the leaders?" said Phillip.

"Sorry, impossible. The security is too tight."

"What if I were to tell you the brotherhood has already planned an attack which, in the words of your fellow member inspector Tobón, is unstoppable," said Prado.

"Forgive me, sir, but I would say nonsense."

"If I told you, Cristiano Da Rosa, under the instructions of el Fundador, accepted delivery of some strange smelling objects some four months ago and kept them in his locker. What would be your reaction?" said Prado.

"How do you know about el Fundador?" said Bustillo looking puzzled.

"Da Rosa told us as much as he could including el Fundador's involvement in the death of Father Julián," said Prado.

"I knew nothing about it."

"Irrelevant," said Prado. "As a member of a brotherhood involved in slaughtering one of the most popular priests in the cathedral, you are an accessory to the conspiracy. If you could be a tad more cooperative, we might look more favorably on any charges against you. Have you at any time received instructions in person or by WhatsApp from el Fundador which could be considered outside of your usual remit as a security officer?"

Bustillo stared at them long and hard.

"What would my sentence be if I refused to cooperate?"

"It depends," said Prado. "If nothing happens on Wednesday, then your role in the conspiracy to murder the priest would earn you some three to four years in prison. Could your dear wife and two sons cope, what would they think of you when you were released, how would your loving and religious parents react to your behavior? However, should the attack go ahead tomorrow morning, you can say goodbye to the rest of your life and remember, terrorists and their accomplices are not well received by other inmates. You'll either be in solitary with no visiting privileges or dead. Is this the legacy you want to leave to your sons?"

"No. I er. I was the next link in the chain, after Da Rosa. I moved the boxes from his locker to a spare one. My instructions were then to ignore their gradual disappearance which naturally piqued my curiosity. With the weight of them and the stink of oil, I wondered what the hell was inside. I kept an eye out at various times of the day and night to see who took them. Eventually, I spotted a man carrying a box from the locker to a large chest situated under where they were working on the roof."

"Did you recognize this man?" said Prado.

"Yes, he was the site manager for the roofing contractors."

"Did you find out his name and company from the security log?" said Prado.

"Yes. He was Jaime Lozano and the company he worked for was Techos Inteligentes and one more thing."

"Go on," said Prado.

"There is still an unused box in the locker."

"Did you look inside?" said Prado.

"No."

"Will you show us now?" said Prado.

Bustillo nodded.

"We'll have to cuff you," said Prado.

"I understand," said Bustillo standing and holding out his wrists.

Prado opened the door.

"Guard, please cuff him and bring him up to reception," said Prado.

Three minutes later they were in a marked police car, blue light flashing as it threaded its way slowly through the midafternoon crowd to the cathedral. White fluffy clouds speckled the blue sky and the thump of base drums from several bands echoed around the streets. They drove as far as they could and left the vehicles in front of the entrance to a locked garage in a side street some three hundred meters from the cathedral. The driver stayed with the vehicle.

As they approached the east entrance, a brotherhood in white tunics and green cloaks were entering the main door at the west end. Prado showed his pass to the security guard who was perturbed by the handcuffed Bustillo and spoke into his radio. They headed for the builder's office. They hadn't gone more than a hundred meters before Guillermo caught up with them.

"Why is Bustillo being kept from his duties?" he said. "We are desperately short of resources."

"He's helping us with our inquiries," said Prado. "Did he tell you he was a member of Hermandad de Corpus Puro?"

"Those weirdos, no he didn't but if the bishop finds out it means instant dismissal."

"He's cooperating," said Prado. "So, hold off for a moment."

"Is this to do with tomorrow?" said Guillermo.

"Could be," said Prado.

"How can I help?"

"I don't know yet," said Prado. "Come with us anyway. Bustillo is taking us to a locker with some unusual objects. You might know what they are."

They continued their way through the building which at the far end was away from the procession activities, empty, almost ghostly.

Guillermo unlocked the builder's office door and turned on the lights. They went in.

Phillip looked at Bustillo and nodded. He went over to a row of fifteen tall metal lockers some meter and half high and a third of a meter square. He opened the locker door of the fourth one from the far end. It was empty except for a white cardboard box at the base. Bustillo nodded. Phillip heaved it out and placed it on the table in the middle of the room. It was taped up and looked as if nobody had opened it previously. Phillip stuck his key into the tape on the top and ran it along. He opened the flaps.

Inside was a row of long thin objects individually wrapped in oilcloth. He delicately removed one and carefully laid it on the table next to the box. He slowly unfurled the cloth laying the edges flat revealing a long thin cylindrical stainless steel, object some twenty centimeters long and one-centimeter diameter. There was a black cable five centimeters long sticking out one end of the tube with a black plastic bulb shape on its end.

"Looks like a detonator," said Guillermo.

"It could be, and the bulb is bound to be the receiver for the timer signal," said Phillip picking up the tube. It was lightly smeared with oil and weighed about a third of a kilo. He looked at both ends then grasped each and paused.

"Won't it explode?" said Guillermo backing off.

"It might," said Phillip twisting. After half a dozen turns, the outer casing was released from its thread. "But as you can see, it hasn't." He slid the casing off to reveal the inner workings. A glass vial full of a clear liquid nestled in the middle surrounded by cotton wool. The wire from the signal cable was connected to the top of the vial which was protected by another bulb-shaped plastic knob.

"Acid," said Phillip. "When the timer sends the signal, this inner bulb twists the glass, breaking it releasing the acid onto the metal, which then dissolves and snaps the cylinder in half, whatever this is holding up will lose its support and fall to the floor."

"And whatever is above will follow it down," said Bustillo. "Ingenious. I've never seen anything like it."

"We used them on bridges in Afghanistan. They were quick and quiet whereas explosives attracted nearby enemy," said Phillip rummaging inside the box, counting the cylinders.

"Twenty-four to a box," he said. "How many boxes?"

"Eight," said Bustillo.

"It means one hundred and sixty-eight have been used somewhere," said Phillip.

"But where," said Prado.

"The roof," said Bustillo. "It must be."

"What were they doing to the roof?" said Prado.

"Replacing some of the timbers and beams, mainly over the area where the cracks were in the floor," said Guillermo.

"Why?" said Phillip.

"When this end of the building slid several centimeters downhill," said Guillermo. "Some roof timbers shifted to the extreme edge of their supports. They had to be replaced with longer beams, and new fixings."

"If these acid cylinders have been used as fixings the roof could be brought down on top of the delegates," said Phillip.

"In the scale of things," said Guillermo. "There's not many. Each beam requires two bolts so only eighty-four would have been changed. When you consider there is a beam every meter totaling thousands in the whole building, the damage would be limited."

"These will be concentrated above the mihrab," said Bustillo. "Where the cracks were."

"The timbers falling on their own won't be particularly lethal," said Guillermo. "Not enough to guarantee killing everybody."

"Is it possible to store things on top of the timbers?" said Phillip.

"Yes," said Guillermo. "There's an attic on top of each run of timber. The floor can't stand too much weight, but a load of bricks evenly spread plus the timbers collapsing from eight meters high would be lethal."

"How regularly do you inspect the roof?" said Prado.

"Once a year," said Guillermo.

"When was the last time?" said Phillip.

"A week ago, after the builders had finished their repairs," said Guillermo. "It was clear."

"We should check again now," said Prado.

"Follow me," said Guillermo heading toward the stairwell.

As they climbed, Phillip glanced at Prado.

Prado smiled grimly.

Four flights later, they went through a door onto a pathway between the outer castellated wall and the first gable. It traversed the width of the building. They went to the end, turned right overlooking the bishop's palace, and went into the first gable. The long narrow triangular space which was precisely on top of the mihrab was empty.

In the center of the second gable, above where the leaders would be standing in front of the mihrab, was an evenly spread pile of builder's rubble. They moved closer and saw it was packed with a deadly mix of metal reinforcement rods and broken bricks. The next two roof voids were full of similar rubble, but the remainder were empty.

"This is a deliberate attempt to kill the religious leaders and their delegates," said Prado checking his watch. "In about eighteen hours."

"Ok," said Guillermo. "What now?"

"We need builders here and fast," said Phillip. "They will have to remove this rubble, locate the acid cylinders, and replace them with solid metal ones."

"It means working all night and canceling the remainder of today's processions," said Guillermo. "Assuming we can find enough builders, we're cutting it extremely close for tomorrow."

"Bearing in mind what Tobón said about it being unstoppable," said Prado "The general will have to summon a host of military engineers to replace the bolts and find the damn timer."

36

Prado summoned the driver of the car who had brought them partway to the cathedral to collect Bustillo and return him to the comisaría. His next call was to el jefe.

"We've uncovered the brotherhood's plan, sir."

"Excellent, tell me."

"The cathedral roof over the area where the delegates will be standing tomorrow morning has been set to collapse. Over one hundred and seventy support beams have had their metal fixings replaced by devices that dissolve when acid is released inside them. It will bring down several tons of builder's rubble piled in the roof void and kill or maim anyone standing underneath."

"What do you suggest?"

"Can the general arrange for military engineers, electric platforms capable of extending to the eight-meter-high ceiling, along with roofing equipment, builders' hoists, and as many laborers as possible? They will need to move the rubble out of harm's way and replace the acid cylinders with the correct fixings. Despite the failure of the general's men and dogs to find a timer, there must be one somewhere in the cathedral. They need to search again and set up a signal blocking device. Hopefully, we would have fixed the roof in time but just in case, the blocking signal should ensure the delegates are safe and the service can proceed as planned. Please liaise directly with Guillermo Rojas. It needs to be arranged immediately, sir."

"I understand. I'll call you back as soon as it is done," said el jefe. "Then join you at the palace."

Satisfied his boss was on the job, Prado and Phillip headed over to the palace and rang the bell.

"Si," answered a male voice Prado recognized.

"Father Ildefonso?" said Prado. "It's Prado, we need to see the bishop immediately."

"Sorry, but he's watching the next brotherhood set off in today's procession."

"Can you message him immediately to return to the palace? It's a matter of life and death."

"Are you joking?" said Ildefonso.

"I'm a policeman, father. I never joke."

"I'll message him immediately then come and let you in. You can wait in his office."

"Thank you."

Several minutes later, the father opened the door just as the bishop arrived panting from his dash up from the Roman arch.

"Thank you, Father Ildefonso," said the bishop. "You may return to your duties."

"Yes, bishop," said the crestfallen priest walking away with slumped shoulders.

"My dear secretary," said the bishop shaking his head. "Needs to control his emotions."

"My colleague, Phillip Armitage," said Prado

indicating Phillip. "He's also the fiancé of my abducted translator."

"Have you found her?" said the bishop as they walked around the cloisters toward the bishop's office.

"At the brotherhood headquarters," said Prado. "Along with a complete membership list."

"Thank, God," said the bishop.

"The list led us to Da Rosa and the security guard Bustillo," said Phillip.

"To cut a long story, short," said Prado. "The roof is set to collapse on top of the delegates in the morning."

"Oh no," said the bishop crossing himself. "We'll have to cancel. What a disaster."

"No bishop," said Prado. "It's exactly what they want you to do. I believe the army will be able to put everything right in time to go ahead but they will need unhindered entrance to the cathedral. We must cancel today's processions immediately and send everybody home. Do you have a procedure for such an event?"

"Only for severe weather."

"Are the Legion in today's event?" said Prado.

"Yes?"

"Do they have a commanding officer with them?" said Prado.

"Yes, I'll have to look him up on my laptop."

They arrived at the bishop's office. He unlocked it, led them in, and turned on his computer.

"Don't you have any officers available for crowd control?" said the bishop.

"Some," said Prado. "We're still resolving who we can trust. If we can at least begin by clearing the riverside of the next brotherhood and inform those due next not to come, it will give us access to and from the building. The builders' entrance is at that end. Those thrones already underway can just be stopped and told to disperse. Any in the cathedral can be allowed to clear through. It should take a couple of hours by when the army should be ready to start work."

"Your theory is fine," said the bishop. "However, to gain the brotherhoods and crowds immediate cooperation, we will need to present them with a solid reason not serious enough to cause panic. Any ideas?"

"Does the city have a gas supply," said Phillip.

"Yes," said the bishop. "We have it in the palace kitchens."

"Then we could declare a minor gas leak," said Phillip. "It will need investigating which means we need to clear the area to grant access to the gas engineers. It's plausible and shouldn't scare people."

"And it happens all the time," said the bishop so nobody will be surprised just annoyed."

"All agreed?" said Prado nodding at Phillip.

"I'll call the legion and brotherhoods," said the bishop reaching for his phone.

"I'll call Guillermo," said Prado. "His team can stop any further entry and start informing the crowds."

***

Two hours later, the streets were empty. Only one person had been injured. An elderly man had tripped over some cobblestones and sprained his ankle.

The sun was setting as the army arrived in a convoy of trucks and low loaders on the embankment packed with mobile platforms, roofing equipment, skips, and two hundred troops.

Phillip, Prado, and the bishop watched them from

the open palace gate as they set about their business.

Then police officers started arriving from the comisaría and relieved the legionnaires blocking off the streets.

El jefe and general Quijano joined them. The general was dressed in military fatigues wearing a beret. He was a medium height man in his early fifties with a pencil mustache, slim and alert."

They shook hands.

"Gas leak?" said the general. "Damn good ruse. Who thought of it?"

"I did, sir," said Phillip. "Nothing original though, it's one of many British army tactics for a rapid disbursement of civilians."

The general nodded.

"There is something critical I need to discuss with everyone," said Prado. "Can we reconvene in the bishop's office?"

The bishop led the way.

Father Ildefonso rushed out of the general office and followed them into the massive conference room where tomorrow the world's religious leaders would gather and sign a document that could be a reboot for humanity.

"Has this room been scanned for devices?" said Prado.

"Every three hours since my team arrived," said the general. "It's clean."

The room was prepared for the event with a long central table covered with crisp white cloths. Notepads, pencils, glasses, and bottles of mineral water lay in front of each chair. Sixty chairs were abutting the table for the main delegates and two chairs behind each for their assistants.

They sat down at one end and helped themselves to water.

Father Ildefonso made to sit with them.

"Thank you, father," said the bishop. "That's all."

The father couldn't hide his momentary flash of anger as he strode out of the door and shut it a tad too firmly behind him.

"Excuse my secretary," said the bishop. "I usually invite him to join us."

"Bishop, General, and gentleman," said Prado. "On the face of it, we seem to have thwarted the brotherhood attack for tomorrow morning. Normally I would relax and go home, a job well done. However, before I go and attempt to reconcile with my wife, I want to share a theory with you and invite your comments."

Prado looked each in the eye. Happy they were taking him seriously, he continued.

"The brotherhood has been thinking about and planning their attack ever since Tobón was asked to be involved in the security of the event. They have gone to extreme lengths to place members in key positions and worked out a strategy right down to the tiniest of details. Yet they had not foreseen their plot might be uncovered. Somehow, they learned Father Julián had at least guessed they were up to something and had to resort to desperate measures to stop him from telling anyone. They abducted the father's sister to blackmail him to keep quiet. They made plans to kill the father. El Fundador even made a rare personal appearance armed with a pistol and was prepared to shoot him. However, they seriously underestimated Julián's resolve to expose them. He hid the office files and wiped his laptop. He sent a cryptic message to the bishop. He chose a specific chapel to kill himself to draw attention to the brotherhood's intentions without revealing anything specific and hopefully save his sister. He jumped before el Fundador had a chance to shoot him. Why?"

Prado paused.

Phillip cocked his ear toward the door.

"Sssh," he mouthed, stood up, and crept silently toward the door. He yanked it open to reveal Father Ildefonso bending over with his ear to the keyhole. Phillip grabbed him, twisted his arm behind his back, and marched him into the room."

The father was terrified.

"He was only listening," said the bishop. "Surely we can be generous and let him go."

"And allow him to report what we were talking about to el Fundador," said Prado taking a set of cuffs out of his briefcase and handing them to Phillip. "We don't have time to deal with yet another distraction. Take him to the general office, attach him to a radiator and return here."

They watched while Phillip dragged the complaining father out of the door.

"You think he might be involved?" said the bishop. "Sorry, but I find it highly unlikely. He's a nice man from a good family and is usually most diligent."

"I have no idea, bishop," said Prado. "But nobody else should hear what I'm about to say, especially if their loyalty to you might be in question and listening at keyholes is hardly conducive to supportive behavior. We'll talk to him later and find out."

Phillip returned and resumed his seat.

"All secure," he said.

"Did the father say anything?" said the bishop.

"He just whined he was being excluded from everything," said Phillip.

"Oh dear," said the bishop.

"Concerning my question," said Prado. "Why did Julián jump before he was shot?"

"He wanted to kill himself on his terms," said the general.

"Exactly," said Prado. "He wanted to fall face down with the cross pointing toward the mihrab to guide us to where the attack would take place. My next question is, why did he choose the Chapel of the Souls of Purgatory to end his life? Bishop, can you think of any theological explanation which might justify his thinking?"

"As I mentioned before, the only relevance springing to mind are souls flying about in limbo preparing to knock on heaven's door."

"In other words, up not down," said Prado.

"Indicating the roof where my troops are now working," said the general.

"Do any other chapels indicate adjacency to heaven?" said Phillip.

"Several," said the bishop. "Some use angels, others the almighty father. Dear Lord, perhaps Julián was indicating something in the roof above that particular chapel."

"I'll call Guillermo to take a look," said Prado picking up his phone.

"Phones don't work in the cathedral," said the general. "We'll have to go look for ourselves."

They trooped out of the conference room.

The bishop glanced into the office on their way to the palace gate.

Father Ildefonso had vanished.

"Always with the distractions," said Prado when the bishop pointed out the missing priest. "We'll deal with him later."

They met Guillermo at the cathedral entrance and followed him in.

Between the entrance and the cathedral, all was quiet but between the cathedral and the mihrab, it was absolute chaos. The noise echoed around the building making conversation impossible.

"What are they doing," said the bishop. "This is a place of God; can they not treat it with more respect?"

"Best not to look too closely, bishop," said the general. "They have an impossible job to complete by an immovable deadline. They know what they are doing, let them carry on."

The bishop frowned as they walked past the Chapel of the Souls of Purgatory. It seemed so innocent with its white sheets and innocuous sign. Guillermo unlocked the door to the stairwell in the corner by the cathedral exit. He led the way up the four flights of stairs and out onto the roof. They could see the empty courtyard and serried rows of orange trees below to their right as they walked the roof path along to gable number four directly above the chapel.

Guillermo opened the door, switched on the light, and invited them to enter.

It was empty.

Except on the floor in the corner to the left of the door, was a neatly arranged backpack and a large, sealed carton.

37

Phillip squatted and slit the tape sealing the top of the robust cardboard box with his car key. He opened the four flaps revealing beige folders with a handwritten note on a single sheet of A4 paper stapled to the top one. Phillip held it up.

"Where do these go next year?" read Prado. "What does it mean?"

"Let me look," said the bishop taking the folder and inspecting the note closely. "It's father Julián's writing." He flicked through the papers inside. "It's the missing paper files and at the end of the year they go to the archives."

"Where are the archives?" said Prado.

"Directly under the conference suite," said the bishop. "It's a climatically controlled, bomb and fireproof vault but I don't understand. Blowing up the archives to destroy people in the conference room would need a massive amount of explosives."

"General, did your men test the archives?" said Phillip

"Several times, the last only a couple of hours ago. The room was clean."

"How many rooms are air-conditioned?" said Phillip.

"The archives are on a stand-alone system, but the conference suite and swimming pool use the same unit," said the bishop.

"If they're not going to blow it up," said el jefe. "How do they propose to kill over two hundred people?"

"There are only so many ways to kill in large numbers," said Phillip. "If not an armed attack or explosives, it has to be poison via catering or gas through the air conditioning ducts."

"The only catering involved is bottled water on the buses," said the general. "Which came directly from the source in Lanjarón. My men supervised the whole process from the bottling plant to delivery."

"Then it has to be gas," said Phillip.

"General, your men need to check the conference room air-conditioning again," said el jefe. "This time you're looking for some kind of timer and a canister, not explosives."

"I'll go and arrange it now," said the general turning and leaving.

Phillip opened the backpack and removed a rich purple tunic, conical silk hat, and mask. He unfolded them and spotted some embroidery on the back. He read it out. "El Fundador," he said. "Hermandad Corpus Puro, 1939."

"I can only assume," said Prado. "This belonged to Jesús Blanco, their founder."

"Anything else in the box?" said el jefe.

Phillip picked up the next item, a framed photo. He held it up for all to see.

"It's Jesús Blanco with two men," said Prado. "The

family resemblance is uncanny; look at the noses."

They crowded around Phillip for a closer look.

Jesús was on the left and what must have been his son in the middle.

On the right was a young Father Demetrio. The dean of the cathedral.

"Surely not," said the bishop.

"May I present the current El Fundador," said Prado. "Grandson of Jesús."

"Da Rosa said he was small, stooped, and walked with a limp," said Phillip.

"Simple enough," said Prado stooping and hobbling around.

"I've known the man for decades," said the bishop. "This can't be right. I must speak with him and hear it from his mouth. Then I might believe it."

"This is an old photo," said Prado. "Taken well before the days of Photoshop. I have no reason to believe it's a fake."

"Let me see," said the bishop.

Phillip handed it over.

The bishop looked at it from every angle. Eventually, his shoulders slumped with resignation.

"The dean's job was the perfect cover," said Prado. "He has a legitimate reason to be everywhere in the cathedral at any time. He had me fooled completely."

"I wonder how Julián found this photo," said the bishop. "Anything else in the rucksack?"

Phillip fumbled around the bottom of the rucksack and pulled up a brown, sealed envelope. Handwritten on the front was 'Bishop.' Phillip handed it over.

"Again, it's Julián's handwriting," said the bishop before tearing off one end. He extracted a folded piece of A4 paper covered on both sides with the same cursive text on the envelope.

He scanned it through quickly.

"It's all here," he said. "I'll read it out."

My dear Salvador,

I write these, my final words with a sad heart and sense of shame but I see no other way out of these tragic circumstances. If you are reading this then you have understood my clues, have probably worked out what is going on, and have found a way to prevent the dean and his evil Hermandad de Corpus Puro from committing their heinous crimes against the church and all humanity. I pray it is so.

I only stumbled on their plans by accident.

After a particularly stressful day dealing with roof problems some two weeks ago, I decided to swim before retiring. I'd missed my usual daily workout. As you know, I'm a creature of habit and this change to my routine was as surprising to me as it was to Father Ildefonso and the dean. I found them in the sauna, embracing and, well, I'm sure you follow my meaning.

Before I could tell you the next day, the dean came into my quarters with a pistol and in no uncertain terms warned me harm would come to my sister should I inform you. I wrongly assumed he was terrified of his sexuality being exposed so said nothing about it to anyone. However, knowing how strongly you feel about abuse in the Catholic church, I resolved to investigate further to see if this was a meaningful relationship between the two of them or something more perverse.

I watched them both carefully, overhearing several conversations, a few of which included the words Cofradia Corpus Puro, Wednesday, and archives. I researched the brotherhood in more detail and to my horror discovered not only were they misogynistic but also extremely racist. Their name means pure Spanish blood. I wondered if they might be planning something terrible at the event on Wednesday and started checking the cathedral for any unusual activity especially in the restoration works. I discovered some odd-looking bolts in a locker in the builders' office, took one apart, discovered the acid, and worked out their plan to collapse the roof. I initially thought this must have been their master plan but when I thought it through, it had no guarantee of success, and all it would take to prevent it is to remove the rubble from the attic and block the timer signal.

I also found where the dean hid his El Fundador robes and family mementos. Please forgive me for stealing some of them. You might find more in his locker in the choir changing rooms, including I suspect more evidence of abuse.

I wrestled with all the possibilities. What were their plans?

They had me flummoxed for a few days.

Then I guessed.

The roof collapse was just a distraction from the real attack. I didn't hear them say where, but the only other possibility was in the palace which had to mean something to do with the archives.

I set out to spoil their plans.

Last Thursday evening, I confronted the dean in the choir changing rooms and accused him of conspiring to kill the Pope.

He called me a fool and ranted on about his grandfather's brotherhood being founded to save and expand the Spanish church using traditional values. He was simply carrying on with his family's obligations to their many members.

I argued with him saying it was those old-fashioned values that were driving worshippers away in droves. Not just the Catholic Church needed modernizing, but all religions are suffering from a lack of interest because they are slow to accept and adapt to modern ideas and diversity. Any attempt to go back would mean the ultimate death of religion. The accord on Wednesday would be a start to putting things right.

He drew his pistol and I thought he was going to shoot me, but Father Ildefonso arrived and stopped him.

I retired but didn't sleep. My mind was a cauldron of indecision. Should I tell you or not. I decided I would despite the fact it may endanger you personally.

However, on Friday morning, Father Ildefonso informed me my sister had been abducted and if I revealed anything, they would kill her.

I racked my brain trying to think of a way out.

I waited a few days to see if the Sevilla police could find her but when there had been no sign of her, I had to make a decision. This pathetic and shameful attempt at pointing you in the right direction is all I could think of in the time available. I pray my death will save my sister and enable the signing on Wednesday to proceed.

It has been a pleasure working with you.

As I go to end my life, I will pray for you all.

Your loyal servant and friend.

Julián.

38

The bishop covered his eyes momentarily before standing and crossing himself. "Sorry," he said. "A moment of sadness for my dear friend.

"He's a hero," said Phillip. "He gave his life so others may live. In the army, he'd be decorated with the highest accolade."

"We need to locate Father Demetrio," said the bishop recovering quickly. "He has a lot of explaining to do. I'll check this locker Julián mentioned and his quarters. I'll call if I need help."

"We'll go to the archives," said Prado heading toward the door. "We'll leave the files for now but Phillip, could you bring the backpack and contents, please."

"I'll catch up with you," said the bishop.

"Will you be alright on your own, bishop?" said Guillermo. "Only the dean is armed."

"He wouldn't dare shoot me and I'll appreciate the few moments alone with him."

They filed down the stairs. Guillermo locked the door at the bottom, and they went their separate ways.

The courtyard was empty of people. The floodlights

lit up the orange trees as if they were sentries standing motionless on guard.

Two armed soldiers had been posted outside the palace gate.

"The general is in the palace basement," said one. "He's left instructions for you to join him."

Guillermo led the way around the cloisters to the main stairwell in the far corner. Another soldier barred the door but stood aside and opened it as they approached. They went down two flights and into a brightly lit corridor. Religious paintings adorned the walls on both sides and there was a faint smell of chlorine from the swimming pool.

The general was standing outside the door with two soldiers. He looked angry.

"The door has been locked and bolted from the inside," said the general. "I've knocked and shouted but nobody answers."

"It's a solid armored door," said Guillermo. "Some four centimeters thick. When shut, the oxygen is sucked out and seals the room into a vacuum. Nothing can get in or out."

"How does whoever is inside propose to breathe?" said el jefe.

"The vacuum takes about ten minutes to reach one hundred percent," said Guillermo. "After that, they'll last about five minutes."

"Won't a vacuum prevent the gas from circulating?" said Prado.

"Yes, but it won't stop the timer," said Guillermo.

"Can we block the timer signal?" said Phillip.

"We can try," said the general. "But transmitting through thick metal will weaken the signal. There's no guarantee we can stop it. Any other suggestions."

"Yes, sir," said one of the engineers, a veteran in his mid-forties. "We'll cut through the door with a thermal lance."

"Do we have one with us?" said the general.

"No, sir," said the veteran engineer. "We'd have to request one from the depot."

"How long will it take?" said the general.

"Two hours to arrive and four or five to cut through," said the veteran engineer. "Plus, a couple more to clean up."

The general looked at his watch.

"It's cutting it fine," he said. "But we have no other choice. Go ahead."

The veteran went back upstairs, radio in hand.

"Who do you think is inside?" said el jefe.

"Has to be somebody on the cathedral staff," said Prado. "To be familiar with the door closing system. Father Ildefonso perhaps and possibly the dean. How are your men progressing in the cathedral?"

"They will finish on schedule, but it will be a close-run thing," said the general.

"Should we cancel?" said el jefe. "We must consider the safety of the delegates."

"We have no option but to proceed," said the bishop joining them. "Too much preparation has gone into this to even consider postponing the signing. It's tomorrow morning or never."

"Can't we move the venue elsewhere?" said the general.

"No," said the bishop. "We've already had that debate. This is not just the signing of a piece of paper. The leaders coming together in the Mosque-Cathedral is a hugely symbolic gesture. Nowhere else in the world lends the occasion the substance it deserves. Also, think about the damage a cancellation or change of venue would do to religion and our country. We'd have to explain why. Imagine what a laughingstock we would be?"

"Then here it will be," said the general. "What are you proposing to do with the brotherhood members not involved in the conspiracy?"

"Good question," said the bishop. "We can't allow them to carry on as before."

"Legally, there isn't much we can do," said el jefe. "It's not illegal to run a brotherhood or be a member."

"Surely, you can't let the judges and public servants continue in office?" said Phillip.

"Again, legally they can," said el jefe. "Providing they don't commit any illegal acts and remain impartial in their work. They have every right to serve."

"It's unthinkable," said Prado. "However, there might be a way to address the issue."

"Go on," said the bishop.

"It's an argument I used with Da Rosa," said Prado. "To persuade him to open up to us. My thinking is the same applying to gangs. If one member commits a crime then by default, the other members are guilty of being an accessory whether aware of the crime or not. I believe the same legal principle can apply to the brotherhood. They too are a gang and together guilty of a multitude of crimes from terror to attempted murder, blackmail, false imprisonment, rape, removing children from their mothers against their will, and conspiracy to kill the world's religious leaders. I suggest those brotherhood members not involved in illegal activity are given the option to resign their position, cancel their membership, and vow never to involve themselves in any other group activities. Those who decline will be charged. Those who accept may disappear quietly."

"Are you including the brothers and nuns at the monastery?" said Phillip.

"No," said Prado. "I'm confident we'll gather enough evidence to lock those brothers up for the remainder of their days. As for the pseudo nuns, it depends on the evidence against each, but some will be needed. We can't just abandon the patients at the monastery and there are too many to absorb into the public health system. It makes sense for the monastery to continue as an asylum for those suffering addictions and poor mental health but under proper supervision."

"Good idea," said the bishop. "Perhaps the newly united religions could play a role in its management. Some good could come from this after all."

"Bishop, gentlemen," said the general. "All hell will be let loose down here in the next hour or so and we would only be in the way. I don't know about you, but I'm starving. May I suggest we find somewhere to eat while we wait? My men will keep us informed when they are ready to open the door."

"Good idea," said the bishop. "I know of an excellent restaurant accustomed to our odd catering hours not far from here. We'll go there."

They headed up the stairs and paused at the fountain while Prado left his briefcase in the general office.

While he was gone, the bishop sidled up to Phillip and took his hand.

"The dean wasn't in his rooms and his locker was empty," he said palming a pen drive. "Except for this. Have a look and decide what to do with the contents. If it's harmless, throw it away."

39

Despite his nagging hunger, Phillip was desperate to see his beloved. Prado arranged a car for him. which stopped directly outside a private hospital on the western fringes of the city about a kilometer and a half from the cathedral.

"I'm on until six am," said the female driver. "Call me when you need picking up. I hope she's OK.

"Thanks," said Phillip climbing out and stretching wearily. Finally, he could spend some time with Amanda. How would she be, he thought. Is she up for the wedding on Saturday? After the past hectic thirty-six hours, he could sleep for a week. From what she had been through the poor dear must be more than exhausted.

"Amanda Salisbury," he said to the middle-aged gray-haired receptionist.

"Id," she said regarding him nervously.

He dug it out of his wallet and passed it over. She checked his photo, picked up the phone, and spoke quietly.

She put the phone down and smiled warmly.

"Seventh floor, room nineteen," she said. "You'll

have to present your Id again to the security guards before they'll let you in."

"I understand," he said. "Could I order some food?"

"Sorry, it's too late for the kitchen," she said. "But there is a vending area on each floor. It's not too disgusting."

Phillip grimaced and headed for the elevators.

Then a thought struck him. He reached in his pocket and took out the pen drive given to him by the bishop. He returned to the receptionist holding up the drive.

"Have you a computer I could quickly use?" he said. "I need to know what's on this. It could be relevant to what happened to my fiancée?"

Her face softened. "Try the ward sister's workstation in the corner," she said standing and leading him over. "Don't worry, she's not on duty."

She came over, activated the machine, and entered the password.

He inserted the drive into a port at the rear of the monitor.

When the icon appeared, he opened it up.

The first folder was thumbnails of choir boys in their smocks and ruffs. He clicked on each and a video played them singing to organ music. It was beautiful. The receptionist hummed along.

"Doesn't sound too incriminating," she said.

The only other item was a folder marked photos.

Inside were fifty-odd photos of Father Ildefonso dressed in his customary black suit in front of varying backgrounds. Most were inside the cathedral, a few in the swimming pool. They were harmless enough, so he extracted the drive and pushed back the chair.

"Thank you," he said heading to the elevator.

"Hope it helped," she said.

He shrugged.

There was nobody to be seen as he walked along the corridor. An elevator car was waiting. He went straight up and on the way to room nineteen stopped at the vending machines, grabbed two soggy rolls filled with jamón serrano and a muddy coffee in a flimsy plastic cup.

Two alert private security officers were guarding Amanda's room.

Phillip sighed with relief. He'd been worrying the brotherhood might try something again with her.

He showed his Id, they smiled and opened the door for him.

Amanda was sleeping.

He checked the monitor; her vitals were normal.

He put the food down and stroked her cheek.

She didn't stir so he sat in the comfortable armchair next to her bed, ate the rolls, struggled through the coffee, and fell asleep holding her hand still wearing his jacket.

He was dreaming of a terrifying incident in Afghanistan when something irritated his chest. He opened his eyes. Amanda was still asleep, her pulse throbbing slowly like a chronometer and so was his phone. He slid it out from his inside jacket pocket. It was five am. Just a little over five hours to go until the buses started arriving with the largest ever group of religious leaders the world had ever seen. He read the message from Prado.

"Breaking through the door in about half an hour. Car waiting outside.

Phillip threw the remnants of his supper in the

trash. Splashed water over his face, bent and kissed Amanda.

Her eyes opened.

Her initial expression of alarm melted. She hugged him with her good arm and kissed his cheek then lips.

"How are you?" he said.

"Groggy and sore but I can walk."

"Strong enough for Saturday?"

"You bet but I'll have my left arm in a sling."

"As long as you can say I do, I don't care what you're wearing," he said.

"Well, I mind. I'll be in my dress whatever it takes. Are you done with Prado?"

"Almost, there's a car waiting downstairs to take me back."

"Do you know who was responsible?"

"Remember the painting in the monastery library?"

She nodded.

"The dean is the grandson of Jesús Blanco. It's him behind the conspiracy to kill the leaders along with Tobón and the bishop's secretary Father Ildefonso."

"How?"

"Collapsing the cathedral roof which the general's men are fixing, or possibly poison gas through the air conditioning. We're searching for a device and canister now."

She held him tight.

"Be careful," she said.

"This is my last thing with Prado," said Phillip. "What with your injury in the Vélez-Málaga case and now this, it's progressively becoming too dangerous. I couldn't bear you being hurt again."

"We'll see," she said tapping her stomach. "You stay safe for us and Sasha."

"The baby?"

"I'm nine weeks, and the baby is fine."

He sat up, held her hands in his, stood, and left. As he walked toward the elevator tears streamed down his cheeks.

He wiped his eyes on his sleeve as he walked out the hospital front door, took a deep breath, and tried to repress his emotions. After boarding school and military service, it was something to which he was accustomed.

He took a deep breath and opened the police car door.

"How is she?" said the same female officer.

"Better than expected thanks for asking."

They sped through the empty streets in comfortable silence while Phillip wrestled to keep his concerns for Amanda under control. As they approached the palace, he glanced toward the riverbank. The troops had commenced reloading their vehicles.

Prado was waiting for him at the palace gate.

"Ok?" he said placing his arm on Phillip's shoulder.

"She and the baby are fine," said Phillip.

"I guess we could say, thank God," said Prado.

"We're in the right place," said Phillip. "So, Amen to that. Anything new?"

"No timer has been found in the cathedral which puzzles me," said Prado. "Why go to the trouble with the cylinders and rubble if they never intended to use them?"

"Perhaps it's not a timer?" said Phillip. "Maybe someone will carry a remote control that works with both devices They'll set off whichever they think has the most likelihood of success?"

"Or both. Then we should assume the person with

the remote control is working independently from those that set up the devices," said Prado.

"And only one person knows who that person is," said Phillip. "And could issue instructions to stop them."

"El Fundador," said Prado.

"Let's ask the general," said Prado as they headed toward the stairwell. "What form a remote timer could look like so we can brief security when scanning the delegates."

"Any developments with the other brotherhood members?" said Phillip.

"El jefe has rounded up the prominent members. One of the businessmen who owns a steel mill with a blast furnace admitted to supplying a canister of Hydrogen Cyanide to Tobón. It's an extremely toxic gas smelling faintly of almonds. Exposure, even at a low density, for more than two seconds can cause death or severe long-lasting illnesses, especially to older victims such as most of the leaders. He's provided the general's men with protection equipment and masks but assures us he had no idea what it was to be used for."

"So, he says."

"At this point, I don't care. We'll deal with him later when we know what the damage is," said Prado yawning. He shook his head and looked at Phillip. "This is way more than you or Amanda signed up for my friend. In future, I'll insist to el jefe, translations only."

"And no sickos," said Phillip.

"No sickos," said Prado as they arrived at the bottom of the stairs.

"How are they going to move the door?" said

Phillip. "It must weigh a ton or more."

"They only cut three sides," said Prado. "So can push it open on its hydraulic hinges."

The noise of the lance was unbearable.

Seconds later it was turned off and there was complete silence.

The operator took off his mask and headphones and nodded to the general.

"Go ahead," said the general.

Two bulky soldiers standing by the wall moved forward and took their place by the door.

"One two three." shouted the general.

The men put their shoulders to the door and pushed. They strained and strained and eventually the door began to open.

As soon as there was a space wide enough, the general entered, pistol in hand. The ceiling lights were still on.

Prado and Phillip followed him.

They found Fathers Ildefonso and Demetrio dead in each other arms on the floor between two racks of files. Demetrio was wearing his purple cloak. Prado searched them both. Father Ildefonso had a bunch of keys and a wallet containing some cash, credit cards, and a selfie photo of him and the dean looking lovingly at each other. The dean had keys, a wallet, and an opened packet of three contraceptives with two missing. In his inner jacket pocket was a pistol. Prado pulled it out with his gloves and examined it. It was a replica. A totally convincing model made of metal, but it had no firing pin, and the chamber was empty.

"Why was the dean using a replica weapon?" said Prado.

"Only he can answer that," said Phillip. "But

probably as a tool to instill fear and force cooperation."

"Can we check for devices again general?" said Prado.

"Already started," said the general.

"I think we've underestimated their resolve to misdirect us," said Phillip. "Unless they made a mistake and didn't know about the vacuum when the door was closed."

"The dean was responsible for the archives being converted into a vault," said the bishop. "The work was completed over ten years ago, long before I arrived. They would have both known exactly what would happen if they locked themselves in."

"If these two men were prepared to suffocate themselves to stop the signing, something powerful must have driven them to it," said Phillip. "The question is, are their deaths the end of it, or were they working with others? Is there someone else with a timer control?"

"Are you suggesting, this is not over?" said Prado.

"I don't know," said Phillip. "But we could be taking a huge risk with the lives of the delegates by assuming it is. We have to find or eliminate the possibility of a gas canister anywhere in or near the conference room."

"Where should we search?" said the general.

"It could be anywhere in the ducting," said Phillip.

"We'll take a look," said the general turning to the veteran. "Do we have a robot with us?"

"Yes, sir, it's in the electronics truck by the river," said the veteran. "I'll send someone to fetch it now."

"Then hurry," said the general looking at his watch. "We only have four hours to find this damn thing and disarm it."

They trooped upstairs to the conference room and stood by the door while three engineers started unscrewing the vent grills.

Fifteen minutes later, the soldier returned with a large plastic case. The veteran opened it up, removed the robot, checked the battery, set the tiny ariel to vertical, and placed it on the stone floor. He opened the handset, turned it on, and when the view from the camera appeared he pressed the remote control. The four-wheeled robot moved forward and then back. He picked it up and inserted it into a vent.

An hour later, every meter of ducting linked to the conference room had been searched. Other than a few rats, they found nothing.

"Do other ducts link into the HVAC unit?" said the veteran.

"The swimming pool," said Phillip moving closer to Prado.

"Leon," he said. "We need to look at some images of a pen drive found in the dean's locker in the choir changing rooms."

"I don't recall you going into the cathedral."

"The bishop found it. He asked me to look. He was worried it might contain abuse images."

"And did it?"

"They seemed innocent enough except there were photos of Father Ildefonso with several different backgrounds. We should also check his and the dean's email accounts and search their rooms. They might reveal something."

"In that case," said Prado. "We'll need the bishop."

While the general and his team took their equipment down to the pool. Phillip, Prado, and the bishop headed for the general office.

The bishop trailed slowly behind them.

They waited at the office door for him to catch up.

"Sorry," said the bishop. "The deaths of three of my main staff members in just under three days have drained me completely. Why didn't I see this coming? The two of them right under my nose plotting against me and the church. I never suspected anything and trusted them completely. How could I misjudge their intent so hopelessly? It's testing my faith; I can tell you."

"Bishop," said Prado putting his arm around the bishop's shoulder. "If we are to prevent a disaster in a little under three hours, now is the time we need your strength and clear thinking. This is no fault of yours. We're dealing with clever men determined to outwit the finest minds in the country. They've been working and planning this for years and yet we've caught up with them in just a few days and all because you had the wits to see through Tobón and involve the right people. Believe me, your actions have and will save the day. All we need you to do now is browse through some photos and help us resolve what they might mean. Could you give it a try, please?"

The bishop sighed and nodded.

"Thank you, inspector," he said and with a determined expression pushed past them, opened the office door, and led the way to the dean's desk.

Prado spotted the handcuffs used to restrain Father Ildefonso lying on the floor by the radiator under the window to the left of the door. He strode over to pick them up but froze before doing so.

"These have been unlocked," he said. "Not cut."

"What does that suggest?" said the bishop.

"Neither the dean nor Father Ildefonso had the

right key on them and there isn't one here. They could have thrown it away before locking themselves in archives or somebody else, possibly police or cathedral security could have assisted them. Phillip, while you and the bishop check the images and email accounts, I'll scan the cuffs for prints."

Prado picked up his briefcase from where he'd left it earlier on Cora's desk, opened it, put on some fresh gloves, and took out his scanner.

He picked up the cuffs, turned on the device, and began to search.

"Where should we start?" said the bishop.

"The photos," said Phillip sitting down behind the dean's desk and taking the pen drive out of his pocket. He inserted it into an available port and turned on the laptop.

"The password is Crónicas1," said the bishop.

Phillip clicked on the image folder and opened the first photo of the father in front of the mihrab.

The bishop grabbed the chair from Cora's desk, slid it over, and sat next to Phillip.

"Flick through them quickly," said the bishop.

"Father Ildefonso doesn't seem to be posing," said the bishop after twenty-odd images had been shown. "Just standing."

"What about the backgrounds?" said Phillip clicking on more images.

"They're concentrated on the area where the service will be held later this morning."

"You mean under where the roof was designed to collapse?"

"Yes."

"What about these in the swimming pool?"

"Every image includes an air conditioning vent at

the far end of the pool," said the bishop. "The wall containing those vents forms one side of the machine room housing the HVAC unit that feeds the pool and conference room. Even with my lack of technical know-how, it's a logical place to locate a gas canister."

"No prints on the cuffs," said Prado. "Or the radiator. I'll go down to the pool and tell them about the machine room. You carry on looking for emails."

"Bearing in mind their complex planning," said Phillip. "I doubt we'll find any trace of emails sent from any of these devices. It's such a basic mistake to make. I'll check now though."

Phillip checked the log that recorded copies of all cathedral activity. The bishop watched as he scrolled down the long list of sent and received emails.

"Just the usual stuff," said the bishop. "What about the trash?"

Phillip clicked.

The list was huge. Nothing had been deleted for months.

"Did the fathers have cell phones?" said Phillip.

"We all do but they're synchronized with the laptops here."

"Do they have personal devices?"

"Not that I know of. Sorry, I should say, I've never seen them with one but after today, who knows?"

"Can we search their rooms?"

"We'll start with Father Ildefonso's, it's next door," said the bishop.

There wasn't much to search.

The father had a cramped bedsit with no cooking facilities and a bathroom with a small fridge jammed behind the door. It contained bottled water. His wardrobe was stuffed with black suits, a cassock, and an array of black shirts with white collars. The chest of drawers contained underwear and socks, the bedside cabinet some family photos, cufflinks, and belts. The floor and walls were solid stone, the ceiling timber.

They found nothing.

It was the same in Father Demetrio's apartment.

They returned dejected to the office to find Prado looking brighter than he'd done for hours.

"There wasn't a device in the archives," he said. "But they have located a cylinder and some kind of mechanism to release the gas in a duct in the swimming pool machine room."

40

They went down the stairs, turned into the pool room, and along to the machine room entrance at the far end where they joined the general who issued them with gas masks. They put them on and watched the two engineers at work through the door. The aluminum cylinder was about half the size of a standard propane bottle and lying on its side inside a two-meter-long duct that stretched from the top of the head-high HVAC unit to a hole in the wall. To its left was a small battery-operated fan to waft the gas in the right direction if the HVAC had been switched off. Access was through a maintenance plate that had been removed.

The veteran engineer was giving a running commentary as he examined it.

"It's a standard poison gas cylinder," he said. "Consisting of one cylinder inside another. The inner cylinder is opened by this tap on the side of the valve. In this case, the tap is open, and the valve has been inserted into a device that keeps it sealed until a signal is received from a remote controller. The fan will also be turned on by the same signal. As a matter of interest, the acid cylinders in the cathedral roof could also have been activated by the same remote controller."

"Can you deactivate it?" said the general.

"It doesn't seem to be fitted with any antitamper device," said the veteran. "First, I'll close the tap."

Total silence prevailed as he slowly twisted the tap to a closed position.

"There," he said. "It's safe."

"I'd like to have our forensics experts examine the timer control," said Prado. "To see if we can identify where it was made and by whom. Can you separate it from the cylinder?"

"I think so," said the veteran grasping the device, and after twisting it a few times it separated. "It was screwed onto the valve. Can you take it please?"

Prado stepped into the room, collected it, and examined it closely.

It was a combination of an electrical and mechanical device. When the signal was received from the remote control, the electronics went into action twisting the cylinder seal from horizontal to vertical. Simple but effective. Prado left the device activated but reset the seal to closed.

They watched as the two engineers lifted the cylinder down from the duct and fixed it firmly on a cart. The soldiers wheeled it off to the riverside. The others dropped off the device at the general office and followed the cart down to the final truck where the cylinder was loaded and would be disposed of back at the barracks. The engineers and remaining soldiers climbed in the rear and the truck departed. The winter rains had subsided, and the river Guadalquivir waters gurgled gently underneath the arches of the Roman bridge. The sun shone brightly, the sky was clear and blue with not a breath of wind. Perfect, God-given weather for such a special day.

The general led the way up the hill back to the palace to find the prime minister and the King of Spain waiting inside the gothic gate with their security teams. The first bus was due imminently.

"I'm convinced that you and the delegates are no longer in danger," said the general in response to the prime minister's question. "Thanks to Detective Inspector Prado and his team, we know the identity and whereabouts of every member of Hermandad de Corpus Puro. We've removed the gas cylinder from the palace pool. The cathedral roof has been repaired and rubble removed. The buses have been closely examined and under armed guard since they arrived at the airport last night. The water drains surrounding the cathedral have been inspected and sealed. Every interior room, chapel, niche, and cranny has been checked and double-checked by the anti-terrorist team and declared safe to use. The delegates including the Pope and security teams have all been scanned before boarding the bus and nobody was allowed to carry anything bigger than a watch and a radio. I guarantee nothing will happen and the event will go ahead without any problems."

"What about the media?" said the prime minister.

"They are er busy elsewhere," said el jefe.

"Thank you, general, inspector, and all involved," said the King as the first bus stopped outside the palace. "Excellent work everyone."

They headed off to the conference room followed by the suited delegates. There was no greeting, shaking hands, or talking. Each knew exactly where to go and moved purposely to their seats.

The conference room looked magnificent. Posies of

flowers had been placed in the center of the table and a huge arrangement placed on a dias at the far end.

At the other were a podium and microphone.

On it was large a parchment document bound into a leather cover.

The first ten pages described the terms of the accord in English, the common language used for the negotiations. Each delegate would sign a page written in their language describing their commitment to the new way of doing things and agreeing to the system of arbitration in the event of misunderstandings or modifications. It was as binding as it could be, but each knew that it wasn't the text that would bond them together. It was the spirit of the occasion. The awareness that if this wasn't signed today, it would never be, and religion would fade away rejected by the modern society it was trying to save.

The camera crew was as discreet as possible. The presenter, the retired Bishop of Liverpool, was mouthing his commentary and would add the voice-over in the studio where it would be dubbed into over a hundred and sixty languages.

When everyone was seated. The Bishop of Córdoba dressed in a black suit and plain white shirt, picked up the microphone in one hand and the leather book in the other.

"I, the Bishop of Córdoba," said in perfect English. "Welcome you to this historic place and momentous occasion." He waved the book. "My job is to pass this book to each of you to sign. The first signatory selected purely by alphabetical order is the Archbishop of Canterbury on behalf of the Anglican church."

As the book went around the table, nobody had any last-minute doubts or interruptions. Just determined men and women joined in a common purpose to do good.

It took half an hour longer to sign than anticipated but it was done.

Prado and Phillip standing outside in the cloisters heard the applause and shared sighs of relief. So far so good.

The delegates stood as one, applauded, then filed out in pairs to the cathedral.

Phillip, Prado, el jefe and the general tagged on behind. Their reward from the bishop for saving the day.

Only ninety minutes previously, the engineers had still been working on their platforms replacing the acid cylinders with the correct bolts. Somehow, they had finished, cleaned up, and cleared out just in time.

They listened to the new form of service.

It was surprisingly light-hearted and enjoyable.

Even the four diehard agnostics agreed it wasn't too shabby.

There was no time for chitchat after the service. Planes were waiting, buses needed to be loaded. By one-thirty it was all over, and the Easter processions could reconvene.

Thanks to Phillip's distraction at the monastery, no media had attended. The first the world would know of the momentous events was when the documentary was broadcast later that evening.

Prado and Phillip returned to the palace office to collect Prado's briefcase.

"Ye gods," he said picking up the gas cylinder mechanism and looking at the seal.

"What?" said Phillip

"Someone activated it," said Prado.

He switched it off, they looked at each other and shrugged. The mystery would probably nag them for the rest of their days. Just as the holder of the remote controller recruited to set it off would wonder why nothing had happened when he or she pressed it.

After bidding farewell to everyone, the bishop went down to the Roman arch to see off the first brotherhood of the day. He heard their band warming up as he approached.

"Morning bishop," said many of the crowd as he passed them.

"Fixed the gas leak?" said one.

The bishop snapped around to see who had posed the question.

But then he remembered Phillip's ruse from the previous afternoon,

"Thanks for asking," he said. "Yes, but thanks to the military only just in time."

"They must have had some divine assistance," said the same voice.

"God moves in mysterious ways," said the bishop smiling.

41

A black Mercedes glided to a halt outside what used to be known as Convento Las Claras situated in the old part of Vélez-Málaga, the principal town of La Axarquía, the mountainous region resembling Tuscany to the east of Málaga. The former convent was unrecognizable. Salome Mendosa, Amanda's university roommate and now retired flamenco dancer had with the help of her architect fiancée Vicente Ayala restored much of the building exterior to its former gleaming glory. The walls were sparkling white. The tower was no longer cracked or leaning to one side, the stained-glass windows twinkled in the bright sunlight.

The driver climbed out and opened the rear door. The Bishop of Córdoba dressed in a black suit with a fuchsia shirt and white collar walked up the steps to be greeted by el Alcalde de Vélez-Málaga, Antonio Ruiz, representing the Spanish Socialist Party - PSOE, who had overseen the Townhall since 2015.

"Bishop," said the mayor coming down the steps. "Thank you for your visit. It's an honor but you do realize that Amanda and Phillip are expecting a non-religious ceremony performed by me and Las Claras is now a Flamenco University, it's no longer consecrated."

"Thank you, mayor Ruiz," said the bishop. "Yes, I am aware of the circumstances and am not proposing to rain on your parade, simply, with your permission of course to add my blessing when you've finished."

"Oh, I see," said the mayor. "I'm sure that will be fine. Shall we go inside?"

"I'd prefer my attendance to be a surprise," said the bishop as he climbed the steps. "Is there somewhere I can wait out of sight and then appear when it's my time?"

"Is this part of your lightening up religion campaign?" said the mayor.

"Not really," said the bishop. "But I am interested to learn what people think and am looking forward to hearing your words. Maybe the church can learn from them."

"That is good to hear," said the mayor. "Shall we go in? I'll show you where to wait and introduce you to Salome."

"Salome Mendosa, the dancer?"

"Yes, she is the owner and is converting the site into a residential flamenco university. The old church will be her dance studio, but local people can still use it for hatching, matching, and dispatching."

"What a good use of an old religious building," said the bishop. "We should do more of that."

Salome came over.

She looked stunning in her matron of honor outfit. A sleeveless cream dress topped with lace clung to her shapely curves and set off her long black hair.

"It's an honor, bishop," said Salome. "Amanda and Phillip will be delighted. I hope you'll say something."

"I will add a blessing after the mayor has finished. Salome, I'm a great fan of your dancing. May I compliment you on the magnificent restoration of this gracious old building? As you know we have hundreds of empty old buildings lying empty. The church would appreciate any advice you could pass on to help rejuvenate them."

"Vicente and I would be honored, bishop. But not today. Could you please take your places, the bride's vehicle has just arrived?"

An old white Rolls Royce stopped at the bottom of the steps.

A tall, elegant elderly man with thinning gray hair and an erect military bearing wearing a light gray suit with a red rose in the buttonhole climbed out of the roadside door and went around to wait on the pavement with Salome and the children.

Sasha was smartly dressed in a gray suit with a red rose. A mini version of Phillip. Phillip's three nieces were in loose cream dresses topped with lace, each with their blond shaggy hair pinned back and a red rose behind their ear.

The driver in a gray chauffeur's uniform and peaked hat opened the rear door, he reached inside and pulled gently.

Amanda winced as she stepped out of the car, her left arm in a cream silk sling that matched her stunning dress. The photographer snapped away as she and her short cream train were maneuvered into position at the top of the steps. She smiled tearfully at her father as she took his arm.

He sniffed, stuck out his chest, and tried to disguise his pride and emotions.

The organ played the wedding march.

They walked slowly into the church.

Everybody stood and closely followed their movement. Ingrid, the wife of Phillip's former business partner Richard was sitting on the front row next to Prado, his wife Inma, retired bullfighter Juan Romero and his wife Maribel, plus el jefe and his wife.

The original statue of the virgin had survived the restoration.

She dominated the southern wall of the former church looking serenely down on the congregation She glowed mystically under the multicolored rays of sunshine kissing her face and shoulders through the huge stained-glass window that didn't contain one single angel or heavenly character, only a host of young flamenco dancers twirling and stamping.

Phillip stepped forward with his best man Richard.

Amanda's father handed her over and stood by her side.

The mayor walked forward from the side of the virgin and stood before them.

Fifteen minutes later, Mr. & Mrs. Armitage turned and faced their cheering wedding guests to see a man in a black suit walking toward them.

As he approached, he held up his hands and the guests quietened.

"Ladies and gentlemen," said the bishop. "I hate to intrude on this special day. I'd just like to add to the mayor's words by offering you my blessing and to thank these two incredible people for their assistance in making sure the landmark event took place this week in Córdoba. In recognition of their contribution, I'm privileged to award them with the freedom of the city of Córdoba. May God bless and keep them."

The bishop extracted two silver medals on green

ribbons from inside his jacket pocket, placed one over Amanda's shoulders, and repeated the same for Phillip. There wasn't a dry eye in the house.

The Author

Londoner, Paul S Bradley has lived and worked in Nerja, Spain for over thirty years writing and publishing lifestyle magazines, guidebooks, and travelogues in English, German, and Spanish. On retirement, he self-published his first book of five of the *Andalusian Mystery Series* on Amazon. More recently, *Reinventing the Wheel*, a biography of America's first mobility-impaired female judge, was published by Rand Smith on June 17th 2024. Current work in progress is *The Fontainebleau,* a journey back to the 1970s when Brits kicked off their enduring love affair with Spain. This will be followed by *Nostalgia Man*, the first non-Spanish novel set in Henley-on-Thames where the author lived during the 1960s.

What did you think?

Reviews, good or bad fuel this independent author's continuous efforts to improve. If you enjoyed this book, please leave a comment on my blog, your preferred retailer, or follow my social media.
See the website for more details. Thank you.

www.paulbradley.eu